Praise for Mary Anna Evans

UNDERCURRENTS

The Eleventh Faye Longchamp Mystery

2019—Oklahoma Book Award Finalist

"The Longchamp mysteries combine history and mystery in a gritty way that makes them feel different from most amateur-sleuth fare—dark-edged rather than cozy. Faye, too, is not your traditional amateur sleuth; she could just as easily anchor a gritty thriller series and give some of the giants in that genre a run for their money."

—Booklist

"Evans expertly juggles a host of likely suspects, all the while breathing life into the city of Memphis, from its tourist-filled center to its marginal neighborhoods and the spectacular wilderness of the state park."

—Publishers Weekly

BURIALS

The Tenth Faye Longchamp Mystery

2018—Willa Literary Award Finalist, Contemporary Fiction
2018—Will Rogers Medallion Award Bronze Medalist,
Western Fiction
2018—Oklahoma Book Award Finalist, Fiction
2017—*Strand Magazine* Top 12 Mystery Novels
2017—*True West* Magazine Best Western Mysteries

"This is a highly successful murder mystery by an author who has mastered the magic and craft of popular genre fiction. Her work embodies the truism that character is destiny."

—*Naples Florida Weekly*

"Evans's signature archaeological lore adds even more interest to this tale of love, hate, and greed."

—*Kirkus Reviews*

"Evans sensitively explores the issue of how to balance respecting cultural heritage and gaining knowledge of the past through scientific research."

—*Publishers Weekly*

ISOLATION

The Ninth Faye Longchamp Mystery

2016—Oklahoma Book Awards Finalist

"Evans skillfully uses excerpts from the fictional oral history of Cally Stanton, recorded by the Federal Writers' Project in 1935, to dramatize the past."

—*Publishers Weekly*

"A worthwhile addition to Faye's long-running series that weaves history, mystery, and psychology into a satisfying tale of greed and passion."

—*Kirkus Reviews*

"Well-drawn characters and setting, and historical and archaeological detail, add to the absorbing story."

—*Booklist*

RITUALS

The Eighth Faye Longchamp Mystery

"A suspenseful crime story with just a hint of something otherworldly."

—*Booklist*

"A superior puzzle plot lifts Evans's eighth Faye Longchamp Mystery…Evans pulls all the pieces nicely together in the end."

—*Publishers Weekly*

"The emphasis on the spirit world makes this a bit of a departure from Evans's usual historical and archaeological themes, but it's certainly a well-plotted and enjoyable mystery."

—*Kirkus Reviews*

PLUNDER

The Seventh Faye Longchamp Mystery

2012—Florida Book Award
Bronze Medal Winner for General Fiction
2012—Florida Book Award
Bronze Medal Winner for Popular Fiction

"In her delightfully erudite seventh, Faye continues to weave archaeological tidbits and interesting people into soundly plotted mysteries."

—*Kirkus Reviews*

"Working in Louisiana, archaeologist Faye Longchamp doesn't expect a double murder and pirate plunder, but by now she's used to the unexpected."

—*Library Journal*

"The explosion of the Deepwater Horizon rig in the Gulf of Mexico provides the backdrop for Evans's engaging, character-driven seventh mystery featuring archaeologist Faye Longchamp."

—*Publishers Weekly*

"Details of archaeology, pirate lore, and voodoo complement the strong, sympathetic characters, especially Amande, and the appealing portrait of Faye's family life."

—*Booklist*

STRANGERS

The Sixth Faye Longchamp Mystery

"Mary Anna Evans's sixth Faye Longchamp novel continues her string of elegant mysteries that features one of contemporary fiction's most appealing heroines. The author also continues to seek out and to describe settings and locations that would whet the excavating appetite of any practicing or armchair archaeologist. Mary Anna Evans then commences to weave an almost mystical tapestry of mystery throughout her novel."
—Bill Gresens, Mississippi Valley Archaeology Center

"Evans explores themes of protection, love, and loss in her absorbing sixth Faye Longchamp Mystery...Compelling extracts from a 16th-century Spanish priest's manuscript diary that Faye begins translating lend historical ballast."
—*Publishers Weekly*

"Evans's excellent series continues to combine solid mysteries and satisfying historical detail."
—*Kirkus Reviews*

"This contemporary mystery is drenched with Florida history and with gothic elements that should appeal to a broad range of readers."
—*Booklist*

FLOODGATES

The Fifth Faye Longchamp Mystery

2011—Mississippi Author Award

"Mary Anna Evans gets New Orleans: the tainted light, the murk and the shadows, and the sweet and sad echoes, and the bloody dramas that reveal a city's eternal longing for what's been lost and its never-ending hopes for redemption."

—David Fulmer, author of Shamus Award
winner *Chasing the Devil's Tail*

"Evans has written a fascinating tale linking the history of New Orleans' levee system to the present and weaving into the story aspects of the city's widely diverse cultures."

—*Booklist*, Starred Review

"Evans's fifth is an exciting brew of mystery and romance with a touch of New Orleans charm."

—*Kirkus Reviews*

"Evans's fifth series mystery…reveals her skill in handling the details of a crime story enhanced by historical facts and scientific discussions on the physical properties of water. Along with further insights into Faye's personal life, the reader ends up with a thoroughly good mystery."

—*Library Journal*

FINDINGS

The Fourth Faye Longchamp Mystery

"Evans always incorporates detailed research that adds depth and authenticity to her mysteries, and she beautifully conjures up the Micco County, FL, setting. This is a series that deserves more attention than it garners."

—*Library Journal,* Starred Review

"Faye's capable fourth is a charming mixture of history, mystery and romance."

—*Kirkus Reviews*

"In Evans's fine fourth archaeological mystery…the story settles into a comfortable pace that allows the reader to savor the characters."

—*Publishers Weekly*

EFFIGIES

The Third Faye Longchamp Mystery

"As an archaeological tour alone the book would be worth reading, but it's the fascinating and complex characters that give the story life and vibrancy."
        —Rhys Bowen, author of the Constable Evans mysteries

"The best one yet….a fascinating read."
        —Tony Hillerman, *New York Times* bestselling author

"Though Evans has been compared to Tony Hillerman, her sympathetic characters and fascinating archaeological lore add up to a style all her own."
        —*Publishers Weekly*

"Starting with racial tension between blacks and whites, Evans adds Native Americans into the mix and comes up with a thought-provoking tale about people trying to live together."
        —*Library Journal*

"A captivating combination of archaeology, Native American tales, romance and detection. A must-read for those so inclined."
        —*Kirkus Reviews*

"Like Randy Wayne White in his Doc Ford novels, Evans adds an extra layer of substance to her series by drawing readers into the fascinating history of ancient American civilizations."
        —*Booklist*

RELICS

The Second Faye Longchamp Mystery

"An intriguing, multi-layered tale. Not only was I completely stumped by the mystery, I was enchanted by the characters Evans created with such respect."

—Claire Matturro, author of *Wildcat Wine*

"The remote setting engenders an eerie sense of isolation and otherness that gives the story an extra dimension. Recommend this steadily improving series to female-sleuth fans or those who enjoy archaeology-based thrillers like Beverly Connor's Lindsay Chamberlain novels."

—*Booklist*

"Evans delivers a convincing read with life-size, unique characters, not the least of whom is Faye's Indian sidekick, Joe. The archaeological adventures are somewhat reminiscent of Tony Hillerman's Jim Chee mysteries. While the story is complex, *Relics* will engage the imagination of readers attracted to unearthing the secrets of lost cultures."

—*School Library Journal*

"A fascinating look at contemporary archaeology but also a twisted story of greed and its effects."

—*Dallas Morning News*

ARTIFACTS

The First Faye Longchamp Mystery

2004—Benjamin Franklin Award for Mystery/Suspense
2004—Patrick D. Smith Florida Literature Award

"A haunting, atmospheric story."
—P.J. Parrish, *New York Times* bestselling author

"An excellent read. I couldn't put it down."
—Lonnie Cruse, author of *Murder in Metropolis*

"The shifting little isles along the Florida Panhandle—hurricane-wracked bits of land filled with plenty of human history—serve as the effective backdrop for Evans's debut, a tale of greed, archaeology, romance, and murder."
—*Publishers Weekly*

"First-novelist Evans introduces a strong female sleuth in this extremely promising debut, and she makes excellent use of her archaeological subject matter, weaving past and present together in a multilayered, compelling plot."
—*Booklist*

CATACOMBS

Also by Mary Anna Evans

The Faye Longchamp Mysteries
Artifacts
Relics
Effigies
Findings
Floodgates
Strangers
Plunder
Rituals
Isolation
Burials
Undercurrents

Other Books
Mathematical Literacy in the Middle and High School Grades:
A Modern Approach to Sparking Interest

Wounded Earth

Jewel Box: Short Works by Mary Anna Evans

Your Novel, Day by Day: A Fiction Writer's Companion

CATACOMBS

A FAYE LONGCHAMP MYSTERY

MARY ANNA EVANS

Poisoned Pen
PRESS

Published by Poisoned Pen Press, an imprint of Sourcebooks
P.O. Box 4410, Naperville, Illinois 60567-4410
(630) 961-3900
sourcebooks.com

Library of Congress Cataloging-in-Publication Data

Names: Evans, Mary Anna, author.
Title: Catacombs / Mary Anna Evans.
Description: Naperville, IL : Poisoned Pen Press, [2019] | Series: A Faye
  Longchamp archaeological mystery
Identifiers: LCCN 2019019250 | (hardcover : alk. paper)
Subjects: | GSAFD: Mystery fiction. | Suspense fiction.
Classification: LCC PS3605.V369 C38 2019 | DDC 813/.6--dc23 LC record available
at https://lccn.loc.gov/2019019250

Printed and bound in the United States of America.
SB 10 9 8 7 6 5 4 3 2 1

This book is dedicated to Dr. Robert Connolly, who has been my friend and archaeology guru ever since he introduced himself at a book-signing for Artifacts *in 2003.*

On those occasions when I have gotten Faye's professional life right since then, it has been due to his advice and expertise. On those occasions when I haven't, it has been because I neglected to ask or was too bullheaded to listen. His stories from the archaeological front lines have inspired the plots of more than one of my books.

When Faye digs up a stone point and I need to be able to describe it, I shoot an email to Robert and he tells me what it looks like, who made it, and how old it is. He has driven me all over northwest Mississippi and east Louisiana to look at ancient earthworks. He and his wife, Emma, have opened their home to me as a base for these adventures.
The best thing about my life as a writer have been the people I've met, and I am most grateful to have met the Connollys.

Chapter One

The man stood tall, backlit by sunset. The sky glowed a brilliant shade of blue only achievable in the desert, and the sun was bittersweet orange. His lean body was framed by craggy stone formations and they, too, were as orange as flame.

In the brightness, he was nothing more than a dark shadow. His silhouette might have been carved of granite, and yet he moved. Still in near-darkness, he turned his face toward the cameras and the film crew and the almighty director who gave them all their orders. His long hair whipped in the western wind.

Resting lightly in his hands was a slender wooden flute. On cue, he raised it to his lips and let loose a slow melody built on a pentatonic scale. The flute was made of nothing but cedar, and it was shaped by traditions as old as time. Cully Mantooth still made his flutes exactly as his Muscogee Creek father had taught him. He wrote his own songs, but they were only elaborations on the old ones. Maybe all songs are elaborations on the old ones.

No one would ever hear this song. The wind would surely spoil the recording. If it didn't, the neighing of the horses waiting just off-camera would do the spoiling. Cully would play it again in the studio, so that movie audiences could hear his music with all the clarity it deserved, but they would never hear this living moment.

Cully had to know that he was playing only for himself and the people around him, but it was obvious to the shrewd old director, Jakob Zalisky, that Cully was putting his soul into the song. Jakob knew that the music's magic would come through in the way Cully's body moved, so he let the cameras run for as long as the song did.

Jakob controlled the bank of fans making the wind that moved Cully's hair so artfully. He controlled the massive lights that allowed him to decide when Cully's face was in shadow and when it was fully revealed. He controlled everything but the music and the charisma of the man who made it.

Rolling the credits over this footage would be a crime against art, but that's what Jakob was planning to do. He knew movies, and he knew how to grab a distracted audience's attention and keep it. After the names of stars, co-stars, and producers had scrolled in front of Cully and his flute, and after Jakob's own name had been displayed in flowing script, there would be nothing left on the screen but the man, the sky, the rocks, and the flute. The theater would fill with this aching melody and the audience would feel the loss of things that used to be.

When Jakob judged that he had let that pain linger long enough, he cued the horses.

A herd of riderless stallions leaped between Cully and the rolling cameras, prancing for joy. They reared, pawing the golden air with their hooves, and then they were gone.

This sequence, devoid of plot or dialogue, would occupy mere seconds of his two-hour film. When editing, Jakob would cut from Cully and the exuberant horses directly to the weathered face of his star, a man who didn't have Cully's talent but whose face did have the capacity to put millions of moviegoers' butts in seats. It was a bankable face—blue eyes framed by a shock of wheat-colored hair—but a face alone couldn't take the owners of those butts back to 1800s Oklahoma. To accomplish that kind of time travel, a director needed tools. Today his tools were Cully Mantooth, his flute, and an acre of horses.

When Cully finished his song and the last note had died, Jakob reluctantly spoiled the magic. Stepping into the horses' dusty hoofprints, he yelled "Cut!" and watched Cully rouse from whatever dream his music made for him. No longer flattered by Jakob's carefully placed lights, harsh sunlight brought Cully's face into focus, and wrinkles showed around his broad mouth. Maybe a lifetime of flute playing had put them there. Or maybe a lifetime of cigarettes had done it.

Somehow, the wrinkles didn't detract a single iota from his good looks. The worst thing that Jakob could say about Cully's looks was that he was almost a caricature of a handsome man. Every curve and plane of him was perfect.

Sometimes, like now, Jakob hated Cully, just a little and just for a second. Jug-eared and potbellied Jakob had long believed that age would narrow the beauty gulf between him and his oldest friend. He saw now, again, that he had been wrong and that he always would be.

Jakob gave that petty resentment the millisecond of attention that it deserved, then he moved on. Sticking out his hand, he started the same conversation they always had after Cully played the flute by saying, "That was glorious."

Cully took the hand and shook it, silently nodding his thanks.

"I want you in all my films," the director demanded of his friend. "Can I have that?"

He got the same response as always. "Until I go home."

As always, Jakob left the conversation there, giving Cully a manly thump on the back and keeping his questions to himself.

No, not as always. He had once been too brash and young to know when to keep his mouth shut. He had pushed the famously reticent man by asking, "When will that be? And where's home, anyway?"

Cully had given him a polite nod and walked away. Then he had refused Jakob's calls for weeks on end until the day when he didn't. Jakob had never asked him about his home again.

The basis of their friendship was loyalty, but they showed it in different ways. Cully knew that Jakob would never stop reaching out, and Jakob knew that Cully would always come back. It just might take him a little time.

Jakob and Cully had been in Hollywood for forty years. Okay, maybe more than that, but they'd both been so young when they met, learning about the movies while they worked on the sets of the last black-and-white Westerns.

Jakob had gotten his start as a grip, slaving over the cranes, dollies, and tripods that let a camera see what it needed to see. Cully had parlayed his face into work as an extra. They'd moved up together. Just as Jakob landed a job as second assistant cameraman, Cully moved into speaking parts, and they accomplished those moves just in time for a seismic shift in Western films. When Hollywood shifted from movies about cowboys killing Indians toward films that recognized that the enemies they called "Indians" were in fact people, Cully was ready for starring roles and Jakob was ready to direct them.

Even more important to Cully's pocketbook, Jakob was the one who had realized that Cully's financial future rested in the slender wooden flutes that were never far from his hands. A run-of-the-mill horse opera became something sublime when Cully wrote the score. Other directors had stolen Jakob's idea, as people do in Hollywood, and Cully's career as a composer had gone into overdrive. It was possible that Cully himself didn't know how many Westerns he had scored.

The two of them had made their fortunes at the tail end of the popularity of cowboy movies, but their money spent just as well as the money made by people working in their heyday. And even during the dry years since then, movies set in the West still got made. More often than not, they got made by Jakob and scored by Cully.

These days, Cully took fewer and fewer jobs, spending most of his time alone in a studio filled with his Stone Age musical instruments and his Computer Age recording technology. Weeks, sometimes months, went by between phone calls, but Jakob figured that if he wasn't Cully's friend, then Cully didn't have any.

By the same logic, he no longer needed to ask Cully where his home was. If California wasn't home, then the man didn't have one.

Imagine his surprise when Cully stepped down from the rocks where he'd just finished playing. Raising his voice so that he could be heard over the nickering and stomping of the horses, he grabbed Jakob's shoulder and said, "I'm going home. Got my tickets bought and my bags packed."

Jakob couldn't imagine anything more unexpected coming out of his friend's mouth but, with his next words, Cully managed it.

"Why don't you come with me?"

There was only one answer worthy of a man who had been filming the cowboy ethos so long that he'd absorbed it, deep inside. Cully's story had taken a turn and he needed a sidekick. Jakob knew that he could act the part.

"Sure thing, pardner. Where, exactly, are we going?"

Cully looked at him as if to say, "How, after all these years, can you not know the answer to that question?" But he didn't say it. Maybe he remembered how thoroughly he had squelched Jakob's attempts to get him to talk about his growing-up years.

Instead, he just said, "Oklahoma," as if it were the only place in the world worthy of the word "home."

Chapter Two

The man standing in front of Faye Longchamp-Mantooth was movie-star handsome, which was only logical. He was, in fact, a movie star, and he'd been one for her entire life. His smile took her back to rainy childhood days in front of the television, wrapped in her grandmother's arms while they watched a steady stream of Western movies.

Faye's Mamaw had considered the films that she'd called "shoot-'em-ups" to be wholesome family fare, so Faye had seen the insides of a thousand fake saloons and brothels before she was ten. Cully Mantooth's manly form had graced more than a few of those establishments of sin.

Cully had never been a star of the first magnitude, because few men of color had managed that in those days, but he had made a career of stealing the show away from the stars whose names came first on the marquee. Faye imagined that the shelves in his home must groan under the weight of awards for Best Supporting Actor.

Mamaw, as a movie-loving woman of color, had possessed a discerning eye for scene-stealers like Cully, and he had been her favorite actor. This meant that he was still Faye's, and now here he stood. When Faye looked up at his familiar face, she was five years old again.

Cully's profile was still as sharp as a freshly struck coin. His stomach was flat and his back was unbowed. A few gray streaks showed in his long black hair and his trim goatee, but they looked like someone had carefully painted them, choosing the exact spots where a glimmer would call attention to his dark rugged face. And maybe someone had. Faye supposed that a movie star might have people whose only job was to paint each individual hair on his head and chin with its own perfect color.

The silver strands made Cully's black eyes sparkle. Even the faint wrinkles etched around those eyes and mouth were perfectly placed to make him look rugged but not old. Maybe he had surgeons who were good enough to make this so, but Faye was pretty sure that God was Cully's plastic surgeon.

Cully looked perfectly at home in the Art Deco fantasy of Oklahoma City's Gershwin Hotel. The hotel's lobby was awash in 1920s architectural details, its sweeping granite curves adorned with finely fretted bronze. It had been built during the years when Oklahoma was establishing itself as a center of the petroleum business, and the oil money showed. This was a lobby built for wheeling and dealing.

Faye supposed Cully must be nearly seventy by now. She did not care. She was a happily married woman, so she entertained no fantasies that went beyond chaste admiration. Still, in the spirit of chaste admiration, she hoped from the depths of her woman's heart that his voice sounded exactly like it did in the movies.

"You must be Faye."

His voice did sound exactly like it did in the movies. Resonant. Deep. Reedy.

"Excuse me," he went on. "I should have said Dr. Faye Longchamp-Mantooth. I hope you'll have time to talk archaeology with me while I'm in town, even though I'm a rank amateur."

Faye grasped his outstretched hand and nodded, still too starstruck to form a sentence. Cully had been dealing with star-struck fans for a very long time, so he covered for her ever-so-gracefully by turning to the hotel manager and asking if she'd mind taking their picture.

The young woman, whose elegant white jacket and crisp navy slacks looked like they'd been chosen to look fabulous in the hotel's gold-and-cobalt interior, folded her own phone shut, then did the kind of double-take that Cully must have seen a million times. Her face morphed from pleasant helpfulness to oh-my-God-I'm-talking-to-a-movie-star, but she recovered quickly. Flashing the lightning-bright smile of an experienced hospitality worker, she reached out a hand for Faye's phone and said, "Smile!"

When Cully Mantooth draped a fatherly arm around her, Faye realized with a sheepish thrill that she was going to have lifelong documentation that she'd been this close to a movie star.

Cully took Faye's phone from the adorably nervous hotel manager's outstretched hand and handed it back to her.

"I'm looking forward to meeting your husband, Joe. I understand that he's Sly's boy."

Faye had never told Joe about her hopeless infatuation with a movie star who just happened to have the same last name as they did, so Joe had never told her that Cully Mantooth was a distant cousin whom he had never met.

She found her voice. "Yes. Yes, he is. And you know—" She paused to study Cully's famous features. "I think he looks a little like you."

Cully chuckled. "Poor man." He held out a long narrow bag made of turquoise-colored flannel. Its mouth was pulled tight with a drawstring. "Your husband wanted me to give you this, but it's from him. An anniversary gift, I believe?"

"It is. Joe's outdone himself this year." She opened the bag and slid out a hollow shaft carved from rosy-brown cedar wood. Its surface was smoothly finished, and a series of holes drilled along one side revealed its purpose. It was an Indian flute, handmade by Cully himself.

When Joe got word that Cully was coming back to Oklahoma

City for his first visit in decades, he'd networked hard, tapping every connection he had in Creek country in hopes of finding someone who could put him directly in touch with his famous cousin. Faye was pleased—and, to be honest, she was spitefully pleased—that Joe's tribal connections had so successfully bypassed Cully's hyper-vigilant personal assistant, who had politely but firmly said no.

Thanks to Joe's persistence and to the all-knowing Creek grapevine, Faye's anniversary present had been this flute, which would be followed by three private lessons with the man himself. In other words, Joe had effectively won at gift-giving for the rest of their natural lives. The only conceivable way Faye could top this was to time-travel her husband back to the Stone Age, so that he could pick up some tips for chipping the awesomest spearhead ever made, directly from the lips of the people who invented stone tools.

The upheaval came as she was admiring her new flute, fitting her fingers over its open holes and testing its balance. In that cataclysmic moment, Faye's logic failed her. This is the way of upheavals.

She cradled the flute like a baby as she went down, sacrificing her own safety to protect it as her right elbow and shoulder and cheekbone crashed to a floor that was lushly padded with its luxurious golden rug, but not lushly enough to spare her the bruises that would come...if she lived.

Her free arm, the one not clutching the flute, flung itself out to her side, its hand scrabbling for something solid to hold her up. It extended past the edge of the rug, so the lower part of her left arm—elbow, forearm, wrist, and hand—struck the marble floor so hard that the pain rang like a crystal bell.

Everyone around her was dropping to the ground, and she had no idea why. Maybe they were all dead. Or dying.

There was a noise, or there had been. Something had overwhelmed her ears and her mind could no longer process sound.

Faye felt a slap across her back from shoulder to shoulder, and she retained enough awareness to know that Cully had reached out an arm of protection as he fell with her. It was the act of a man accustomed to protecting children. This made her realize that she had no idea whether Cully was a father or a grandfather. This was a thing that mattered when death loomed, creeping near enough to make her consider who would grieve for her if she died.

Joe would grieve her, of course. So would their children, Michael and Amande, and Joe's father, Sly, and her friends.

Loved ones had gone on before her—her mother, Mamaw, the father who had never come home from Vietnam, her loving mentor Douglass. Was she a moment away from seeing them again? And Cally, the great-great-grandmother whom Faye worshipped for freeing herself and a hundred others from slavery in 1800s Florida? Was there a place in Heaven where she would finally meet Cally?

Her brain gave up on making sequential memories, giving her only snapshots taken during the instant that she spent falling.

A woman, her coat collar still flipped up against the early fall chill, who stumbled as she made her way to the reception desk where a uniformed clerk waited.

The two clerks at the reception desk, a red-haired man and a graying woman, who disappeared behind the desk so suddenly that Faye couldn't tell whether they were falling or diving for cover.

The sweet-faced hotel manager, whose open phone dropped from her hand as she crumpled flat on the carpet.

The middle-aged woman wearing a cell phone earpiece, who was speaking to the air in one moment and collapsing to the ground in the next.

The man emerging from an alcove on the far side of the lobby, cowboy hat pulled low over his eyes, who took flight without warning, arms flailing as if to stop gravity from dragging him back down.

The two women wearing blue-and-white maids' uniforms

and carrying mops, one of them crumpling by the hotel's grand staircase and the other one miraculously upright as she stumbled over the shuddering floor.

The people standing in friendly conversational clumps who toppled to the floor, perfectly synchronized.

Faye wanted to wonder what was happening, but even wondering was beyond what her brain could do. It was rattled and still rattling. If her brain had been in working order, she could have come up with a long list of reasons why she might be lying facedown on the ground, gently keeping her flute from harm and cradled in the arms of a film star.

An earthquake.

A tornado.

A mass shooting.

A meteor strike.

A bolt of lightning.

A plane crashing through the roof of this magnificent building.

Catastrophic failure of the beams supporting that magnificent roof.

Any of these things might explain the rumbling beneath her and the deafening noise and the screams, but Faye's mind was too frayed to hold more than one thought. In Oklahoma City, where in 1995 a cold-blooded murderer brought down a tremendous building on the heads of hundreds of people who were peacefully living their lives, she had only one thought as she watched strangers cry out and collapse.

In Oklahoma City, when a human mind is trying to make sense of apocalypse, the first word that comes is "bomb."

Chapter Three

Evil must be obliterated.

This was the First New Commandment. He had repeated it to himself as he got on the bus, as he rode across town, and as he navigated a city sidewalk crowded with people. His backpack was heavy, but the First New Commandment had given him the strength to carry it as if it were made of feathers. Whenever his vitality flagged, he whispered it again and felt God lift him up on the wings of eagles.

Evil must be obliterated.

A doorman had opened the old hotel's heavy door for him, enabling him to pass through it quickly while intent on avoiding bellhops who might try to relieve him of the backpack. A maid and her mop were wetting down a segment of floor nearby that was marked by yellow signs reading, "Wet—Do Not Walk." The wet floor had been an unexpected obstacle, forcing him to walk down a path prescribed by someone else, but good fortune pointed that path in exactly the direction he wanted to go.

No, not good fortune. He was doing the work of the Lord, and the Lord was not going to let him be impeded by a thin skim of water on old marble.

Once past the unexpectedly wet floor, he had let himself slow perceptibly, because he couldn't afford to be singled out for behaving oddly. His goal had been to be unnoticeable, even innocuous, until that moment when it was impossible for anyone to ignore the momentous thing he had done.

He had adjusted the cowboy hat and lowered his chin, just as he had rehearsed. He'd been told where the security cameras were, so he had practiced using the hat's brim to shield his face from the government agents who would soon be looking for him.

He had forced himself to meander, drifting first to the glass-fronted showcase by the elevators. It was full of musical memorabilia—George Gershwin's watch, Ira Gershwin's notebook, a photo of their childhood home—and he'd lingered there as if he were interested in century-old trash. Then he had paused to admire a bronze statue and a monumental floral display and a glossy black piano, each stop taking him closer to his destination. Finally, he had drifted toward another display case that was tucked in an out-of-the-way alcove because it was full of less interesting memorabilia from the history of the old hotel—quaint china, monogrammed napkins, telegrams from famous people.

He'd lingered there until another hotel maid, barely ten feet from him, finished mopping the marble floor and moved away. Again, the wet floor acted in his favor, keeping others from passing close enough to see his next move, which was to tap gently on the wall. He'd been told exactly which spots to tap on the richly gleaming mahogany paneling, and the instructions proved sound. The panel slid into the wall, revealing an old brick staircase leading down into darkness.

Two steps had taken him through the opening and two more taps on the wall had closed it behind him, shutting him into the catacombs that had rested beneath Oklahoma City for almost as long as there had been an Oklahoma City. Local children had told stories about the monsters lurking under the city for decades. They'd had no idea that the monsters weren't real but that their tunnels were.

His heart had been light because he had known that vengeance was coming. His steps had been light, too, as they took him down the stairs, toward the door that he had been assured would be unlocked, as it had been in 1992 when he last saw it from this side.

And it was indeed unlocked. The door had opened easily, with only a slight grinding of wood on sandy brick. This was the gateway to his victory.

Once through, he had stood in front of two more doors, one in front of him and one opening into a corridor at his left. He had paused to fumble for his compass. Where was it? Not in his backpack, no. He had no desire to disturb the device there, built to help him do God's work.

The device—crafted of a pressure cooker and powered by black powder—was designed to destroy everything above the spot where it exploded. He had built it by instructions available to anyone on the internet, crafting an ignition device from a cell phone and a string of Christmas lights. Though he would gladly have sacrificed his life to bring down this particular building, the device was built to be detonated remotely. He was at no risk. His mission was to place it, get clear, and then use the cell phone in his pocket to set it off.

Poised on the brink of victory, he had pulled the compass from his pocket and studied it. Not liking the direction of its needle, he had tapped it firmly with his index finger, then tried again. The needle didn't budge.

There had been two available paths, a door ahead of him and another to his left. His instructions were to take the door to the left, but the compass reading had told him that the IRS building was behind him and to the right. Could the maps he'd been given be this far wrong? This was an important problem, important enough to abort the mission until he could be sure of hitting the target.

But first, before aborting his mission and going back topside, he had wanted to see the work of his hands again. He had opened the other door, the one directly at the bottom of the stairs, and taken three steps through it. His eyes had traveled the room's walls, the floor, the ceiling, everywhere but the bench to the right of the door. He never wanted to think of the things that he had put there, not ever again.

But every other surface in that room, every square inch of it, was still covered with his paintings, and their colors shone as brilliantly as ever. He had soaked in the beauty of his work, the lush countryside of his farm and the faces of his family. He had given thanks that the plan had never involved setting a bomb off in that sacred spot.

Then, he had spun on his heel, feeling the heft of the backpack and its cargo of death. Passing back through the doorway, he had closed the heavy door behind him, for no reason other than that he was an essentially orderly person. The wasted seconds that he spent closing it saved a half-dozen lives.

Taking the stairs slowly, he and the bomb had risen toward the surface. His deliberate motion had consumed more seconds, and thus saved more lives.

He had reached out a hand, tapped the door, and watched it slide into the wall again. The maid standing nearby had dropped her mop and run hard at the sight of someone materializing out of nowhere, and this bothered him. He'd been told that the alcove would be clear and that he wouldn't be seen.

A single step had put him barely through the doorframe when the bomb went off. In the few milliseconds left to him, he just had time after the world-rattling blast to wonder how the bomb could blow when he hadn't touched the cell phone rigged to trigger it.

Nevertheless, it blew. Nature was merciful enough to throw him quickly into shock, but not so merciful that he didn't feel an impact like a runaway freight train hitting him from behind and not so merciful that he didn't feel the horror of impending death, even if only for an instant.

The alcove's stout walls, constructed at a time when everything was built stoutly, had contained much of the explosive force in three directions, behind him, to his left, and to his right, focusing the blast in one direction. The blast carried him out of the alcove where the bomb did most of its damage, blowing a hole in an exterior wall that opened the hotel's lobby to the autumn breezes. One of the walls enclosing the alcove was obliterated, too.

The nails packed into the homemade bomb burst out into the world, accompanied by twisted pieces of the pressure cooker itself. Small fires erupted around the spot where he'd been standing before his body went airborne. Plaster fell from walls and from the ceiling high above him. A tremendous chandelier plummeted, adding its crystal prisms to the flying nails.

The bomb landed a fierce attack on the old building, which suffered grievous damage, but the people in it were protected by its thick masonry walls and by fate. Perhaps this was the worst insult fate could have dealt him. No one other than himself was killed by his rage, and this was a terrible end for a man whose life had been consumed by the hatred in his heart. He had used its flame to emotionally maim everyone who knew him, and now he had missed his chance to physically maim a lobby full of innocent people.

The world was still rumbling when he died. Ashes were settling around him, but his thoughts were no longer coherent enough to remember the phrase, "Ashes to ashes and dust to dust." He had no more thoughts at all.

His hatred winked out of existence when he did. He simply was, and then he was not, and the world kept turning without him.

Chapter Four

"Sorry, but I gotta shine this in your eye."

Faye wasn't sure how long she'd been waiting on this city sidewalk to see the paramedic who was checking her pupils. It had been an hour, maybe two, because others had needed help far more than Faye.

At first, the medical personnel had struggled in the chaos of rubberneckers. Even after the first responders had moved bystanders out of the way and established a perimeter to control access to the site, and even after an impressive convoy of FBI vehicles had sped to the scene, there had been the problem of locating survivors. Many of them had picked themselves up off the floor, running blindly as far and as fast as their injuries would allow. Now they had to be found before they could be treated or interviewed as witnesses. Some of them had evaded medical personnel completely until they were located by the FBI agents sweeping the area around the Gershwin Hotel, looking for accomplices. Or for additional bombs set, God forbid, to blow up the survivors as they fled. Considering all the confusion, Faye thought that an hour or two was probably an appropriate amount of time for someone with no obvious injuries to wait for emergency services.

Nevertheless, however long Faye's wait had been, she should have waited longer. Cully was pushing seventy. He should have been checked out before her.

She opened her mouth to say so, then she saw Cully's solicitous face looming over her. He came from a generation that did things differently. The psyche of a man of his age was tattooed with the chivalrous notion of "Ladies first." Cully would have died before he got between a woman and emergency medical care. He would literally have lain on the ground and bled out before he let that happen.

Faye had her own brand of chivalry and it told her to stuff the desire to say, "Did you notice how old this man is? Look at him first!"

Faye eyeballed Cully herself. He was walking without a limp, so at least he hadn't broken a hip. His eyes were focused and their pupils weren't dilated. He made sense when he talked. She remembered him lifting her from the rubble-strewn carpet with two strong hands. Maybe he was okay.

Cully saw her scrutinizing him and waved away her concern. "I've probably got some bruises, but everything works," he said, and he demonstrated it by breaking into a jig. Faye was pretty sure she'd seen him dance a jig in *Beyond A Golden Sky*, distracting the bad guys while his buddy got away. She was also pretty sure that *Beyond A Golden Sky* had been filmed before she was born.

Cully didn't dance long. He was obviously favoring a knee and he was breathing a little hard when he was done, but just those few steps had succeeded in attracting a few dozen people. They stood just on the other side of the crime scene tape that separated the witnesses and victims from the curious bystanders. They stared, murmuring, "Is that...? I think it is!" Most of them were of retirement age, but not all. Cully's fame had filtered into the next generation, and the next. Faye thought that Oklahoma City was probably a hotbed of Western movie fans, and this made her wonder why it had been so long since Cully visited his childhood home.

He gave his fans a smile and a nod, but his attention was focused on Faye and he was revealing himself as a micromanager. "She hit the ground hard. Face-first. Did you check her neck? And she hasn't had much to say. I mean nothing, really. Do you think she has a concussion?"

Faye was pretty sure that all composers were micromanagers. Who else would be interested in telling every last person in an orchestra what to do and when?

"Probably shock," the paramedic said. "Can you say something for me, ma'am?"

Faye was pretty sure Cully was exaggerating until she tried to speak and nothing came out but "Check ma flllt."

The paramedic looked concerned. "Maybe she does have a concussion."

Cully understood her, and he responded like a father whose teenager had turned bullheaded. "Don't be stupid. Your flute is fine. I'm worried about your head. I can always make you a new flute."

Faye felt the power of speech returning. "Yeah. But I like this one."

She remembered hitting the floor, then a timeless instant of nothing. She had opened her eyes while smoke was still rising and people were still pushing themselves up on all fours. Those who could run were still running, so the moment of blackness obscuring her memory couldn't have lasted long. She was conscious before the sirens began to scream, with no thought in her head beyond, *I have to get out of here before things get worse.*

When her head began to clear, the need for flight became even more obvious. Any fool could have seen that running was the smart thing to do. People were sprinting down the grand staircase and running for the huge, heavy doors of the lobby's monumental entrance. Faye saw one of them literally hurdle an old man lying stunned on the floor.

She remembered trying to work herself to an upright position, planning to run as far as her feet would take her. Unfortunately, those feet had turned out to be attached to legs made of jelly. Without Cully's hands grasping her armpits and lifting her to her feet, Faye would still have been lying on the plush golden carpet, covered with ash. By the time he got her upright, she was clearheaded enough to realize that they couldn't leave yet. They needed to check on the people still lying facedown in the debris.

Together, she and Cully had staggered across the lobby to check on those people, one by one. Across the room, she saw a young woman doing the same and the gray-haired hotel clerk and a teenaged boy. Miraculously, the five of them had found that all of the wounded and stunned people still lying on the floor were alive. Even more miraculously, they'd all been more or less ambulatory. Working together, everybody had been able to get out of the building.

All but one.

Only when she found herself standing next to the only corpse in the room did Faye know for sure what had happened. The condition of the body, the pattern of the damage radiating outward from it, the remnants of a backpack still attached to the remnants of his torso, all of these things had told the story of a bomber. Presumably a suicide bomber. Looking up at the ceiling stretching two stories above the lobby, painted with the stars of a western sky, she saw the soot of a tremendous blast. Only a bomb could do that.

Faye knew that she was literally shell-shocked. Looking at the bomber's corpse had made her hope with all her heart that her memory would be affected by the blast. She would have happily sacrificed a few brain cells to ensure that she lost the memory of that one torn body. She wanted to hate the dead man for the thing he had just done, and she knew that she eventually would. At that moment, though, she'd just wanted to run hard from the scattered pieces of him.

"Squeeze my hand," the paramedic said, bringing her back to

the sidewalk and chasing away, for a time, the memory of a body utterly destroyed. Faye looked around, nervous, until she remembered that a bomb squad had swept up and down this street, so she could be pretty sure that there wasn't a second bomb waiting to annihilate the people who survived the first one.

"He wants you to squeeze his hand," Cully repeated.

"I heard him," Faye snapped.

"Wonderful," someone said. "She can still snarl. She'll be herself again any minute now."

Faye looked toward the voice and saw a familiar face that she'd thought she might never see again. She had worked with FBI Agent Tom Bigbee to solve a very cold case in east Oklahoma—and by very cold, she meant twenty-nine years cold—just a few months before. Ordinarily, Bigbee had a face like a beige rock. It was the kind of face that made suspects talk because its very stillness freaked them out. Today, Bigbee was smiling, and that was just weird.

He rushed toward her, right hand thrust forward to shake hers.

"I'm so happy to see you sitting out here, safe. Are you all right?" He looked her up and down. "No bleeding. No broken bones." He gave the paramedic a nervous glance. "Right?"

The paramedic nodded, then gave him a dismissive hand gesture that said, "Would you get out of my way?"

Bigbee stepped back and let the paramedic resume prodding Faye. "I saw your name on the triage list *and* on the list of witnesses to interview, so I volunteered to be the one who took your statement."

He let his face return to its rock-like normal state and turned it toward the paramedic. "You've done a full workup? A careful one? You'll never meet a sharper mind than this one, so you might not notice if she were having neurological problems. If it weren't for Dr. Faye, a murdered woman in Sylacauga would have never gotten justice."

The confident young man stammered in the face of Bigbee's

judgment. "I'm not a doctor, but—um—I don't think she has a concussion and—um—I see no signs of internal injuries or broken bones."

Bigbee kept his blistering stare on him and said, "The FBI wants to know how this woman is."

The stammering resumed in earnest. "Um—I'm—I'm not a doctor, so I can't render that kind of opinion but—" He caved under Bigbee's glare. "She seems okay to me."

The federal agent waved the words away. "I don't want to hear 'seems okay.' I want to hear your professional opinion. Is this woman physically and neurologically okay to work?"

The paramedic gave up trying to play by the rules. "Yes. She is."

"I came looking for you for a reason, Faye," Bigbee said. "Well, I wanted to make sure you were okay, but I also had a professional reason. The bomb uncovered something that's historical for sure and, in a way, I think it's archaeological. You're already in the Bureau's system as a consultant and I know personally that there are none better than you. I've recommended you to Assistant Special Agent in Charge Micah Ahua, and he agrees that we can use your skills. Can we hire you to consult on an extremely oddball situation?"

"Oddball seems to be what I do best."

He beckoned and walked away without looking behind him. Faye shot a nervous glance at Cully and the paramedic, then she followed.

———

As Faye grew nearer to the site of the bombing, she got a closer look at the people investigating it and at their tools. She could see the FBI's Mobile Command Center, a tricked-out gray semi that she imagined to be full of high-tech gadgets and serious-faced agents. Another truck, black and almost as big as the command center, boasted in big gold letters that it housed the FBI Bomb

Squad. The Technical Hazard Response Unit had its own vehicle, and so did the Evidence Response Team. It comforted Faye to see how many resources the FBI could put on-scene and how fast they could do it.

"The SWAT team and the Bomb Squad made fast work of clearing the hotel and the buildings in the vicinity," Bigbee said. "Now the evidence response people are doing what they do and things will be moving a lot more slowly. It takes a long time to clear out a bombing site when the piece of evidence that will solve a crime might measure a centimeter across."

Faye thought of the way she excavated an archaeological site, sometimes removing soil a few grains at a time, if that's what it took to do the job. Evidence retrieval was the same kind of destructive technology. When you're doing the kind of work that can't be undone, you do it slowly.

The SWAT Team and the Bomb Squad hadn't found any other bombs or any other bombers, so the FBI had cordoned off an area in the immediate vicinity of the Gershwin Hotel. Outside of that area, the rest of Oklahoma City was now free to get back to normal, or at least to try. She knew this because Cully had been streaming newscasts on his phone since they were detained in this no-man's-land reserved for witnesses, away from the bomb site but not free to go.

Faye hadn't seen her own phone since the blast, so she guessed it was one more piece of evidence on the floor of the Gershwin Hotel's bombed-out lobby. She could only watch the FBI agents at work. Years of training were obvious in the confident way they moved, like dancers who knew their choreography cold. You can't fake competence, and these people were utterly competent.

Cully and his phone were behind her as Bigbee led her toward the Mobile Command Center. Once there, she was greeted by an intimidating array of computers and other high-tech devices she didn't recognize, all of them being operated by people who looked far too busy and competent to bother with her. As it turned out, the one person who didn't consider himself too busy doing important things to give her the time of day was, in fact, pretty darn important.

He was a thin, dark-skinned man in late middle age. His hair was trimmed so closely that the curl barely showed, and his expression was sober. Sitting in front of a computer display, he had the shiny shoes and close-to-the-vest poise that screamed FBI agent. As it turned out, he was an FBI agent plus some.

He stood up, extended a hand to shake hers, then gestured toward an empty chair next to his. As Faye sank into it, her weary legs failed and she hit the seat with an uncomfortable thump.

"Dr. Longchamp-Mantooth," he said, "I'm Micah Ahua and I'm an Assistant Special Agent in Charge for the Oklahoma City field office of the FBI. I know you've been through a lot this morning, but we could use your help."

"I'll do anything it takes to find out what happened today."

"I'm told you saw the bomber?"

"Only for an instant when he was alive." *And in one piece.*

"That's what all the witnesses are saying, but Bigbee says you're the kind of person who will remember more detail."

"Maybe, I think I may remember seeing him just as the bomb went off, but he wasn't anywhere near the rest of us. I think he was the man I saw across the room, wearing a cowboy hat. It's hard to be sure, considering the difference between what he looked like before the bomb went off and what he looked like afterward."

"That's good information. The other witnesses are too shaken up to remember even that much."

Faye tried to picture the hotel lobby, with its grand staircase and ostentatious bronze elevator doors. "If I'm remembering the right guy, he wasn't near the desk where people were checking in. He wasn't in the main lobby where there are lots of chairs and sofas. He wasn't by the stairs. He wasn't near the elevators. He was in an empty alcove where there was…well…nothing that I could see. Maybe some display cases, but nothing else. Nothing to do, nothing to see, and no place to hide. No reason to be there."

"Well, bombers don't usually do their thing in the middle of a crowd."

"Yeah, but what was he going to do? Just put the bomb on the floor and walk away? Even the Boston Marathon guys hid their bombs in a trash can. Was he a suicide bomber? Even if he was, that alcove makes no sense as a place to blow yourself up on purpose. If you want to take somebody with you, doesn't it make sense to go stand where the people are?"

"I don't know the answers to your questions. I do know that I wish all my witnesses had your powers of observation. And that they were half as logical."

Faye laughed. "When I'm stressed, I fall back on logic. And I'm pretty stressed. See me sitting here all calm and collected? This is what I look like when I'm having a nervous breakdown."

A disembodied voice emanated from behind a computer display. "Are we having nervous breakdowns? Is it time for mine?"

Even Bigbee smiled, but he didn't loosen up enough to admit that he might enjoy a small breakdown.

"Not yet, Liu," Ahua said. "And I hope you'll put your breakdown on hold, Dr. Longchamp-Mantooth. I didn't call you in here so I could ask you the same questions that people have been asking you all morning."

"All morning?? Has it been that long since the blast?"

He gave a single nod. "Time is a weird thing during a catastrophe like this. The mind shuts down from time to time, just to try to make sense of things. At least, that's the way I think of it. An expert might describe it differently. Sometimes, it can make it really hard to gather consistent testimony from a group of traumatized people. In any case, our evidence recovery team uncovered something really weird while they were conducting interviews and I'd like an archaeologist's eyes on it."

Faye had been wondering why Ahua had called her into the FBI's inner sanctum.

Ahua used the computer keyboard in front of him to pull up a photo on a large computer display. On the screen was a photo of the damage done to the side wall of the Gershwin Hotel's lobby.

The bomb had taken out a chunk of the hotel's stone wall, but the rest of the ninety-year-old wall looked sturdy and strong. On either side of the open hole, buttresses of hand-laid stones provided enough support to keep the wall vertical. They were helped along by more buttresses built at regular intervals down the entire length of the side wall.

In the screen's lower right-hand corner, Faye saw a tremendous cornerstone chiseled with the names of people who were probably very important in 1927. It had done its job of holding the corner level and square, supporting more stone blocks than Faye could count.

Ahua pulled up another photo, shot through the open hole in the wall. Faye could see through it and into the hotel lobby, and this outside-in view was disorienting. The floor was heaped with chunks of metal, glass, charred wood, and stone, all of it twisted and blasted into bits.

The camera had caught two crime scene technicians at work. One of them was squatting down to mark a barely visible clue with a cone. Another one crouched on all fours, his face close to the floor but not touching it. Faye couldn't quite make out the evidence he was studying, but it looked like something that was mere millimeters in diameter.

Above the technicians, Faye could see that a section of the bronze gallery railing encircling the lobby was warped and twisted. Blackened carpet showed that there had been a fire at ground level, but it must have been quickly contained, because only the portion of the cavernous room nearest the blast was scorched. Farther away, heavy tables lay on their sides where they had been heaved. A fallen chandelier had sprayed crystal prisms everywhere.

Now Ahua pulled up another photo, taken at the epicenter of the destruction, just inside the hole in the wall. Faye could see that the bomb had blasted away several of the floor's marble tiles. This was no surprise, given the strength of the blast. The surprise came when he pulled up yet another photo, taken by a camera pointing straight down into the hole. The crime scene photographer had done a great job of using flash for illumination, but she couldn't see the bottom, because the hole just kept going.

It extended into a darkness almost deep enough to hide a staircase that the missing floor tiles had covered. Faye, too excited to craft actual words, flapped a hand at the screen.

Ahua used the computer keyboard to enlarge the high-definition photo to show details of brickwork so intricate that it was surely built when labor was really cheap. Judging by the age of much of downtown Oklahoma City, Faye would have guessed that the staircase was built after World War I and before the Great Depression.

Ahua flipped to another photo, an extreme closeup of a single brick's orange-red and crumbling clay. As Faye had suspected, the brick itself was obviously made by hand. She said, "Would you look at that?"

"So it's old?" Ahua said. "As old as the hotel?"

"Oh, yeah," Faye said. "It's not even out of the question that those bricks and that staircase are older than the hotel. Can you show me where the stairs are in relation to the rest of the lobby?"

Ahua picked up a felt-tip marker and moved to a whiteboard. With a few deft strokes, he drew the square lobby and sketched the monumental entryway at the bottom of the whiteboard. He drew the staircase near the middle of the left wall and looked up expectantly.

"Wait," Faye said. "I need to fill in some details. The front desk is here, right?" she said, pointing to a spot near the top of the whiteboard. "The elevators and fire escapes are behind it. The grand staircase is here," she said, pointing to a spot near the center of the square room. "Or it was. Is the staircase still standing?"

Ahua nodded and drew in those details. "The building didn't sustain much structural damage. Buttressed stone walls are pretty sturdy and the bomb wasn't built to take down a building. It was a people-killer."

The word made Faye shiver.

"The Technical Hazardous Response Unit was able to clear us for entry fairly quickly," Ahua continued, "because they judged that the building wasn't in any danger of collapse. When they sent me these photos, I knew I wanted to get some expert eyes on them. Bigbee told me that somebody who did this kind of work was sitting right outside and…well. Here you are."

Faye was studying his sketch. "The alcove? The one that was on top of the old staircase?"

"Some of those walls are gone, but they weren't load-bearing." He roughed in some walls, marking the destroyed sections with dotted lines. Faye was relieved to see that her memory of the lobby's layout was reliable, despite the fact that the bomb had given her brain a big jolt.

"Can we go look at the underground staircase? I really want to see it in person." Faye asked, knowing that the realities of crime scenes and evidence protection meant that the answer would be no. Still, she burned to see those stairs.

"I'm sorry," Ahua said, confirming what she already knew, "but we have to protect the integrity of our data collection efforts. All I can do is show you these pictures, but that staircase is in a very significant spot, and it's obviously very old. What can you as an archaeologist tell me about it?"

Faye kept silent and thought for a minute. Ordinarily, she would have guessed that the staircase's purpose was to access the hotel's basement, except for the fact that it led away from the center of the room, extending under the plane of the exterior wall. From there, it kept going, heading toward the hotel next door. It didn't make sense for there to be a basement running outside the Gershwin Hotel's footprint, underneath the narrow sidewalk between the two buildings. Nevertheless, there the staircase was. It had to go somewhere. And Faye had a pretty good idea where.

Agent Liu had gotten up from her station and come to peer at the photos with them. Ahua hadn't asked her to join them, but he didn't ask her to leave, either.

Liu didn't seem to be big on keeping silent and thinking. For an FBI agent, she seemed almost chatty. "You know," she said, "that staircase has gotta be more than seventy years old. I guess those stairs could even be older than the hotel, in theory, if it was built on the site of an older building with a basement."

"Could be. Or it could have been dug after the building was built. This hotel's been here since before the Depression and that was a long time ago," Faye said. "I don't know why you'd dig a hole through the floor of an existing building and build a staircase to…somewhere…but it's as likely as any other theory. Or unlikely. There are a lot of unlikely stories about underground Oklahoma City."

Nobody bit at the bait Faye was dangling. It was hard to make a dramatic revelation when the people around her didn't respond to conversational cues.

Liu caught her eye, so Faye thought that maybe one person in the command center had heard of the crackpot theory she was about to parrot.

"Why would someone want to get into one building's basement from the first floor of its next-door neighbor?" Ahua asked.

"Maybe the two buildings were owned by the same person and he saved money by building a single basement?" Faye offered. Then she decided to go for the gusto and blurt out her implausible theory. "Another possible explanation involves one of Oklahoma City's oldest urban legends. And this legend has the advantage of being true."

Ahua was watching her silently as she spoke. It suddenly struck her that it must be very hard to be married to someone who controlled information so well. His expression gave her the oddest feeling that he already knew what she was going to say. The feeling was especially odd because what she was about to say was something flat-out weird. "In the early twentieth century, a community of perhaps two hundred people lived underground in this part of the city."

One of the agents working at a computer station at the other end of the command center snickered. "Like moles?"

"No," Faye said. "Like people who lived in basements because they were Chinese and they had trouble getting landlords to rent them apartments with amenities like…you know…daylight. Not to mention that they were working for people who wouldn't pay them enough to afford anything *but* a cold bare room in somebody else's basement. Still, they were hardworking people. And enterprising. They found a way to do better for themselves."

"By living underground?" the disbelieving agent asked.

"You're not from around here, are you?" Liu asked.

He shook his head.

"Historians think that they started out by simply enlarging their basement apartments, digging out into the surrounding dirt," Faye explained. "Eventually, their burrows starting encroaching on each other and became tunnels. Then they enlarged the tunnels and made rooms that were really pretty big, according to eyewitnesses, when you consider that they were carved out of dirt. We have government records that say this is true."

Liu asked. "I've heard of the Chinese underground all my life. Most of us in the local Chinese community know about it. It's a small community. When we have urban legends, everybody knows them. Still, I didn't know there were actual documents saying that it was real, other than stories told by people like my grandparents."

"Yep," Faye said. "The health department went down there in 1921 and wrote a report that said two hundred were living down there in very clean conditions."

Ahua didn't react.

"It's true," Faye insisted. "We have the health department report from 1921, and we have newspaper photos taken of the space in 1969, years after it was abandoned."

"I believe you," Ahua said. "I'm not from the Chinese community, but I was a nerdy little kid living here in 1969. I'd forgotten all about it until you and Liu started talking, but I remember seeing a picture of a mysterious underground staircase in the paper. It looked like this one, but they're not the same. I guess that makes sense. There must have been more entrances to a space that big."

Smiling like a man with a secret, he clicked the mouse and another photo covered the screen.

It was a closeup of the top two brick stairs. A handful of papers, yellowed and blotched with water stains, lay flung against the side walls of the stairwell. Attracted by their obvious age, Faye took a step closer, as if by doing that she could reach down and pick up a sheet.

Squinting at the screen, Liu too moved nearer. "That's Chinese script. Cantonese."

Faye didn't read Cantonese, so she stepped aside and let Liu study the pictographs.

"My friend Stacy Wong is going to have a coronary when she sees this," Faye said. She reached in her pocket for her phone, so she could take a picture of the picture and remembered, again, that she hadn't seen it since the blast. "Stacy teaches in the university down in Norman, not an hour from here, but she may be in town by now. She's a speaker at the conference I'm supposed to be attending tomorrow."

Faye figured that the odds of the conference taking place approached zero, so her trip to Oklahoma might have been for nothing. "Stacy's official specialty is the history of the petroleum industry in Oklahoma," she said, "but she's got a private historical obsession and Oklahoma City's underground Chinatown is it."

Ahua said, "I'll want you to get an interview with Dr. Wong, Bigbee. Her knowledge sounds useful."

"I've never met Stacy Wong in person," Faye said, "but I'm looking forward to it. She and I have been internet buddies for a long time. Stacy's not the only one obsessed with Oklahoma's underground Chinatown. We've both done a deep dive into the available information, and it has been really fun to compare notes with her."

"Don't all academics have those non-academic private obsessions?" Liu asked. "I think they crop up right after somebody hangs the title 'PhD' on them."

"We know we're supposed to have a specialty," Faye said, "but we want to have *all* the specialties. I guess we're just afraid of missing out."

Liu walked even closer to the photo, bringing the Cantonese script right up to her eyes.

"Can you read it?" Ahua asked.

"A little," she said. "It's a flyer advertising a laundry, which tracks with what we know about the underground community."

"Tell me what you know. Both of you," Ahua said.

"In the late sixties," Faye said, "there was a lot of urban renewal going on in downtown Oklahoma City. They were getting ready to build a convention center, not far from here."

"I was a kid, but I remember when they put in the convention center," Ahua said.

"I wasn't born yet," Liu said, "but I've heard all about it from my family. Some of my ancestors go back to the 1800s in Oklahoma City."

"Lucky you. My ancestors are of no use to us here," Ahua said. "They're all in Nigeria, except for my mother and father. They came to the U.S. before I was born, but we didn't move to Oklahoma City until I was five, after my father finished his surgical residency in Chicago. I do remember those newspaper pictures, though. I distinctly remember a photo of an old oil stove that people had used to cook and stay warm."

Bigbee held up his phone. On its face was a black-and-white photo from a 1960s-era newspaper. A man in a suit held a flashlight to illuminate an iron cookstove, its oven door hanging open. Faye had studied the photo on her own phone so many times that she didn't need to look at it to know the details it showed.

"That's the exact picture," Ahua said. "The internet is amazing."

Faye waved her hand at the brand-new photo of the laundry flyers. "Maybe they used the stove to heat water for washing clothes."

"Maybe," Ahua said. "I also remember a picture that showed papers tacked to the wall that looked a lot like the one you're holding. The newspaper said that those flyers advertised a gambling hall."

Faye remembered that photo, too.

Liu was scrolling through her phone for more pictures. "My grandparents said that there were huge rooms down there and tiny cells where people slept, one after another after another."

"Where's that stairway?" Ahua asked. "The one that they found in the sixties. Could it be a back door into this crime scene? Did the bomber use it to access the hotel lobby?"

Faye shook her head. "There's no way to know where those stairs were. Just a few days after the developers found the entrance in 1969, city leaders decided to go ahead with construction. They built over the only known entrance to underground Chinatown."

Ahua looked stricken. "I'm really glad nobody told me that when I was a kid. The underground city was as real to me as Jurassic Park was to my kids."

"The Chinese underground community was real," Liu said. "The rooms where they lived were real. Growing up, I knew people who had actually been down there, even lived down there."

"They're still real," Faye said. "Stacy and I talk about this all the time. All the city did was seal one entrance, but there were others. We know that from eyewitness testimony. The city wouldn't have expended the time and expense to fill the tunnels in, not when they had a convention center to build. The underground rooms are still down there. They have to be."

"No wonder you said Dr. Wong would have a coronary when she saw this," Ahua said.

"May I send her a picture and ask her to come take a look?" Faye asked.

"I can't let you send anybody a picture, but you can call Dr. Wong and tell her I have some questions for her. Tell her to hurry. I don't want to be just another idiot destroying history while I'm cracking this case."

———

Cully Mantooth supposed that the FBI had gotten all the information from him that they thought they were going to get, so he had been released. He had nowhere to go, since they still hadn't released his hotel suite to him, but there were worse problems to have on a day when he might have been maimed or killed by a bomb. He was perfectly happy to homestead the sidewalk bench where he sat, watching people walk by and admiring the well-preserved historic structures and modern buildings of this city that had once been his home. It was also a vantage point for trying to see what was happening at the Gershwin down the street.

Every now and then, a passer-by recognized him and gave him a smile, but now one of them had worked up the nerve to come ask for an autograph. His pleasant interlude was officially over. A small crowd began to gather.

It was strange for Cully to realize that these people were happy to see him, excited even. When he was a kid growing up in Oklahoma City, he'd never felt that anybody was happy to see him.

No, that wasn't true. His mother was always happy to see him, every day of their life together. It was the happiness of a quiet woman who had been taught to keep her emotions to herself, but it showed in her eyes and in her gentle touch. His father was never a talkative man, either, but he'd lavished time on his only child and he had laughed a lot. From where Cully sat, he'd say that was good enough. He'd never had any reason to doubt his father's love.

Cully's father had started teaching him to play the flute when his fingers were barely big enough to cover the holes. When the time came, he had taught him to make flutes, too. Only a person with a finely tuned sense of musical pitch and a real knack for working with wood could make a flute with good intonation and a pleasing tone. Cully had inherited both from his father, not to mention the ability to sit down at a piano and play any tune he'd ever heard. He was also a fearsome sight-reader, because his dad had hired the church pianist to make sure his son learned to play the music inside him and then write it down for everybody else.

What had he inherited from his mother? If he were to be honest with himself, probably everything else. He was quiet, for sure. He was a good enough actor to smile and be affable with strangers who never seemed to notice how rarely he laughed. Like his mother, he was capable of a deep and abiding love that didn't show unless you looked really closely. Like her, he could make a killer pot of *yan du xian*, though he had never learned her secret for frying chicken feet. But perhaps he was most like her in his sense of otherness. In the tiny Chinese community of Oklahoma City, having a Creek father made him feel set apart.

There were plenty of Creeks in Oklahoma, so his father's world was assuredly not tiny. It was made of what seemed like a million old friends and distant cousins. Cully knew a lot of them, and he liked most of them, but he couldn't be a registered member of the Muscogee Creek tribe without the requisite paperwork. And his Chinese mother was a complication in the Creek nation's matrilineal culture. Not that the paperwork and the matrilineal thing were the be-all and end-all of being Creek. And not that there weren't a lot of Creeks, with and without the paperwork, who had ancestors from Europe and Africa and probably China, too. Despite those things, Cully felt set apart.

Maybe Cully's alienation came from inside him and not from the Creek and Chinese communities that were, in truth, very loving toward him. Somehow, all that love never stanched his feeling that he was different, deep-down, and there was nothing he could do about it.

Outside the walls of his childhood home, he'd been a community of one. His father had seen this and he'd tried to fix it, but sending him to a Creek boarding school had been a really bad idea. Cully had made trouble there for a few years, then he'd run away to California at the first opportunity.

And now here he stood, surrounded by people who wanted his autograph and didn't seem to care whether he preferred chicken feet or fry bread. Each of them returned his smile, and he'd wager that none of them noticed that he never laughed.

Chapter Five

Evil must be obliterated.

I learned those words at my father's knee. I was taught to use them in prayer and in worship, but I never found them particularly useful in the day-to-day world. At least not until now.

Certainly, I have seen evil. Ever since childhood, I have known it for what it was, but what can a child do against utter darkness?

Nothing. Absolutely nothing.

To successfully strike out against evil requires an adult's ability to plan. It requires an adult understanding of the world as it is, and it requires an adult's craving for a different world, one that makes sense.

Like most things in this flawed and nonsensical world, it requires cold, hard cash.

Still, I have done it. I acquired the cash. I formulated the plan. I implemented the plan, manipulating a doomed man into believing that he was going to take down the freaking IRS with a wholly inadequate bomb. I successfully implemented every step of my plan, even to the point of wandering around underground.

All along, I pretended to get my orders from some unnamed commander. Lonnie never bothered to hide the fact that he thought I was stupid, when he was the most demonstrably stupid person in his own life. And now, at the end, he came close to killing innocent people because he failed to follow through on the single task I gave him to do. Now I am burdened with cleaning up the mess he left behind and making certain that no clues remain to lead the FBI to me or to the innocents I must protect.

Despite these concerns, I must pause for a moment and allow myself some self-praise. I have obliterated the evil that has shadowed my entire life.

And yet there is still evil. I sit, even now, with a newspaper draped across my lap like an apron, and its pages are drenched with evil. The faces of refugees, some of them children and all of them hungry, look out of its pages. Wounded civilians limp across those pages. Beside them are wounded soldiers with very young faces who deserve to be at home with their families. I see photos of mass murderers, corrupt government officials, petty thieves, and I don't know how to obliterate them all. I have only ever known how to obliterate the one evil man, and I have done it. I have nothing left but emptiness.

Now what?

Chapter Six

Joe Wolf Mantooth didn't know where his wife was, and he was beside himself. He'd been hours east of Oklahoma City when he heard about the bombing. He hadn't known what to do when she didn't answer her phone, so he had gotten in his dad's truck and drove. Hours had passed since then and all he'd heard from Faye was a text from a strange number. She'd said that she was okay but that she'd lost her phone when the bomb went off and that's why she'd borrowed his cousin Cully's phone. She'd said that she was having trouble getting a call out, probably because the cell system was clogged up with people trying to find each other, but she thought maybe a text would go through.

And it had, but only after a delay that meant that Faye wasn't standing next to Cully and his phone when Joe was finally able to read and answer it. All he'd gotten was a return text from Cully.

> Hello, Cousin Joe. I still can't get a call out, so here's a text. Faye looks just fine and the paramedics agree, but it'll be a while before I can get your message to her. The FBI has decided that they need an archaeologist on their team. I have no idea why, but I would think that being with the FBI would be the safest place to be.

This sounded to Joe like Faye had been way too close to the bomb for comfort. And also, he wasn't sure how much he trusted the FBI with his wife's safety.

He didn't know exactly where his wife had been when the bomb blew, but he knew where she'd woken up that morning. She'd taken advantage of their business trip to Oklahoma to visit her friend Alba Callahan, driving from Joe's dad's house into the city the evening before and sleeping in Alba's guest room. Unfortunately, Joe didn't have Alba's number.

But he did have her son Carson's number, because Carson was the reason they were in Oklahoma to begin with. Carson was a Ph.D. archaeologist like Faye and he was Joe's childhood friend. When he'd called Joe to say, "I'm putting on a big conference and I need speakers," Joe had said, "I'll put Faye on the phone."

Carson had spoken just quickly enough to keep him from handing the phone over to his wife. "No, no, no, I want you to come do a presentation."

There was only one question for Joe to ask, and that was "What the heck for?" He and Faye owned a cultural resources firm together, and he had a bachelor's degree and all, but Faye was the doctor.

"I'm calling it The Oklahoma Conference for the Study and Celebration of the Indigenous Arts. I want you to come show people how to chip stone."

Joe had tried to say some things like, "Aw, you don't want me," and "Nobody wants to hear me talk about how much I like rocks," but Carson was having none of it.

"I've seen your work, Joe. In my opinion, it's museum quality. There are a lot of people who want to learn how to do what you do. There are also a lot of anthropologists and archaeologists who want you to show them how ancient people did what they did. You'll be a big draw and it will help me make this conference a success. Please say you'll come."

Joe thought Carson was just being nice when he said he'd be a big draw, but it was a chance to do something nice for his friend and a chance to take Faye and the kids to visit his dad, so he had said yes. He and Carson had talked to each other more over the past three months than they'd talked since they were kids, only now they were doing it on cell phones. Joe pulled his phone out of his pocket and hit Carson's number, which now resided on his Favorites screen. Before the fourth ring, he heard Carson's affable voice saying, "How ya doin', Joe?"

"You don't talk like a PhD."

"Does your wife?"

"Sometimes. Speaking of Faye, I can't get her on the phone. The radio says that the FBI ain't letting anybody into the hotel where we're supposed to stay tonight, since it got blown up and all. So I can't call her there. Do you know where she is? Or maybe does your mom know?"

"I've been trying to reach Faye, too. Actually, I've been trying track down Faye and the entire faculty for my conference. Let me tell you, it hasn't been easy. My contact at the hotel is in touch with the FBI and she's in touch with me, but the information isn't flowing all that well. All I know for sure is that Faye and Cully were in the lobby of the hotel when the bomb went off and they're both fine."

Joe was too well-mannered not to ask "Is everybody else okay?" even though he wouldn't be feeling truly mannerly until he found his wife.

"They are. Dr. Nick Althorp, the basket expert, was at the coffee shop down the street when it happened. He was having breakfast with Sadie Raincrow, who actually knows how to weave baskets. Dr. Althorp is a Sadie Raincrow groupie, so I'm sure that they were deep into a discussion about natural dyes and river cane when the bomb blew. I'm not surprised to hear that he'd already cornered her before breakfast this morning and dragged her out for coffee. Who knew that Dr. Althorp's fan-boy tendencies and Sadie's desire to eat at a Native-owned place would save both of them from the bombing?"

Joe also had a basket fetish, so he was a little jealous of Dr. Althorp's face time with the renowned Sadie Raincrow. And he wished Faye shared his fetish, because maybe she too would have been at a coffee shop far from the epicenter when the bomb went off.

Carson kept telling Joe about the health of people who weren't Faye. "Dr. Gilda Dell, who studies traditional music, is local, so she's still sitting in her university office thirty minutes south of here. Dr. Stacy Wong, the Oklahoma historian, is also a professor at the university in Norman. She is taking a historical walking tour and having a fine old time. I talked to Dr. Nathan Jackson, who studies African and Native American influences on modern American cuisine and he's still at the university, too. And yeah. He's gonna cook for us," Carson said, victorious in his belief that keeping his attendees full and happy would ensure his conference was a success. "He's promised to bring pots and pots of egusi soup with bitter leaf to his presentation. And fry bread, because we're in Oklahoma."

Joe's patience was too thin to keep listening to Carson burble about a conference that had probably been bombed out of existence, so all he said was, "Faye."

Carson must have heard Joe's strangled tone, so he got focused. "Like I said, the feds say she's okay, and that tracks with what I'm reading on the web. All the news people are saying that the most serious injuries were broken bones, and I'm hearing that Faye's and Cully's bones are just fine. Faye's bones must really be fine, because I'm also being told that the FBI has hired her as a consultant. They like their people able-bodied, don't you think?"

"She's working for the FBI? Why?"

"I have no idea. Listen. I'm supposed to meet the hotel's assistant manager downtown this evening to hear about her plan to save this conference of mine that is currently homeless. I'm at Mom's now. Why don't you come spend some time with us and ride back to town with me when I go to that meeting? Surely the

FBI can't keep Faye a prisoner—or an employee or whatever—all night. I bet you hear from her by then."

Carson's mother Alba lived in a suburb of Oklahoma City, close to downtown but apparently far enough out that the bombing's aftermath hadn't disrupted her cell phone service. Or maybe, as Joe thought of it, the FBI had co-opted the city's cell towers for itself during the crisis.

Alba's house was a perfectly reasonable place to wait for Faye to call, but it was too far away to suit Joe. "Thanks, Carson. I really appreciate it. But I can't go that far from where Faye is. If I can track a bear, and I can, surely I can find my wife. Even if the FBI wishes I'd stop trying."

———

Ahua had stepped out of the command center to do something that was probably pretty important, since Faye figured that Assistant Special Agents in Charge delegated trivia and kept the important stuff for themselves. While she waited, Agent Liu pulled her aside for a private talk. Liu was a thirty-ish woman with a starchy demeanor, but Faye could see that excitement had rubbed some of the starch off of her.

"My grandparents told me stories about those old tunnels," Liu said. "They knew some of the people who lived down there. My grandmother even said that she worked underground in a laundry for a few months before she was married. I always believed that the stories were real, because my grandmother wouldn't lie, but I never thought I'd have a chance to see the place with my own eyes."

Agent Liu's excitement, though charming, was insufficient to distract her from the task at hand, which was investigating the bombing. She seemed determined to repeat the interview Faye had already done when Bigbee pulled her off the street and into the FBI's lair. Faye figured that this was one way they tripped up liars who couldn't keep their stories straight.

"Bigbee says you were in the hotel lobby at the time of the blast?" she asked. "Did you see the bomber?"

Faye wanted to be snarky and say, "Like I said already, yes," but being snarky to the FBI sounded like a really dumb thing to do. She went with a simple "Yes. I think I caught a glimpse of him."

"You say that you didn't recognize the bomber?"

Faye realized two things. First, she was liking these yes-or-no questions, and second, she liked them because she was very, very tired. All she had to do to answer a yes-or-no question was nod now and then, or shake her head. That is, until Liu started focusing on people she cared about.

"So tell me about this conference. How do you know the organizer, Dr. Callahan?"

"He's my friend."

"You've known him how long?"

"Just a few months, but—"

"And Cully Mantooth. He's a relative of yours? You know him well?"

"We're only related distantly and by marriage. We met a couple of minutes before the explosion, tops. So no, I don't know him well, but I have no reason to mistrust him."

"Dr. Wong?"

"Until an hour ago, I only knew her online, but we've exchanged professional correspondence for at least a year."

Liu checked her tablet for the names of the other conference speakers. "Dr. Althorp? Ms. Raincrow? Dr. Dell? Dr. Jackson?"

"Nope. Don't know any of them."

"But you do know Joe Wolf Mantooth." Liu's eyes flicked down to the narrow band on Faye's left hand.

"He's my husband and I really need to talk to him. He was at his father's house outside Sylacauga when the bomb blew. I'm sure he got on the road right away, so surely he's here now. I think it's a four-hour drive. Maybe?"

"Then I should hope here's here by now."

"I would know that if someone would help me find a phone that worked so I could call him." Faye couldn't believe she was raising her voice to the FBI.

Perhaps Liu saw Faye's overreaction to her noncommittal response. A trained interrogator should have seen that the subject was having trouble keeping still, but Liu wasn't picking up those cues. Fortunately Bigbee was, because he approached them and said "Faye? Are you okay?" as he held out a bottle of water.

All of Faye was trembling, even her voice. She knew this made her look like she was guilty of something, though it could hardly have been planting the bomb that might have killed her. Also, she was as certain as certain could be that if she were a suspect she would never have been in the command center. Strangely enough, this didn't make her feel any better.

She felt a shivering deep at her core, as if she were standing in a prairie blizzard instead of sitting in a government vehicle with marginal air conditioning.

"I'm sorry," she said. "Are you saying it has been more than four hours since the blast? Is that true?"

Was she losing time? Did she hit her head that bad? It didn't seem so.

Bigbee moved closer. "What time do you think it is? Has anybody even showed you the bathroom?"

She gestured toward the back of the command center where the bathroom was and said, "Yeah. But I don't know what time it is."

"Have you eaten?"

"Not since breakfast."

He handed her a bag of peanuts. "Somebody should have made sure you were taken care of. We're all busy, but this is important."

"I think somebody might have offered me food at some point, but I wasn't hungry."

Maybe that's why she was so confused. She hadn't had lunch and she wasn't hungry. Therefore it couldn't be afternoon yet.

"If I've really been cooling my heels for that long, then I need to talk to my husband before he loses his mind."

Bigbee said, "We can help you get a call through to him. Do you need anything else?"

"I need—" She stopped herself from saying, "I need to sit down," because she was already sitting down and the question would get her an immediate neurological workup. Instead, she crossed her arms on her legs and laid her head down on them. Curled up like a startled armadillo, she sat there and concentrated on not fainting.

Faye was a scientist. She knew what she was feeling, but knowing it didn't help at all. Her trembling collapse was fueled by the adrenaline that had been pumping since someone detonated a bomb in her immediate vicinity…and it had apparently been pumping for more than four hours.

No, longer than that. Faye's adrenaline had first shot up that day for the most innocuous of reasons. She had laid eyes on a movie star. It seemed like a million years had passed since her first moments with Cully, when nothing was more pressing than scheduling some lessons so that he could teach her to play her beautiful new flute.

She looked down at her hands. They still cradled the flute, just as they had all morning. She had nothing else to do with them. Maybe the feel of its polished cedar was keeping her sane. It certainly seemed that way.

The memory of Bigbee's "Do you need anything else?" was still echoing in her ears, but it must have been doing that for a while, because now the words, "Are you all right, Dr. Longchamp-Mantooth?" were coming from several mouths and they were joining "Not exactly," in some kind of weird harmony.

Faye yanked herself back from the edge, refusing to faint in front of the FBI. Slowly, she raised her head.

"I'm fine. Just fine."

Hands reached out and opened the bottle of water, which

she tried to sip. Another set of hands—maybe the same ones—opened the bag of peanuts. She wasn't hungry, but she nibbled at the peanuts anyway, hoping to get her blood sugar to settle down.

Ahua's voice rang in her ears as she faded back into reality. He must have walked back into the command center while she'd been trying to get her brain to wake up. "If you're truly fine, please know that I need you. I've had a text from the Evidence Response Team. They have discovered something odd in one of the rooms at the bottom of the stairs. That's why I asked you to come talk to us. I need expert advice and I want your eyes on it."

Something about Ahua was different. There was a set to his lips and a darkness in his eyes that chilled Faye. This was no ordinary text from the Evidence Response Team.

"Are you sure about this? You can't just let her traipse through the crime scene." Liu asked Ahua. "The bureau has regulations for a reason."

Liu seemed to be something of a loose cannon, but she also seemed to be someone who could get away with questioning the boss, so maybe she was a crackerjack agent. Faye thought she had a point. She said, "I've done consulting work for local law enforcement, and I did that FBI case with Bigbee this summer, but I honestly don't think I belong in a high-profile crime scene, Agent Ahua."

"You don't. And that's not where we're going. Not exactly. Even I don't belong there. With these big feet, I'd crush something irreplaceable every time I took a step. But the Evidence Response Team also found a potential back door into the crime scene, so I sent some people to check it out and now they're back. They did find a back way into that chamber. There's something down there that I want your opinion on, and I know how to get you there. Are you willing to come help me out?"

Faye tried to process these cryptic comments. Where, exactly, would the back door to an underground room be, and how would one get to it? She had no idea.

Not that she didn't know people who could come up with some awesome theories about that. Faye kept up with a bunch of amateur historians' blogs and she'd also spent an embarrassing amount of time in online discussion groups for "urban explorers." If she asked those people, they'd say that there could be a way to get to Ahua's "back door" through a secret door in someone else's basement. The trouble came when you tried to find out whose basement had the secret door.

Faye had a soft spot for urban explorers, a community of brash thrill seekers, mostly quite young, who liked do the city dweller's equivalent of cave exploration. They could be found in abandoned buildings, behind "Posted—Keep Out" signs, in storm sewers, and atop buildings without authorized roof access, always in pursuit of going places where regular people never got to go. Stacy had gone exploring with some of them, but Faye was not that foolhardy. She took risks, yes, but not when the people leading the charge were fifteen years old.

Both she and Stacy had clung for years to the hope that Oklahoma City's urban explorers would find an entrance to the underground Chinatown, but they never expected it to be uncovered by a bomb. If the urban explorers hadn't found a back door after years of trying, was it possible that the FBI had found one in a single morning?

Who knows? Maybe the FBI *could* work that kind of magic. Maybe the "F" stood for "flippin' amazing."

The very serious voice of an actual FBI agent intruded on her thoughts. "Are you up to coming with us?" Ahua asked. "We're trying to get access to a place that's very old. We don't want to destroy history, no more than we want to destroy evidence. And some of that evidence could have been buried since the 1920s. Your expertise as an archaeologist could be critical."

"Why me? There have to be others who have worked with the FBI before."

"I don't know them. I don't know you, either, but Bigbee does, and he can't say enough good things. And also, you're here and they're not, and time is critical. I had some of my people do some calling around. Can you guess the first thing they heard from everybody they asked about you?"

"That I'm stubborn?"

"That trait was definitely mentioned, but no. Every single person said that you were level-headed and utterly calm in a crisis. You're the one that I want."

Faye thought about the subterranean staircase. She wanted to see where it led so bad that she could taste it. Her fluttery heart settled in her chest and the dizziness receded.

"Level-headed? You flatter me, Agent Ahua, but I guess flattery works. I'll do it."

She handed her flute to Agent Bigbee. "Do you remember where Cully Mantooth was sitting? Can you get this to him?" He nodded.

Then she turned to Ahua and said, "The answer is yes. I'm in."

When he handed her hip-waders and latex gloves, then asked if she was up-to-date on her tetanus shots, she wondered if she should rethink that answer.

Chapter Seven

Cully sat on his bench, pleased that the FBI had released him, although he still as yet had no place to go. The cell phone companies had gotten their act together enough for him to speak to his cousin Joe. Joe was on his way to join him, so he was committed to homesteading this bench until he arrived. And probably afterward, because the bench was really pretty comfortable.

Oklahoma City had changed. It had grown, surely. Actually, it had metastasized into an urban, modern place that he didn't recognize. But he did recognize the immense sky, piled high with richly textured clouds, and he recognized the constant wind that was blowing his hair around. He enjoyed being home again far more than he would have expected.

Out of the corner of his eye, he saw someone approaching quickly, but he didn't move like a young man, so he wasn't Joe. Cully recognized the short quick steps and the slightly labored breathing, and he knew that the newcomer was his old friend Jakob.

"Nobody would tell me anything. The FBI set up a barricade blocks from here and I've been stuck behind it for hours," Jakob said to Cully. "I thought you were dead. I was asleep in my room when the bomb woke me up. I don't know how long I banged on your door before a security guard made me leave. He opened your door for me when I told him I couldn't find you. When I saw that you weren't there, I remembered you saying that you were going to the lobby to meet your cousin Faye early this morning so I knew you were right in the middle of things."

"And you couldn't call me to make sure I was okay because you forgot your phone on your bedside table," Cully said.

"No, I didn't forget it on my bedside table. I forgot it in Beverly Hills, but what difference does that make? How would it help if you were dead?"

Cully pointed to his own face. "Look, Jakob. I'm not dead. When you find your phone, a long time from now when you're back in California, you'll see that I texted right away to tell you I was okay."

"That's a very twenty-first-century thing for an old man to do."

"Speak for yourself, old man."

"We're both old and we're gonna go one day. But not like this."

"And not today." Cully crossed his arms, cocked his head, and looked up at his friend. He knew that Jakob had seen him give that look to dozens of men on the silver screen, so his friend knew exactly what it meant. It was a look that said, "I'd take a bullet for you, buddy, but sometimes I'd also give anything to smack some sense into you."

Cully inclined his head toward the teeming crowd lining the street. "How'd you find me?"

Jakob crossed his own arms and returned Cully's arrogant look with one that said, "Go ahead and try smacking me. I just might have some tricks up my sleeve."

Cully kept giving him his I-love-you-buddy-but-you-make-me-nuts-sometimes attitude and Jakob crumbled. "Oh, okay. It didn't take any tricks to find you. I looked for people about our age or a little younger and I said, 'I heard that Cully Mantooth was around here somewhere.' By the time I did that a couple of times, people were coming up to me to tell me that they'd just seen you. Some of 'em even showed me your autograph. You're too famous to hide, you know."

———

Someone kind had heard Faye say that she needed to call her husband. She studied the receiver in her hands, wishing she could avoid this call, but she couldn't. Joe deserved to know that she had agreed to spend some time way underground with the FBI. She punched in his number.

He skipped hello and went straight to "Are you really okay?"

"I'm fine, Joe. Really. But there's this thing I need to tell you."

His answer was slow to come. "I'm not going to like it, am I?"

"Probably not. The FBI has asked me to help them. As a consultant."

"What do they want you to do? Just because they're promising to pay you, it doesn't mean you have to do it. We're not totally broke. And even if we were, there's no sense in you doing something dangerous."

She paused to think of the right thing to say, but she paused too long.

"It's dangerous, isn't it?"

"It shouldn't be—"

"'Shouldn't,' you say? That's just great."

"You think it's great?"

"Nope. I don't."

"Do you realize that somebody set off a bomb this morning and the FBI doesn't have a clue who he is or why he did it? Don't you think I should help if I can?"

"Yeah. I listen to the news. That's all I can do when I can't find you. Listen to the radio and worry."

Faye's easygoing husband didn't lose his temper often, but Faye thought she was probably about to experience her second explosion of the day. She tried to stave it off with a half-truth.

"We're not going to be working anywhere near the explosion. The Feds have found an underground room that seems both historically important and important to the investigation. They want me to take a look at it, but they won't be taking me through the blast area. They've found way to get there by going underground somewhere far away. We can approach it safely from a different direction without contaminating any evidence."

"How far away?"

Faye hated the way her voice got high and tentative when she was dealing with an angry person. "Maybe a mile?"

The second explosion of her day came, and it was loud. "You're going to be moving around underground *for a freakin' mile* because the FBI *thinks* it knows what it's doing down there? Did you think about the fact that you have two children waiting for you at Dad's house? I had to tell Dad to keep Amande and Michael away from the TV so they wouldn't see you talking to a reporter about bombs and explosions and dead people. Forget about me. What about them?"

Faye could only say, "I'll be fine, Joe. I believe it, or I wouldn't go. I would never take the chance of not coming home to them. Or to you."

"You like to think you're rational all the time, but you ain't, Faye. Not always. You're not gonna listen to anything I say, but put me on record as saying that this an awful idea. Awful. And you know it."

She thought he was going to hang up, but she was too upset to let go of the phone, so she heard his parting shot. "I'll be waiting for you when you come back. Like I always am." And then Joe was gone.

Chapter Eight

Cully Mantooth and Jakob didn't have the sidewalk to themselves any more, not since Carson Callahan found them. Cully knew Carson, since the archaeologist had picked him up at the airport, but he didn't know the small, thirty-ish woman with him.

"I hear that the FBI has hired his wife, Faye, to help them with this case," Cully said. "I know she's not the only archaeologist in town, because *you're* an archaeologist. Why Faye?"

Carson and his friend's faces fell, and Cully could tell that they both would have happily traded places with Faye.

"I'd love to get that gig, but I guess I didn't make the cut," Carson said. "Stacy here isn't an archaeologist, but she's a historian and she could have done the job, too, but honestly? Faye's the one they want. She's just that good."

"Cousin Faye's the biggest expert?" Cully was poking the big man's ego on purpose. Carson's response to this question would reveal an awful lot. "Bigger than you and this lady, here?"

"I'm sorry. I should have introduced you. Cully Mantooth, meet Dr. Stacy Wong. When I heard that the FBI had hired Faye for her experience in working with law enforcement, I was disappointed, but I'm not gonna lie. Faye's good at working with law enforcement. I've seen it with my own eyes. She solved the FBI's case for him, if you want to know the truth of the matter."

Good for Carson. He had sufficient ego to aim for a Ph.D. and get one, but he could still admit that other people were highly qualified, too. Cully was willing to entertain the possibility that Carson hadn't bombed his own conference, but he wasn't ready to trust anybody and he was still in the mood to prod the archaeologist a bit. The historian, too. "Bet you both still wish the agent had picked you."

Stacy's face grew sullen and still. She said nothing, but Carson said, "Nobody's saying much, but we're both pretty sure they want Faye to check out some underground structures uncovered by the bomb. Oral history says that they're down there. So if you're asking if I'd love to tour the legendary underground Chinese city that Stacy's been bugging me about for years, then yeah. You bet I wish Bigbee had picked me. I'm an archaeologist. I like to go down in holes in the ground, get dirty, and look at old things. Faye's gonna get to do that, while I sit up here and talk to a movie star. No offense."

Cully's face tingled and his vision dimmed. After all he'd been through that morning, was he really going to faint now? Was it really that much of a shock to hear that the bomb had uncovered a place that he'd spent a half-century trying not to remember?

Yes, it was. He remembered the darkness and the cold, and he remembered his last sight of Angela down there. He would give anything to have her back. Failing that, he would give anything to forget her.

"Are you okay, Mr. Mantooth?" Carson's voice brought him back from that dark place.

Cully covered his distress by clearing his throat, then he asked "What legendary underground Chinese city?" as if his mother hadn't told him a thousand times about the years she'd lived down there as a child. As if he hadn't spent the worst night of his life hiding down there.

It knocked him back on his heels a bit to hear Carson mention the damnable place when he'd just been talking about it himself for the first time since the day he lost Angela. Barely a day had passed since he'd been on the plane from LAX to OKC, telling Jakob things about his Oklahoma childhood that he'd never shared in the half-century they'd known each other.

Why had he told Jakob about his mother's year underground? He'd never even told the man that he was half-Chinese. He supposed he'd been overcome with nostalgia while riding on the plane that would finally take him home after all this time. The only thing he'd kept to himself was that awful night on the run, the one that had started with Angela by his side and ended without her.

Carson was still rambling. Good Lord, this man could talk. He was saying, "I think Stacy's talked to every old person of Chinese descent in Oklahoma City. She's a regular at all the nursing homes. To be honest, I can't make myself believe half of what they've told her. They say the place went on for a mile, all the way south to the river, but come on. That seems a little over-the-top. Still, we do know that it was real. The newspaper published pictures in the sixties, and we have health department records. Now that the bomber's opened the place up, I'd like to see it."

Most people with Cully's family ties would respond to this by asking Carson why he couldn't believe the stories of old people without documents to back them up. Was it because those old people weren't white? He thought about telling his mother's story and daring Carson to call her a liar.

But he wasn't being fair. Carson was Creek himself, despite his wavy blonde hair, and Cully could see that he meant no harm. Nevertheless, Cully was raised by a woman who taught him to keep his stories to himself. He just smiled and nodded. Stacy and Carson never knew that they could have collected a fascinating oral history from an old person of Chinese descent then and there, if they'd only asked.

Except for the part of his history that involved Angela. Cully was resolved that her name would never pass his lips again.

———

Faye was ankle-deep in river water. Or was it really river water? She was standing at the point where a large concrete pipe discharged water into a concrete ditch that took it to the Oklahoma River. According to Ahua, this pipe was a major outfall for the city's stormwater drainage system. When rain fell on pancake-flat Oklahoma City and people's houses didn't flood, it was because a system of drains shunted the rainwater here.

In other words, she was wading in water that had been really clean when it fell from the sky. Since then, though, it had rinsed the streets and sidewalks of a major city's business district and carried away the excess lawn fertilizer from the neighborhoods that surrounded it. This made her really grateful for her hip waders.

She stood between Ahua and Liu, who were each wearing their own hip waders. A man named Agent Goldsby, who said he was with the Evidence Response Team, was briefing them on their upcoming journey under Oklahoma City. Beside him stood Patricia Kura, who introduced herself as an engineer with Oklahoma City's Department of Public Works.

Ms. Kura had unrolled a series of blueprints and spread them across the hood of the vehicle that had brought them to this spot. Her explanation helped Faye to form a mental image of what they were about to do.

"We're starting here, at the outfall that drains rainwater from downtown Oklahoma City into the river. We can easily walk into the pipes that bring that water here. They'll get narrower, but we should still be able to get through to the spot where Agent Ahua wants to go. If our as-built drawings are accurate, this will work. But when you're dealing with a system this old, you can't always count on the drawings reflecting reality. Understand?"

They had all nodded, then Ahua had pulled Faye, Liu, and Goldsby aside for a briefing on new evidence.

Goldsby had chimed in with a report from his Evidence Response Team. "We've only partially cleared the stairs beneath the Gershwin. We've tracked footprints to the bottom of the stairs, where there's a landing and two doorways, one to the left and one straight ahead. There are only a few footprints on the stairs and the landing, but they match the bomber's shoes, so we know that he got that far. There's no sign that he went through the door on the left. Everything on the lower level is covered with a heavy layer of undisturbed dust, so we're pretty sure about that. The other door opens into a small room. Based on his tracks in the dust, we know that he opened the door, walked a few steps into the room, turned around, and came back out, shutting the door again."

"Then he walked back up the stairs and detonated the bomb?" Faye asked.

"Exactly right."

Faye had waited for him to explain how this story related to the fact that she was wearing hip waders. He did not. She had also wondered why the Assistant Special Agent in Charge was devoting a precious hour to this underground adventure. She doubted that he made a habit of donning hip waders.

"We think the room that he entered is key, but we're hamstrung on getting in there and looking around until Goldsby and his people finish gathering evidence," Ahua said. "Because of the dust, we're pretty sure that the bomber is the first person to go through that door in many years. So our question is this: Why? Actually, why did he go downstairs at all if he wasn't trying to blow apart a building's foundation?"

"Was it an elaborate suicide scheme?" Faye asked.

"We don't think so," Ahua continued. "The bomb was made to detonate remotely. Either he meant to leave it down there and detonate it once he was top-side, which begs the question of 'Why?' because there was nobody down there to hurt and we don't know of anything that he might want to destroy. Or he meant to detonate it in the Gershwin's lobby, only without blowing himself to bits. Again, we have to ask 'Why?' There was no obvious target there."

Faye thought that there was one obvious possibility. "Was the bomb stored down in the room he entered?"

"Good thought, but no. If he or an accomplice had hidden something down there, more than one set of tracks would have been obvious in the dust, but that's not the case. There's just one set of tracks, recent ones. They head into the room, turn around, and leave. We think that room is important in some way, so Goldsby's group expects to be working in there for days, trying to figure out why."

"How does that relate to all this?" Faye gestured at the massive concrete pipe, the river, the agents beside her, and her hip waders.

Goldsby, the only one who had been to the bottom of the stairs, had the answer. "When you stand in the doorway to that room, you smell water. You hear running water. And you can see a metal door, maybe two feet across, high on the far wall. We compared notes with the city's public works engineers, and they're pretty sure that metal door opens into a storm sewer pipe."

This explained the presence of Patricia Kura.

"Well, it's certainly not a regular sewer pipe, carrying regular old sewage," Ahua said. "You'd know by the smell."

"Exactly," Goldsby said. "Stormwater is just rainwater diverted from the streets and sent to the river. You wouldn't want to drink it, but it doesn't smell like sewage. We want to know for sure what's on the other side of that door, and we don't want to wait until the Evidence Response Team has worked its way across the floor, millimeter by millimeter. Hence this trip through a wet pipe."

Finally, an explanation for the hip waders.

"And also," Ahua said, "the walls of that room are more interesting than usual. If we can access it from the metal door, we can get a good vantage point for viewing the parts of the walls that are hard to see from where we're currently working, without—oh, I don't know, flying in a drone or using a humongous selfie stick. If I crashed a drone in Goldsby's crime scene, I'd be dead and he'd be looking at a murder charge."

Goldsby laughed, but that didn't mean that he wouldn't kill Ahua for mucking up his crime scene.

"What's so interesting about the walls?" Faye asked, wondering whether Ahua was telling everything he knew about that room. Nothing that he'd said explained why someone of his rank had assigned himself to the menial task of crawling through sewers. And nothing that he'd said explained the new darkness in his eyes and the new heaviness in his step.

Ahua had looked like this ever since he got the text that prompted this underground junket. When a case took a turn that burdened an experienced FBI agent to this extent, it had to be a bad turn. Faye was worried.

Goldsby held out his phone. The photo on its screen was painfully colorful. It showed walls covered with floor-to-ceiling murals—trees, vines, and faces. Many faces.

"This is why I wanted to bring you with us, Faye," Ahua said. "Those paintings look recent to me. Well, not yesterday-recent, but I don't think they've been there since before World War II, which is when people were living down there. I know it's not your specialty, but I thought you might be able to give us an idea of their age. I'd also really like to know when that door was cut into the storm drain. And why."

With that, he had beckoned to Ms. Kura and they had walked to the storm sewer outfall and stepped into ankle-deep water.

———

Goldsby led the way into the darkness, followed by Ahua. Faye walked behind them, then the public works engineer, Ms. Kura. Liu brought up the rear. The concrete pipe arched over their heads and the murky water splashed at their ankles.

"Ms. Kura knows the design of these sewers backwards and forwards. She's going to help us stay safe while we're down here."

The city engineer spoke up. "Call me Patricia, please. Before we go any farther, let me remind you of something. We've got to be especially careful from the get-go, because we might find animals living in the stretches of pipe closest to the surface. People, too, actually. That's more common than you'd think."

Ahua nodded. "Yes, and that's not good. You have to remember that these things aren't just designed to catch rainwater. They're designed to catch *all* the rainwater. There was a family living near here who thought the storm drain would make a good tornado shelter. They're dead now."

Faye felt a very slight current tugging at her ankles. On a day like today, with its zero percent chance of rain, it was hard to imagine the deadly torrent that would come during a rainstorm.

They were making good time, so she guessed that they were far enough into the pipe to be clear of predators, animal or human. There was no hint of sunlight left, either direct or reflected. They were dependent on the headlamps attached to their safety helmets. Still, Faye was comforted to know that Liu, who was nearly twice her weight and heavily armed, had her back.

Goldsby, by contrast, scared her a little. She was pretty sure that if she mistakenly messed up an important piece of evidence, he would beat her with it.

Patricia didn't seem scary, but she too might turn vengeful if Faye hurt her storm sewers.

Ahua had given Faye a recorder to use for her narration of their expedition. "We're walking through a large pipe, apparently recent and well-preserved," she said as she walked.

The five continued to walk along a pipe that slanted ever-so-slightly upward under their feet. She resumed recording. "We just passed a spot where two lateral lines entered this pipe, one on each side. Shortly after that, the main pipe took a left turn."

"Uh-oh," Goldsby said, and she didn't like the sound of it.

He seemed to be responding to a narrowing of the pipe. They had expected this, but it was still disconcerting. It wasn't like the new diameter was tiny. Faye, Patricia, and Ahua could still walk upright, but Goldsby and Liu now had to stoop a bit.

"We'll see the diameter decrease at least a couple more times before we get where we're going," Patricia said. "Once we get past that point, it's hard to be sure. For one thing, the river has been re-routed several times since the old part of this system was built."

Faye took some deep breaths to calm herself. She was only a little claustrophobic—and in the end weren't most people?—so she could generally get past it enough to do what she needed to do. Still, traveling for a mile in an ever-narrowing corridor was making her pulse race. Observing and recording were both calming activities, so she went back to talking to the recorder.

"Here's another pair of lateral lines bringing water into this main line. They're smaller than the pipe where I'm standing, but I could get through them on my hands and knees, if I had to. I'd rather not have to, though."

On cue, the concrete walls around her closed in a little bit more. Technically, she could still walk upright, but the concrete was snagging on her hair and brushing against her sleeves.

"There's a teeny bit of good news," she continued. "The water's getting shallower upstream of those lateral lines. They were each bringing in more water. It barely splashes as I walk through it."

Patricia interrupted her to say, "Would you look at that?" The others gathered behind her to add the light of their head lamps to hers.

In front of them, the pipe changed dramatically. It narrowed again, and it changed color and texture. They were stepping from a modern-looking concrete pipe into a very old storm sewer line, constructed of brick. Even its shape changed into something odd and unfamiliar. This sewer pipe wasn't round. It was wider at the top than at the bottom. Faye didn't know the technical term for this kind of pipe, but she would have said it was teardrop-shaped, only the teardrop was upside down.

"This is old," Liu said. "Do you think it might date to the period when people were still living underground, Dr. Longchamp-Mantooth?"

Thrilled for her expertise to finally be useful, Faye said, "Very possibly. I'd say this brickwork looks a lot like the brickwork in the photo of the staircase underneath the Gershwin Hotel."

They all mumbled their agreement as they checked out the soft red clay bricks set in aging mortar. Then they ducked their heads and stepped into the odd old teardrop-shaped pipe.

Faye reached a hand up and dragged her fingers over the rough bricks above her. This kept her from bumping her head and it helped her remember which way was up in dark, strange surroundings that were thoroughly disorienting.

It was hard to gauge distance as her fingers bumped over the bricks, but she judged that she'd traveled the equivalent of eight or ten city blocks away from the river when Goldsby stopped again. His headlight illuminated something rectangular that had a metallic glint. It was set into the bricks at about shoulder height.

Goldsby let out a low whistle. "That's it. That's the door into the room with the murals. It has to be. It's the right size and shape, and it's right where the city's engineers said it would be. And, just like they said, the pipe's still big enough that all four of us squeezed through." He checked the pedometer on his phone. "We've walked almost a mile, also,just like they said."

Patricia took a small bow. "You sound like you didn't believe us," she said.

"Our people took laser measurements of the staircase and the chamber at the bottom of it and your engineers overlaid that data onto your maps," Goldsby said. "You're all very good at what you do. I'm not surprised."

"Now we've got to get that thing open," Liu said. "If God is good, there will be a handle on this side and it won't be locked."

God was indeed good. The five of them crowded behind Goldsby as he carefully photographed the door before turning the handle with his gloved hands. It operated a latch that screeched loud enough to make Faye worry that dust, rust, and time had left it useless.

Goldsby banged on the handle with the heel of his hand and tried again. Then he did it again. And again.

Finally, the sound of metal on metal echoed off the bricks surrounding them. Its squeal hurt Faye's ears, but when the piercing sound faded, the door was open.

Squeezing behind Goldsby so that she could look over his shoulder, she saw a room that was unmistakably the one that he had shown Faye on his phone screen. The Evidence Response Team had set up lights in the room's doorway, illuminating the windowless space. After walking a mile in darkness that was only punctured by their headlamps, the chamber was bright enough to hurt her eyes.

It wasn't large, perhaps fifteen feet square. Every square inch of its walls and ceiling was painted in eye-poppingly bright colors, brimming with life. It reminded her of prehistoric cave art, even to the bold red handprints that served as a recurring motif.

Scattered through the painted faces and flowers were the symbols of many of the world's religions. Faye saw a cross, a Star of David, and the smiling face of the Buddha. Here and there, she saw Arabic calligraphy that she presumed was associated with Islam. Among the religious symbols, she saw the faces of happy people—men, women, and children. And snaking through it all was more calligraphy, this time in English, saying over and over again, "Evil must be obliterated."

Faye, Patricia, and two of the FBI agents jostled each other for space, all of them trying to get a look, but Ahua hung back while they each took a turn.

"Hey, guys. Look up," Patricia said. "Is that electrical conduit pipe? Surely they didn't have—"

"You don't think they had electricity down here?" Liu's voice emanated from the darkness behind her. Faye stepped aside to let her see. "Of course they had electricity. At least they had it as soon as Oklahoma City got it, around the turn of the twentieth century. My grandmother said that they had electric lights when she worked down here, for sure. A Buddhist temple, too, and gambling halls. They even had rooms where they grew sprouts and mushrooms for their above-ground restaurants."

"Seriously?" Goldsby said, but Faye didn't feel as doubtful as he sounded. It had been a long time since she'd been in a place that was so far outside her everyday experience. She had the sense that anything could happen here.

This feeling extended into the past. Faye had the sense that this was a place where anything could have happened and probably did.

"Didn't you notice the overhead pipes in that picture of the oil stove?" Faye asked him.

"I didn't," Goldsby said, and he sounded embarrassed.

"Looked like electrical conduit to me, and maybe even water pipes, and they looked just like those." Liu squeezed an arm past him and pointed at the chamber's ceiling. "Look around you. Everything's still in good shape. The people who built this were smart enough to figure out how to do things. I bet they tapped into the power lines of people who never even knew they were paying for somebody else's lights."

Faye was haunted by the people who cut the hole she was peering through. She stepped back to give Patricia some space and looked at its metal-rimmed frame, designed to keep water out. The fact that real, live human beings made the fantastical choice to move underground said a lot about how bad life was for them on the surface. Faye was sort of glad to think that they'd stolen electricity from their oppressors. And this door had solved another big problem for them.

Agent Liu kept talking, happy to reminisce about her grandmother's stories while they stared at the bizarre chamber. "All those things—temple, laundries, mushroom farms, and all—were on the level right under the street. Which, I guess, is where we are now. Storm sewers are pretty close to the surface, right?"

"Makes sense to me," Ahua said. "But are you saying there were other levels?"

"Yep," Liu said. "The second level down was supposed to be mostly sleeping rooms. On the third level down—"

"Oh, come on," Ahua said. "You're not going to tell me that they dug three levels below the ground. I never doubted that they did something like what we see here, not after I saw those photos in the paper when I was a kid—"

"You certainly can't doubt that now. You just saw it."

He actually hadn't, because he had yet to take his turn at the door.

"Yeah, but three levels?"

"Not everywhere," Liu said. "But my grandmother said there was a third level down, smaller than the rest, and that's where the cemetery was. And another temple."

"Get outta town," Faye said, hoping that her recorder had caught everything Liu had said.

"Everybody says that when the health inspectors came down here in 1921 for a surprise inspection, it wasn't much of a surprise. Everywhere they went, people knew they were coming before they got there. The stories all agree that they didn't have telephones down here. So how did word go ahead of them like that?"

"Walkie-talkies?" Patricia's joking tone was doing a lot to distract Faye from thinking about how many tons of dirt were over their heads.

"Very funny," Liu said. "The inspectors believed there were ladders between levels, and my grandmother said that they were right. According to her, while the health department people were inspecting one room, somebody went downstairs and hurried to get ahead of the inspectors—"

"Like chipmunks?" Patricia asked, still checking out the murals.

"Yes, like chipmunks, if you want to be snarky. They'd pop up like chipmunks and warn their neighbors to be ready because the inspectors were coming. That theory argues for more than one level belowground."

"Or they could've gone upstairs and run ahead to another surface access point," Ahua said. Liu's snort said that she was finished arguing with nonbelievers.

Faye resumed her conversation with the recorder. "Every inch of the walls is painted with scenes of people interacting with nature. They're climbing trees, swimming, tending gardens, and sharing meals. There are also a lot of religious symbols. The scenes are divided by tree trunks and ivy vines. The floor is painted to resemble grass. The ceiling is sky blue and dotted with clouds. Somebody spent a lot of time down here with a paintbrush."

"Do you think those paintings were done eighty or a hundred years ago, while people were still living down here?"

She paused the phone's recorder to answer Ahua. "Gut feeling? No. They look too recent. To confirm that, I'd recommend taking some paint samples and sending them to a lab."

Ahua nodded and typed a note on his phone.

"It should be possible to tell whether the paints are modern," she said. "If there are multiple layers of paint, the bottom one would give you an idea of when the room was built. Or first painted. Even if the murals are recent, it doesn't mean that they were painted when the room was new. I don't think they were, because everything but the paint looks really old."

Goldsby said, "Good plan. I'll make sure we get paint samples to a lab. We'll take brick and mortar samples, too. And wood samples from the door. Now, step up and take a better look. Give me the archaeologist's perspective. It's incredibly useful."

It took Faye's eyes a moment to fully adjust to the well-lit room and the brilliant colors on its walls. A few moments passed before she noticed that the room wasn't completely empty. Crude wooden benches were pushed against the three walls that she could see, giving the space the feel of an auditorium, lecture hall, or church. Even the benches were painted with bright, busy images that were like camouflage. The benches blended so completely into the walls that they were hardly noticeable, and so were the objects resting on them.

When she made the effort to focus on the benches, their straight lines took her eyes straight across the room from right to left, leading them to the only unpainted things in sight. Three cream-colored bundles rested on the benches that met in the left corner of the room.

When Faye finally saw them, she heard the words "Oh no oh no those can't be real" leave her in a single breath.

But she knew they were real, even though blankets covered the children's faces. Anyone who had ever swaddled a baby would know that these were real. One of the bodies was wrapped a bit less tightly, allowing a few locks of dark hair to escape. Those curls broke her heart.

Faye stood there, trapped by the bodies of her companions, unable to step away and only able to look at the small, shrouded bodies. She had to resist the urge to crawl through the small opening and stumble across the room, folding the blankets back gently to reveal the faces of three young children. The FBI would have something to say about her ruining their crime scene, though, so she couldn't hold the small bodies in her arms. She couldn't tell them how sorry she was that someone had put them down and walked away.

"Who would do this?"

Faye heard the four words hanging in the air, then she realized that she had spoken them herself. She pointed at the bodies, because she'd said all the words that she could manage.

Goldsby squeezed past her for a look, then backed away, shaking his head and silent. Liu did the same and had the same reaction.

Ahua finally stepped forward to peer into the strange room. The look on his face told Faye that he had known all along that the children were here. Their bodies were the reason that a Special Agent in Charge had made the long slog from the river.

"You already knew," she said. "Somebody on the Evidence Response Team leaned into the room, looked hard to the right, and saw something awful."

Goldsby turned toward Ahua and said, "Is that true? One of my people saw this and told you?"

Ahua said only, "Affirmative. And then I sent a team to do exactly what we just did, only they were also sweeping for bombs. When they texted to say that there really were three dead children down here, I organized this party and now here we are."

In the moment that the Evidence Response Team saw the bundles and realized what they were, Ahua's investigation had become something more than an attempt to discern the motives of a bomber who was dead and gone and who was presumably working alone. It also became the investigation of a very cold case involving the deaths of three small children.

Ahua stood looking into the painted chamber for a long moment. Finally, he was able to speak. "I have no idea who left those little bodies here. If they're still alive, I want them in prison for the rest of their miserable lives."

So did Faye. She had begun the day scared and angry. Being given a chance to help find the man who had tried to kill her and everyone else in the Gershwin Hotel had felt cathartic. It had been a way to resolve that anger. But now?

Now her anger had ripened into the kind of rage that powered holy wars. She, too, wanted the person—people?—who had done this to rot in prison until they died.

Chapter Nine

Joe Wolf Mantooth, for the first time, stood face-to-face with Cully Mantooth. He wasn't clear on how they were related, although his father Sly had done his best to walk him through the tangle of relatives who connected them.

"My mother could have explained it better," Sly had said when he finally gave up, "but she's been gone since before you were born."

He and Cully had the same last name, so Joe figured that their fathers had been kin. Since Cully was born just a few years after Joe's grandfather, Joe thought that maybe they had been cousins, but were he and Cully blood-kin? Probably, unless somebody along the line had been adopted or unless somebody's mom had been fooling around with the milkman. When the lines of kinship were stretched this far, the blood ties were so thin as to be unimportant. Joe had been taught that family was family, and that was that.

He stretched out his hand to and said, "Hello, Cousin Cully."

It would never cross Joe's mind to approach a family member as anything other than an equal, so it didn't occur to him that Cully might find it refreshing to meet someone who didn't look at him and say, "Hey! Movie star!" Joe only noticed the genuine warmth in the older man's handshake, and it told him that they would be friends.

Cully introduced him to his friend Jakob Zalisky, who was friendly but quiet. This was odd, because Jakob didn't seem like a man who kept to himself.

"So you're Cousin Faye's husband?" Cully asked.

"I am, and I'd really like to lay eyes on her right about now. She needs to rest up from what happened to her and stop rushing into something else dangerous."

"You don't look real happy about her underground adventure."

Joe was by nature a truth-teller. Right now, he was struggling for a way to tell the truth about what he was thinking without throwing his wife under the bus. "I just don't think she tells herself the truth when she sets out to do this kind of thing. Faye wants to think she's immortal."

"I only just met her, but I already think I understand your point. That woman would rather eat dirt than admit she couldn't do something."

"So you *have* met my wife." Joe felt himself laughing. He wanted to keep being mad at Faye, so this laughter made him even madder.

"Indeed, I have. Why don't you sit next to Jakob and me on this bench while you wait for her? I've been homesteading it for hours. An advantage to being old is that a lot of people will give up their seat to you. If I see a lady with a baby, I'll get out of this comfy spot. Until then? I'm going to enjoy the fruits of age."

"Don't mind if I do."

"This is a handy place for Jakob and me to do absolutely nothing while we wait for the FBI to tell me whether the conference that brought me here is still going to happen and whether either of us has a place to sleep tonight." Cully said. "I for one appreciate the company."

"As do I," said Jakob.

"Don't worry about a place to sleep. We'll find you both a place to sleep, even if we have to drive to Sylacauga and sleep at Dad's."

"That is very kind of you," Cully said. "My guess is that Faye will be back from her trip down below with her new buddies, the feds, before anybody remembers that Jakob and I are here. This is the disadvantage of old age. You get kind of invisible."

A fan fluttered up and asked for Cully's autograph, putting the lie to his claim of invisibility.

"Jakob here directed three Oscar-nominated films," Cully said to a man in his twenties who wanted some time with a movie star. "And he won once. Want his autograph, too?"

The man did, so Jakob added his signature to the scrap of newsprint that Cully had just signed.

Joe settled himself beside Cully. Before his butt hit the bench seat, he asked, "How much do you know about where Faye went? She didn't tell me much and what she did say didn't make a damn bit of sense."

Joe was still hurt that his wife wasn't waiting for him with arms spread wide, but he had known who she was when he married her.

"Well, Cousin Joe, would you believe that the bomb opened up an entrance into an underground lost city? And that your wife was handy when the FBI decided they needed Indiana Jones to go down there with them, but he wasn't available?"

"Faye's smarter than Indiana Jones. More ethical, too. Usually."

"You've gotta cut Indy a break," Jakob said. "He was working a long time ago. Us old guys, we do the best we can."

Joe wondered if Cully and Jakob knew any of the actors who played the indigenous people who had faced off against Indiana Jones. Hollywood was a small town and the two men had been working there a long time, so Joe figured they probably did.

Cully stretched his long legs in front of him and rested his capable-looking hands atop his thighs. For the first time, Joe noticed what he was holding.

"Is that the flute? The one you made for Faye?"

Cully nodded and held it out to him. "She's pretty possessive of it already, but she got a fed to bring it to me while she went exploring. Guess she figured that since I made the thing, I'd keep it safe."

Joe took the instrument, resting his fingers on precisely drilled holes and preparing to fit his mouth to a mouthpiece that a European would say was more like a recorder's than a flute's.

"You hold that flute like a man who knows what he's doing. I'd just given it to her when the bomb blew. She hasn't even had a chance to try it out."

"I play a little," Joe said, pulling the instrument away from his mouth. Faye should be the one who played it first.

"I know she liked it," Cully said, "so you did good with your gift giving. When that bomb went off, it was like somebody cracked open the gates of hell. I thought it was Judgment Day, and I'm here to tell you that I'm not ready to go. I've got some burdens on my soul that I need to lay down before I face judgment. I'm ashamed of them but the truth is the truth. Your wife? She must have a clean heart, because she hit the ground with a face as calm as an angel. And she was clutching that worthless flute to her chest the whole time, like it was made of platinum."

"She's really okay?"

"She's really okay. Well, she's underground with some people who are certainly packing heat, and they're underneath a building that was just bombed and is probably still smoking. And nobody's got a clue why it got bombed, but yeah. She's okay. I get the sense that Cousin Faye will always be okay."

"She's okay in a mysterious underground city from the past?"

"Yeah. In a mysterious underground city from the past."

"Then we might as well get comfortable on this bench. My wife won't be coming back until she's seen all she can see."

"It's what Indiana Jones would do."

Chapter Ten

It wasn't supposed to go like this. All my careful plans blew up along with the bomb that I aimed at nobody but Lonnie. Lonnie has been obliterated, according to plan, but now the whole world is involved. His death was supposed to stay secret.

Lonnie was supposed to be underground when the bomb blew. And he should have been. End of story.

I planned his route carefully. I told him that he would be planting the bomb beneath the IRS's Oklahoma City offices, and he loved that idea, but I actually sent him to a place where even an underground explosion wouldn't hurt anybody but him. And if a bomb that small turned out to be too undersized to kill him right away, it was certainly big enough to injure him too badly to find his way back to the surface. It would not have pained me to know that he suffered alone until death took him.

His death would have been marked by people on the surface by a shuddering vibration and nothing more. These days, Oklahoma City is shaken regularly by supposedly harmless little earthquakes brought on by fracking. Most people wouldn't have known that this one was different.

Geologists probably would have noticed something was wrong when their seismographic charts showed a pattern that couldn't be natural. They might have been able to pinpoint the blast but, with no knowledge of the old network of tunnels, they would have been hard-pressed to find its source. Would they have tried to track it down using ground-penetrating radar or some such technology? Possibly, but the cost would have been tremendous, and the end game would have required excavating a chunk of downtown Oklahoma City.

This is a city that couldn't be bothered with exploring the Chinese catacombs the first time they were uncovered, much less preserving them. Like so many other problems, city officials covered them up and pretended they were never there. Why would anything be different now? Nobody would support spending so much money to investigate a single unexplained tremor, but if they did? What would they find? The rotting pieces of Lonnie, who fully deserved to be blown into pieces and left to rot. And absolutely no evidence that would lead them to me.

Lonnie was too stupid to realize that he wasn't carrying a bomb big enough to destroy the offices of his sworn enemy, the IRS. He was carrying a person-killer, packed with enough black powder and nails to obliterate him, but not nearly enough firepower to bring down buildings.

On the off chance that I was wrong about how much damage my little bomb could do, I sent him to a place under an alleyway where there were no buildings above him to collapse and hurt people. It took me hours of studying maps and searching my memory for the routes of the underground passageways, but I found the safest place to set off the bomb, and that alleyway was it.

If Lonnie had followed the plan, he would have been standing in just the right place when I placed the call that triggered the bomb.

Why didn't Lonnie go where he was supposed to go?

The pieces of Lonnie have now been scraped off the floor of the Gershwin Hotel's lobby, and they are resting in a morgue. Eventually they will be autopsied, if that hasn't already happened. Is it possible that the medical examiner might find a way to identify him? And could that lead the FBI straight to me or to the people I care about? I don't see how.

Lonnie must have had a birth certificate, which was more than could be said for most of his children. He once had a driver's license and a birth certificate was a necessary part of getting one of those. But no valid license exists for him now and it hasn't in a long time.

Lonnie was a homeless grifter from the time the family broke up, and more than twenty years have passed since then. He earned no criminal record, held no passport. He held no job in the years since background checks and fingerprints became part of the hiring process for the kind of menial work he was qualified to do. At least, he never held a job where his employers kept up with those legal niceties. Lawn care and handyman work put food in his mouth, and that was all Lonnie needed.

To my knowledge, Lonnie was never even arrested, which was a true joke when one considered the things that he had done. If anybody had ever dug up the rotting pieces of Lonnie out of the catacombs where he was supposed to have died, I can think of no way they could have identified them.

Even now, after the plan has fallen apart and Lonnie has died aboveground and in a crowd, I see no way for the FBI to ever figure out who he is. Or rather, who he once was. This is important, because there is more at stake than my freedom, much more, but I can find no reason to worry about being caught.

If there has ever been a perfect murder, this was it. And it couldn't have happened to a nicer guy.

Chapter Eleven

Faye was more happy to be sitting down than she could possibly say, even if her mouth weren't full. She was sitting on a sidewalk bench between Cully and Jakob, grateful for the sandwich that Joe had pushed into her hand. Joe sat at her feet on the curb with his own sandwich.

"There's a guy with a restaurant a couple of blocks away," Joe said, waving his sandwich in the air to punctuate his story. "He told me that he came running as soon as he heard the blast, but the fire department was already here and they wouldn't let him go into the hotel to help search for survivors. So he went back to his restaurant and started making food for the workers and for the people stuck on the street. He said he figured that it was something that he knew how to do, and everybody needs food. He opened up his bathroom to all those people with no place to go, too."

"People can be really good," Faye's voice was muffled because her mouth was full of ham, bread, lettuce, and mayonnaise. Jakob handed her a napkin so she could wipe her face.

"Yeah," Joe said. "He walks up and down this street with a big tray of sandwiches and cups of water every thirty minutes or so. I saw him come and go at least three times while you were down there. Faye, I was so scared. First when I heard about the bomb, then the whole time that you were deep underground. I was so scared that I couldn't even eat."

Joe was now demolishing his roast beef sandwich like a man who hadn't eaten in a while, so Faye supposed that this was true.

"I wish you hadn't gone down there, Faye. There was a bomb. Remember? What if the ceiling had caved in on you? I wouldn't have been able to get you out."

Faye said, "The fire department and the city engineers said it was safe," and she realized how naive she sounded when Cully rolled his eyes and clutched his heart.

Joe grunted. "They're just people like you and me. They can make mistakes. The bomb tore that hotel up. I saw the pictures on the web and they're bad. If you're trying to say that it was just a tiny little bomb because it didn't kill anybody but the bomber, well, just don't. I won't believe you."

Faye had seen the damage to the hotel, up close and personal, so she had no intention of telling Joe that it wasn't all that bad. "Well, I'm back now, and I'm all in one piece."

"But you're going back down there. Aren't you?"

Her husband knew her well. If the FBI thought she could help crack this case, then yes. She was going back down there. She wasn't allowed to tell anyone about the children's bodies that they had seen down there, so there was no way to tell Joe why she was so determined to help. He was going to have to trust her.

The thought of dying and leaving her own children without a mother was the only thing that made her waver in that determination. "Do you want me to say no?"

"I'd say no," Jakob said, "but nobody asked me."

Faye was more interested in what her husband thought. "Joe, do you want me to tell the FBI to find some other archaeologist to help them?"

"If you did that, I'd take your pulse and ask you if you were okay. It's your nature to say yes to an adventure and worry later."

She supposed she should let him keep thinking that this was just an adventure, but she wasn't sure how long she could manage it.

Long enough. She was sure that she could keep her secret long enough.

Carson's bear-like form appeared at the end of the block, ambling toward them with a sandwich in each hand and a companion on either side.

"I could tell the FBI that they should hire Carson," Faye said.

"You're going to do this job, because it's who you are. And also," Joe said, speaking quickly so that he could finish before Carson was close enough to hear, "Carson's my friend and I love him, but he ain't half the archaeologist you are. And he ain't got your experience dealing with crime. The FBI needs to find out who set that bomb 'cause they might do it again. It would be pretty dang selfish of me if I told the person who might actually be able to help them that I didn't want her to do it."

———

Faye, not wanting to be rude, hauled her aching body to her feet so that she could shake hands with Carson and his companions. Faye was pretty sure that they were two of the scholars he'd invited to speak at his conference. It seemed right to stand out of professional courtesy.

Cully and Jakob rose, too. Jakob let out a little groan as he maneuvered his portly, seventy-something-year-old body to standing. Faye, thirty years his junior, did the same thing, but Cully sprang up like a dancer.

Joe hopped to his feet, too, which was no surprise, given his young bones and his habitual courtesy. In this case, that courtesy was serving him well. Being invited to present at Carson's conference was a major professional opportunity for Joe, and becoming friends with Cully Mantooth and Jakob Zalisky certainly wouldn't hurt.

Faye stopped worrying about three dead children long enough to wonder whether the conference would be canceled because of the bomb. Of course it would, and that was a bad thing for Joe.

Faye had always thought that her husband should be a hot ticket as a presenter at archaeological conferences, where there were hundreds or even thousands of people who would be fascinated to spend a little vicarious time in the Stone Age. He just needed to get in front of the right people and show them what he could do. A goodly number of the right people were registered for Carson's conference. Faye was only just realizing that the bomber had robbed Joe of that opportunity. This was definitely not the worst thing about the morning's disaster, but Faye hurt for her talented husband.

"This is Dr. Stacy Wong," Carson said.

"Oh, I know Stacy!" Faye said, reaching out to shake the historian's hand. "I've just never met her in person."

"Faye," Carson said, "if Stacy doesn't get to pump you for information on what you saw underground, she's going to explode."

After an awkward pause, Carson said, "Okay, that was a bad metaphor, especially today. Stacy will not explode. But she may scream. Anyway, I need to introduce Kaayla Jones before Stacy starts screaming. Kaayla's the assistant manager for the Gershwin Hotel and she has just managed to save our conference. This is not the most pressing problem of the day, but I invested most of the past year planning the thing, so the thought of saving it makes me really, really happy."

"I recognize you now," Faye said to Kaayla. "You took our picture right before the whole world went kablooie."

Cully nodded. "Yes, you certainly did. How are you? Were you hurt in the blast?"

Kaayla said, "No, nothing to speak of," but Faye saw a deep cut along her hairline. There was blood in Kaayla's dark brown hair, and it had dripped onto her snowy white jacket. An emerging bruise cast its blue shadow along her cheekbone.

Faye's hand strayed to her own cheekbone. It felt bruised in the exact same place. She remembered going down, hitting her knees, then the right side of her pelvis, then her right shoulder, and then feeling her head crash down, driving her cheekbone into the floor. She realized that all of those contact points must be bruised, and this knowledge caused each of them to begin throbbing. Knowing that Kaayla had been standing very close to her at the time of the blast put a strange picture in her mind of the two of them falling identically, their moves choreographed like the motion of dancers. She felt a weird bond with the hotel manager, as if they were sisters in disaster.

She considered the blood on Kaayla's jacket and was glad that none of her own tender points had bled. Joe would have had a major freak-out over any sign of bleeding, no matter how small. And also, she'd just spent a lot of time wading in questionable water. That would have been idiotic if she'd had any open wounds.

"I'm fine," Kaayla said. "I'm just so grateful that nobody was killed. If it weren't for my housekeepers, we might have had guests standing a lot closer. And if my housekeepers had been just a few feet closer to the blast..." Tears welled in her eyes and she swallowed hard. "I would probably have lost some people who are very special to me."

Faye's memory fired and she remembered the two women in maids' uniforms, one of them falling and one of them running from a familiar place turned suddenly into hell. "How did your housekeepers keep other people from being closer to the blast?"

"They were working near the area where the bomb went off. One of them was really close. She'd just stepped out of the alcove where the bomb blew, and I get terrified all over again when I think about it. But here's what saved other people. They'd both set up signs to keep people off the freshly mopped floor. If the 'Wet Floor' signs hadn't been where they were, we might have had hotel guests right at the epicenter of the blast. My workers were just starting to walk away to take their breaks when it happened. Otherwise, they'd have been at the epicenter themselves."

"They were very lucky," Cully said. Jakob, standing beside him, nodded.

Kaayla's answer was simple and characteristic of the steadfast faith that was so common in Oklahoma. "God provides for His own."

"Has the FBI spoken to your employees about what they remember?" Faye asked. "And to you?"

Kaayla nodded and Faye felt like an idiot. Of course they had. Ahua was an experienced and high-ranking FBI agent, and he wasn't the only experienced and high-ranking agent overseeing this case. If she thought she could run the investigation better than the FBI could, then she was having delusions of grandeur.

"I hate to be selfish at a time like this," Carson said, "but one good thing happened today. Kaayla says that there's no reason that the conference can't happen this week, as planned."

Faye looked down the street toward the Gershwin Hotel. Knowing the condition of its interior, she couldn't imagine it being cleared for human habitation in time for the conference to start in sixteen short hours. She also couldn't imagine when the FBI's forensics people would be finished working a crime scene that encompassed its entire lobby and maybe more. Not to mention a substantial area that was underground. Carson wanted the impossible.

Carson was laughing at the look on her face. "You're making the same mistake I did."

"The original historic hotel is a small part of the property," Kaayla explained. "You never had a chance to see your room before the disaster, but it's in one of our two modern towers. They're located in the Tower Annex, just a short walk down the block from the old hotel. Mr. Mantooth knows. He checked into his suite yesterday. So did Mr. Zalisky."

She pointed at two glass and steel buildings looming down the street from them. "The historic hotel houses a limited number of guest rooms, but it was never a large establishment. It has wonderful ambiance, but the heart of our business—both accommodations and conference facilities—is in the Tower Annex. We can easily move the conference there. Most of Carson's guests were already staying in our tower accommodations, anyway."

Faye was confused. "You mean people are actually staying in town after the bomb? Wouldn't you think everybody would run for the hills?"

Kaayla said "Oh, no no no no no" like someone who wished, for her employer's sake, that Faye would shut up. "We've gotten calls from people who wanted to cancel their reservations, certainly, but when we explained that their rooms are nowhere near the bombing site and that the FBI has checked out the premises thoroughly and—"

"And that you're throwing in free champagne and spa treatments."

Kaayla's ultra-professional demeanor cracked slightly and she smiled. "How did you guess? People like luxury and they like a good deal. When we offered them enticements not to cancel their trips, many of our guests decided not to let a little thing like a bomb change their plans."

"Many?" Faye said.

"Many," Kaayla said firmly.

Faye had to admire Kaayla's tenacity. She hoped her employer paid her what she was worth. Her very expensive shoes said that they might.

Kaayla was still rattling off information about her hotel. "Carson's guests will have everything they need, even if our historic building stays locked down. I've put conference attendees into rooms in the North Tower. Recreational facilities—gym, pool, bars, indoor playground—are there and I'll set up a temporary office there for myself. Our convention center is on the bottom three floors of the South Tower. One of our restaurants, George and Ira's Place, is also in the South Tower, and it's a good thing because the bomb seriously damaged Rhapsody, our fine dining restaurant. If we didn't still have a working kitchen at George and Ira's Place, I'd never be able to get all of your people fed."

"George and Ira? Did the musical Gershwin brothers have something to do with founding this place?"

Kaayla's laugh was sweet and a little shy. "Oh, no. In the 1920s, oil was booming, and a man named Waldo Gershwin was looking for a place to put his money. Waldo was no relation at all to the musical geniuses, but he *was* the biggest investor in the hotel, so his partners named the place after him. My employer is a pretty big hotel chain—worldwide, actually, but you probably know that. When they bought the place ten years ago, they took the Gershwin name and ran with it. The old building still had its Art Deco décor, which really fits the Gershwin brothers vibe, so they didn't even have to redecorate. They just polished the place up and made sure they weren't breaking any historic preservation laws. I like the Jazz Age theme because the piped-in music I listen to all day is pretty awesome."

"So," said the single-minded Carson. "You were telling us that you have a working kitchen."

"We do. And we have an extra meeting room where we can cater meals for the conference. You and your VIP guests will unfortunately miss out on the special banquet in Rhapsody that was going to happen tonight, but everything else should be fine."

"Serve us peanut-butter-and-jelly, then let us go to bed at eight," Cully said. "Like seven-year-olds. After a day like today, that will make us all very, very happy. And hey! I've got enough room for the VIPs in that humongous suite you gave me. We can all eat our peanut-butter-and-jelly together. It'll be like a conference banquet without the rubber chicken."

"The Gershwin does not do rubber chicken," Kaayla said, sounding horrified. "Nor do we do peanut-butter-and-jelly. We had rock Cornish hens on the menu for this evening."

"Oh, man," Jakob said. "I love those."

"Glazed in sorghum syrup, with roasted butternut squash and braised chard."

"Oh, man," Jakob repeated, softer this time. "As you can see by his waistline, Cully doesn't care much about food, but I sure do."

"Give my chefs a couple of days to regroup and you'll have your rock Cornish hens. If the FBI follows through on their plan to release the towers to us this afternoon, you can start your conference without missing a beat. Even better, you'll all be able to check into your rooms very soon."

Faye felt good about the way Kaayla was handling things. Going ahead with the conference, no matter what, was the way that scientists and sociologists said, "The show must go on!" It was their way of shaking a fist in the face of the bomber.

This thought stopped her short. She had been too busy surviving the explosion and then exploring a storm sewer to even think about why the bomb was set in the first place.

"Has anybody claimed responsibility?"

"The news stations say no," Cully said as he looked at his phone, which was finally working.

"And if they know who he was, they're not saying," he said, thumbing his screen repetitively like a man hoping to stumble on some good news somewhere.

"So we don't know why this happened," Joe said.

"Not a clue."

Everyone in the group—Carson, Kaayla, Stacy, Joe, Cully, Jakob, and Faye—stood silent for a moment. Had the bomber truly acted alone? If so, then surely he'd left a note somewhere, but Faye hadn't heard any of the investigators talking about one. Nor about a social media post, or even a manifesto in the darkest corner of the internet. Somebody needed to find out why he did what he did, so that the world would make sense again.

Faye laughed at her naive belief that the world ever made sense, but what better definition of a scientist could there be than "a person looking for a way to make sense of the world"?

Faye's need to know why someone had blown up the Gershwin Hotel knew no bounds. She felt certain, admittedly for no solid reason, that answering this question would also answer the question of what had happened to the three children beneath it. The world was not going to make sense to her until the dangling question of "Why?" was answered.

Three children were dead. A man carrying a bomb had died, and many more might have died with him. And for what?

Stacy Wong had been silent while her companions obsessed over what they knew about the bombing. Now she was beckoning Faye to join her for a one-on-one conversation, saying "Come tell me all about it! We've found the Chinese underground, after all these years. I can't believe you were actually down there! And with the FBI, no less."

Faye wasn't sure she felt up to being questioned by an academic on the trail of an intellectual obsession, but it didn't look like she had much of a choice.

Meeting Stacy in person was like seeing an old friend after a long time apart. Faye had the sense that she was as smart and funny in person as she was online, and she was clearly just as obsessed as Faye was with the Chinese underground.

Stacy's curiosity was relentless. "Tell me again. Was the staircase under the Gershwin Hotel stone or brick? Did you take pictures?"

Faye wasn't allowed to show Stacy pictures and she still didn't have a phone to do it with, anyway. She wasn't supposed to tell her anything at all.

"I can't tell you anything."

"You can't even tell me what the stairs were made of?"

"Nope."

Faye could see that it was a struggle for Stacy to keep from badgering her for answers, but the historian successfully shut her curiosity down and said, "I just can't believe you were down there."

Faye couldn't quite believe it, either. "To tell the truth, it was a little surreal."

"No joke. If only I could have been with you."

Faye thought that maybe Stacy didn't know what she was wishing for. Her bruised cheekbone ached.

"Did you see anything like this?"

Stacy held out her phone, which made Faye miss hers. As it turned out, Cully had rescued it, scooping it up off the floor as they fled the bombing. While she was underground, Joe had taken it to a repair shop that had promised to have it repaired or replaced within twenty-four hours. They'd given her a loaner that would have seemed like a miracle device when Faye was in college, but not now. It hung in her pants pocket like a foldable brick.

Stacy's phone screen showed the famous photo taken underneath Oklahoma City in 1969. It was black-and-white, and it featured a man in a 1960s-era business suit, crouching slightly and holding a flashlight. The floor was bare and the walls were bare, but in front of the crouching man was an old metal stove standing on four curved legs. Above him, conduit pipes hung overhead, which were the only things she'd seen while she was underground that she could honestly say were much like this photo. But she couldn't say that to Stacy.

"I'm sorry, Stacy. I just can't talk about what I saw."

Stacy looked at her like she'd been slapped, but she didn't respond. She just went on raving about the photo as if she and Faye hadn't talked about it online about a million times. "Would you look at that stove? And the people who went down there in 1969 said that they saw almost nothing else. Just a few flyers with Chinese writing on them."

Faye, who also loved historical photographs, put on her glasses to get a better look. "They must have taken everything they could carry with them when they moved out. It would be pretty hard to carry a cast iron stove up to the surface, but they got it down there somehow. And it was a really expensive thing to leave behind.

Maybe they kept building after the stove was already down there, and the doors they built were too narrow to get it out."

"Or they were all moving into apartments with modern kitchens and heating systems," Stacy said. "If they moved underground in the early twentieth century and moved back topside around, say, 1940, the whole world would have changed. Even cheap apartments would have had electric or gas heat by then. Refrigerators, even. Imagine how plush those things would have seemed to people who had been living underground, maybe since the turn of the century." She reached out a single finger to the photo, maybe to point at it or maybe just to touch the past. "If they went underground early enough, they would have left a world without universal indoor plumbing."

Now Faye was thinking about plumbing and it wasn't a pleasant thought. "Do we know what they did about…you know… sewage?"

Stacy gave her an appraising look. They'd talked about the oil stove a million times, but Faye had added a new wrinkle by asking what the underground residences had used for bathrooms. Stacy didn't say, "That's a new thought. What made you come up with it?" She just accepted it at face value, or she pretended she did. Faye had known "Intense Stacy" online, but she was beginning to think that she and "Thoughtful Stacy" could come to be real friends.

"I've never heard anybody mention anything about what they did for bathrooms. Latrines, maybe? Or slop buckets that they dumped…somewhere. In a faraway tunnel or someplace topside. They were smart. The health inspectors gave them a good rating for cleanliness. They must have figured something out."

"I heard about those health inspectors. Can you just imagine it?" said Faye, who was thinking that she knew what the underground community had done about their waste disposal problem. She was thinking that they probably took their slop buckets to a room with a small metal door in the wall, where they could throw the contents into an old brick storm sewer.

"In their way, those health department records are hilarious. Six health inspectors and a policeman descended on 200 people living in conditions that could have been really awful, but they ended up saying that the community was 'in good health and surroundings and as sanitary as all get out.'"

"Except for that crate of live chickens waiting to be killed and cooked."

Faye's deadpan comment made Stacy laugh. "Yup. They may have figured out the bathroom problem, but the crate of live chickens was just a little too much for those inspectors. They got demerits for that."

Stacy looked at the photo again. "I wish the people exploring the place in 1969 had taken more pictures. We don't have much beyond eyewitness accounts. But you know that."

She shot Faye an accusing look that said, *And you're keeping your eyewitness account to yourself.*

Ahua approached and Stacy said, "He's the one in charge, right? I saw him on the news."

Faye cringed a little. She was pretty sure that Stacy was about to beg Ahua to take her underground. And she was right.

"You need me, Agent. You just don't know you need me. I can help you—"

"It's a crime scene, Dr. Wong. I have to limit access. It's just standard procedure. When we release the scene, I'm sure you'll have a chance to go down there."

"But who do I ask? The hotel? The hotel next door? The person who owns the alley above the stairs, whoever that is? The city maybe? That's who destroyed the other entrance back in 1969. I don't trust the city. Not at all."

"I'm sorry."

Ahua had enough gravitas to shut down Stacy's pleading, but Faye thought that she might need to plaster both hands over her mouth, just to keep the words in.

To be honest, Faye felt a little sorry for the woman, who

seemed retiring and nondescript when she wasn't talking about her passions. It would be easy for people to ignore Stacy, and that was an insult to a woman with her intelligence and ability. When Ahua released Faye to talk about what she'd seen underground, she vowed to have a cup of coffee with Stacy and share everything she knew.

She was seeing evidence of Stacy's invisibility right in front of her eyes. As soon as the woman did what Ahua wanted and stopped talking, he turned his attention to Faye as if Stacy had never existed.

Faye didn't want to talk to him. She didn't want to talk to anyone. She wanted to find a place to hide until her hotel room was released to her, and then she wanted to crawl under the covers and stay there. She was as surprised as anyone when she broke into heaving, sobbing tears and couldn't stop for a long, long time.

Chapter Twelve

Faye sat on the easy chair in her hotel room, wrapped in a comforter. She wasn't cold, so she didn't need it to keep her warm. It served more as a barrier between her and a world where people did terrible things. If she were a knight, it would have been her coat of armor. If she were a superhero, it would have been her force field. If she were an astronaut, it would have been her space suit.

If she were a toddler, it would have been her security blanket.

Once that thought had burned across her mind, Faye had no choice but to rip the comforter off her body and hurl it across the room. She wanted it to sound a crash as it fell. She wanted it to break something, but all it did was sink gently to the floor. Whenever the image of three dead children, wrapped in blankets and abandoned, crept back into her mind, she wanted to make noise. She wanted to shatter something.

Joe picked the blanket up and folded it at the foot of the bed. "The doctor said you needed some rest. Those pills he gave you are beside the bathroom sink, if you need to take one."

"I don't remember that. Why would I want to sleep?"

Ahua had called a doctor when she suffered her little breakdown on the sidewalk, after coming up out of a space that had served as a mausoleum for children. He did this just before he told her that she shouldn't tell the doctor or anyone else about the children, so she had to make up a reason why she was crying uncontrollably.

Reliving that moment, she remembered that Joe was correct. The doctor had prescribed rest, giving her a few pills to help her sleep.

Joe ordinarily slept like a felled tree, so he couldn't quite wrap his brain around the concept of insomnia. He figured that if he couldn't sleep, then he wasn't tired. And also, he was deeply suspicious of pharmaceuticals, as young and extremely healthy people tend to be. If Joe was suggesting to Faye that she indulge in a little chemical sleep in the middle of the afternoon, then he was worried about her.

"You're upset about something you saw down there, Faye, something you can't tell me. But it's more than that. Did you forget that you were right next to an exploding bomb just a few hours ago? You've hardly stopped moving since then. If you got hurt in the explosion, I'm not sure you'd even know it yet. I can see those bruises all over you, even if you want to pretend like they're not there."

If anybody but Joe had said this to her, she would have indulged in some cheap-but-emotionally-satisfying sarcasm and said, "Really? Tell me again where the bruises on my aching knees and elbows and face came from? I forgot." But aiming sarcasm at Joe would have felt like...oh, dear, now she had let the phrase "like slapping a child" cross her mind and she was going to need to start crying again. Maybe one of those pills would be a good idea, after all.

She remembered saying to Ahua "But you say you need me. Why are you sending me off to sleep?" knowing even then that her bruised and tear-stained face answered that question for her.

He had said, "Because I've got plenty of investigating to keep me and my people busy, and because you look like you might collapse any minute. You just did collapse, actually. I'm not interested in breaking any archaeologists. Tomorrow, we can talk more about that room we saw."

"What about Liu?" she had asked. "She didn't take finding those bodies too well, either. Are you sending her off to cool her heels, too? That's her family history down there. I think you'll have to fist-fight her if you don't loop her into everything you do that relates to the Chinese underground."

"Too true. I told her to rest because I'm going to need her later. I hope she takes my advice." His eyes had raked over her face, giving it the kind of once-over that she figured he usually reserved for suspects. "Go take one of those pills the doctor gave you and just let go of all of this. Leave the world for a while. Then come find me in the mobile command station tomorrow morning. Come early, like seven o'clock early, because I like to make the most of my days. If I were you, I'd find a way to sleep and make the most of my night."

So Faye did. Sort of.

She took half a pill and ordered Joe to wake her up in three hours, just in time to go to Carson's makeshift welcome dinner for his conference speakers. Carson's day had been hellish, too. On a day like today, she wanted to support her friends. Just as the pill started making her feel loopy, there was a knock on the door.

She should have let Joe answer it, but she was closer to the door and admitting weakness had never been her strong suit. She jumped to her feet and swayed, hoping the head rush would settle down before she keeled over. It did settle down, a little bit, so she staggered to the door.

If she'd been completely sober, she would have looked through the peephole to see who was knocking on her door unannounced. She wasn't completely sober, so she flung the door open.

A woman in a crisp maid's uniform stood there with one hand on a housekeeping cart and the other on the handle of a vacuum cleaner. She was fairly young, probably in her late twenties or early thirties. "I am so sorry to be late vacuuming your room, ma'am.

It should have been done before you checked in. The problem
this morning…" Her voice trailed off.

"The bomb slowed you down." Faye spoke slowly, trying not
to slur her words. "Of course it did. Don't worry about cleaning
our room. We're just about to take a nap. Just a li'l nap."

As the woman turned to go, Faye blurted out, "Do you have
any of the little mints? The ones that go on the pillows at bed-
time in hotels like this one? They're delicious. I'd kinda like
mine now."

The young woman reached a hand in her apron pocket and
held out two mints. Faye was embarrassed now that she'd asked,
but she felt like she should take them, so she did. She said, "Thank
you," then she couldn't think of anything to add.

Joe's hand was on her elbow, ready to steer her to bed. Then
the maid turned to go and Faye saw her in profile. The woman's
prominent nose and teeth were familiar, and so was her luxuriant
hair, swept up onto the top of her head into a bun. Her name tag
said that her name was Grace.

"I remember you," Faye said. "I saw you this morning, running
from the bomb." Grace was the maid who had been working
closest to the blast.

Grace said, "Ma'am?"

Her voice was cool, but the expression on her face was not. She
looked like someone scalded by the memory of red-hot chunks
of metal and incandescent gases reaching out for her body and
just barely missing. Her hand strayed to the wooden cross at her
throat, and the reflexive search for comfort brought Faye to tears.
She was seared by the memory of this young woman running for
her life with a mop in her hand.

Here Faye was, drugging herself so that she could take a nap
and forget what she'd seen that morning, and there was Grace,
working. There was Grace, offering to vacuum Faye's floor. There
was Grace, making ready to scrub her toilet.

Faye didn't know what to do, so she reached out for Grace's

hand. Holding it tightly, she said, "I'm so glad you're okay. And I hope you get to go home and rest sometime soon."

When the door closed between them, Faye lurched toward the bedside table, looking for her purse. It wasn't there. She lurched to the desk and to the easy chair that sat invitingly in the corner. No purse.

Joe followed her, asking, "What are you doing? What are you looking for?"

Tears were rolling down her face. "My purse. I need my purse. I can't find it anywhere. Where is it?"

"It's right here by the bed, where you put it. Why do you need it? You were going to sleep. Faye, you need to sleep."

"I need to leave a tip for Grace. A really, really big tip." Now she was full-out weeping.

"I'll do it. Don't worry. It'll be a really, really big tip."

"And I need to call your dad and the kids. All day, I was going to call them and tell them I was okay."

"I told them. You can call them tomorrow. Dad understands and the kids don't need to hear you like this."

Joe's hand was back on her aching elbow, steadying her as he pulled back the bedcovers and guided her to a seat. She lay back on the pillow and let Joe ease her bruised legs onto the bed. He pulled the covers up to her chin and she tried not to think of motionless children swaddled in old, dusty blankets. She ignored the echoes in her head of brilliant light and terrible noise.

Then the drug took her away. Darkness dropped over her like a blanket and she was glad.

Chapter Thirteen

Faye rose from her too-short nap, almost rested and almost sober. Her problems seemed far away, as if she were separated from them by a pane of bulletproof glass. She didn't dread having dinner with Carson and his VIPs the way she had before her wonderful nap. Sleep truly was miraculous. So, apparently, were mind-altering drugs.

Floating in a golden numbness, she got on the elevator with Joe and they rode it all the way up. Cully had been so kind to host the dinner. She was looking forward to seeing how movie stars entertained.

Faye didn't know what she'd expected, but when she got an eyeful of Cully's suite, she knew for a fact that she had gone into the wrong line of work.

The suite took up the entire top floor of the Gershwin Hotel's North Tower, so Faye guessed she should call it a penthouse. This must be where oil barons stayed when they came to Oklahoma City to do business.

The penthouse had a full kitchen, and she wondered why. Surely movie stars and oil magnates didn't cook when they traveled. Then she noticed that the kitchen was a separate room with doors to close it off from the rest of the penthouse, and she understood. This layout was unfashionable in Faye's world where open-concept kitchens were all the rage, but people who could afford caterers—or servants—didn't want their guests to see how the party magic was made.

The living room was made for partying, with two huge leather sectional sofas, an abundance of cushy chairs, and a concert grand piano. A dining table sat sixteen, and its sideboard was fully stocked with liquor. A wall of floor-to-ceiling windows brought in a view of Oklahoma City's single brightly lit skyscraper, looming over downtown and obscured only by patchy mist and light rain.

Through a doorway, she saw a plush conference room that also sat sixteen. It had a bar cart, also fully stocked, because heaven forbid that an executive be forced to walk into the next room to freshen his Manhattan. She would bet money that, somewhere down the long hall, a Jacuzzi also sat sixteen.

Cully greeted her with a kiss on the cheek. "Did you bring your flute?"

She began by saying, "I didn't want to disturb people nearby," but quickly converted it to an awkward "No, I didn't" when she realized that nobody is nearby when your penthouse occupies an entire floor. Given the size of the piano, she guessed that the floor was soundproofed to stifle the noise from partygoers being serenaded by a pianist who, like the suite, was top-flight and rented for the evening.

"Don't forget that your anniversary gift wasn't just the flute, Cousin Faye." Faye's heart fluttered at Cully's reminder of their tenuous family relationship. "It was three flute lessons from me. Come by tomorrow after the conference is over for the day and we'll get started. Until then—" he said, grabbing a flute lying on an end table "—let me give you a taste of what you'll be able to do. Put your fingers over the holes like this."

He centered the middle three fingers of each hand over the wooden flute's six holes, using his thumbs on the back to help support it. Then he placed his mouth over the whistle-like mouthpiece and blew gently as he put each finger down. Then he picked them up again in sequence.

There was nothing fancy about what Cully played. Faye recognized it as a pentatonic scale, no different from the same sequence of sounds played on a guitar or a piano, but the flute's pure tone was so haunting that the room fell into silence.

He pulled a cloth out of his pocket to wipe the mouthpiece. "Your turn."

Great. Now she was going to have to make squawky noises in front of a crowd when Cully Mantooth had just made the same flute sing.

When he saw that she had to stretch to reach the lowest holes, he said, "This is mine and it's in G. Joe said your hands were small, so I made one pitched in A for you. Whatever you're able to do on my flute, you'll be able to do better on yours."

She blew into the mouthpiece, embarrassingly aware that Cully Mantooth's famous lips had just touched it. At first, she heard nothing but wind. Then she made a weird sound like two incompatible notes fighting with each other. This went on for a while until, for no reason that she could tell, the sound resolved into a birdlike tone. It was wavery but it was there.

She tried to do what Cully had done, putting each finger down and then picking each one up. Her tone would break at times and she'd have to struggle to get it back, but she loved the process of making the sound better. Faye wouldn't mind if she never saw another sleeping pill, but she was as hooked by this flute as a newly minted addict who had just discovered heroin. If she'd been alone, she would have kept noodling until her lip muscles made her stop.

"That was lovely." Cully's eyes were smiling. "And you enjoyed it, didn't you? I could tell. My flutes soothe my mind. They keep me sane."

Faye heard Jakob snort and say, "Others might think different."

Cully ignored him and kept his eyes on Faye. Joe, too, was

watching her with the goofy grin of a man who is certain that no man will ever buy his wife such an awesome anniversary present.

"It's like meditation, isn't it?" she said to Cully.

"Playing the Indian flute is about the music, but it's not just about the music. It's about all the people who ever played it before you. But you know that already. I can tell. For now, pick up the flute every time you walk past it and do what you just did. I'll teach you some more tomorrow."

And then the moment of peace was gone and she was left with no comfort but the bleariness left over from her sleeping pill. The other partiers erupted into the kind of party talk that makes the air hum. Dr. Dell pushed her aside to take a look at Cully's flute, exclaiming over its craftsmanship. When she finally gave the flute back to Faye and left to refresh her drink, Stacy Wong rushed up and resumed obsessing about the underground Chinese community.

"When I saw you this afternoon after you toured the underground city, there were wet splatters on the shoulders of your shirt, so I'm thinking hip waders. Is it flooded down there? God, I hope not."

Faye wouldn't have called what she did a "tour," and she wouldn't have called what she saw a "city." Something about Stacy made Faye want to back away, but she resisted the urge. Maybe she was just suffering an emotional hangover from the day and a chemical hangover from the pills. She shouldn't be hard on a woman with a quirky obsession, because she had a few of her own.

Stacy took a big step into Faye's personal space and said, "They said on TV that you found some bodies down there. Children. Three of them. They're asking for anyone with information about missing children from the 1990s to come forward."

The 1990s. So Ahua had found out some things while she was asleep. Good. That's what he was supposed to do. And somebody had told the press about the children, so she was apparently now released from secrecy where they were concerned. Still, she figured it would be wise just to tell people to watch the news if they wanted answers.

"Did you see the bodies up close, Faye? Can you tell me anything at all about them?"

This time Faye couldn't help herself. She did take a step back from Stacy and her ghoulish questions. Maybe the drug had addled Faye's brain, but she began to wonder whether Stacy had arranged for a man to kill himself with a bomb so that she could have access to the place she'd obsessed about for years.

Stacy didn't seem to notice Faye's step back. "I'm so intrigued that you found bodies from the 1990s down there. Do you think maybe that room was built later by somebody else entirely?"

Faye was asking herself the same questions, now that she knew that the children might have been left there in the 1990s. Nevertheless, she wasn't about to share her thoughts with Stacy.

She closed her lips over the things she might have said, like: "I'm not sure why there were colorful drawings on the walls of that room" or "I'm curious about whether they cut that door into the sanitary line as a place to dump their sewage."

Instead, she said, "I don't have a lot to tell you, Stacy," and escaped to the dining room. There, she ransacked the ridiculously overstocked bar for something nonalcoholic that wouldn't fight with the remnants of her sleeping pill.

———

The party didn't last long. Faye wasn't the only one who had started her day with mental and physical trauma. After an hour or so, Faye saw Jakob settle into one of the cushy chairs and doze off.

Cully was still proving his acting chops by playing the part of a gracious host, but there was a sag to his shoulders. His smile, though still infectious, was slower to come. His charisma might be boosting his guests' spirits and his showman-like ability to draw energy from an audience might be boosting his, but he was headed for a crash. His guests all needed to leave so that their host could stop pretending he was still thirty-five. Joe could see how things were, and he rose to his feet to signal their departure. Faye was so grateful.

Stacy, Dr. Jackson, and Sadie Raincrow had missed the morning excitement. Faye could see that they were far from ready to go. Dr. Dell practically ran to the bar when she heard Joe and Faye make their goodbyes. Faye had known people who saw open bar situations as a challenge to drink up. Some of them were alcoholics and some of them were just cheap, but few people over thirty were this obvious.

Faye, on the other hand, had been nursing a Coke for the entire party and wanted to be rid of its watery dregs. The golden-haired young man who had been bussing their glasses was nowhere to be seen, so she headed for the kitchen.

Pushing open the swinging door, she saw someone at the sink, a woman wearing the hotel's navy-and-white uniform and an air of authority. On the countertop were neatly arranged trays of hors d'oeuvres, ready for her assistant to whisk off the plastic wrap and carry them into the party. At her elbow was a tray of empty glasses, waiting to be washed.

Faye knew that she must have seen this woman throughout the party, making sure things ran smoothly, but her presence hadn't registered in Faye's mind. Service professionals were trained to be invisible, and this woman had paid attention to that part of her training.

Faye lingered for an awkward moment and listened to a sink full of glasses clank as the woman washed them. She felt terrible for having ignored a human being for at least an hour. The least she could do was say thank you.

"You did a wonderful job with this party. I really appreciate it."

The woman half-turned in Faye's direction, somehow accomplishing this without taking her hands out of the suds. She turned just far enough to reveal the name tag pinned to her uniform, and Faye saw that it read Lucia.

"Thank you, Lucia," she said.

Lucia's black hair was twisted into a large knot at the nape of her neck and covered by a hair net. Her thin face was dominated by prominent cheekbones and a pair of wary eyes that took in information while giving none away.

She said only "Thank you, ma'am," then she turned back to her dishwashing.

Lucia's accent was faint, as if she had learned English as a young child or perhaps had been raised by Spanish speakers, but Faye recognized it as Mexican. Faye read Spanish well and had even done some translation for her work, but she wouldn't consider herself a fluent speaker. She toyed with the idea of speaking to Lucia again in Spanish, since she was always looking for an opportunity to practice, but Lucia had made it clear that she didn't want to chit-chat. Faye knew she should respect that. She just set her glass at Lucia's elbow with the other dishes waiting to be washed.

As the glass clinked on the counter, Lucia flinched, and Faye said, "I didn't mean to startle you. I just wanted to put my glass someplace that was easy for you to reach."

Lucia didn't answer and Faye said no more, but she didn't even try to stop staring. She kept her eyes on Lucia from that moment until she pushed her way back through the kitchen's swinging door.

Lucia's narrow shoulders, slim hips, and long thin legs were familiar and they were unmistakable. Faye had seen her just that morning, crumpled on a floor she'd just mopped while it was heaving beneath her.

———

Faye shed her clothes as soon as the hotel room's door closed behind her. She did all the usual going-to-bed stuff, from showering to toothbrushing, before she took the other half of the sleeping pill. Apparently, though the doctor had told her it was only a mild sedative, this particular chemical spelled instant unconsciousness for Faye.

Ready for sleep, she washed the pill down with tap water. It was only then, when she left the bathroom and stood by her bedside, that she saw her pillow. Grace had left a fistful of the mints that Faye liked.

Maybe Grace was thanking her for the big tip, and maybe she was angling for another one. But Faye liked to think of the mints as a statement of solidarity, a hand reaching out to hers. She liked to think that Grace was saying, "I know what you went through this morning, because I went through it, too. We both could have died today. Here's a bit of comfort."

Faye picked up a piece of candy and listened to its foil crinkle as she unwrapped it. She laid it on her tongue and let the dark chocolate coating melt off of its cool, creamy mint filling, and she spent that moment of sweetness thanking God that she was alive to taste it.

Chapter Fourteen

On the day that my third brother died, I knew.

I knew what evil was and I knew whose heart harbored it. And evil must be obliterated.

Until that day, I didn't even know where Lonnie had laid my other two brothers to rest. All I could do when they died was watch him drive away with them while I begged him to take me, too. But by the time Orly died, I was old enough to be stealthy. I was old enough to hide under the tarp that lay crumpled on the bed of Lonnie's pickup truck.

It was late at night, so nobody saw him park near a concrete-lined drainage ditch at the river's edge. Nobody but me saw him carry the blanket-wrapped body and a flashlight down into the ditch. Nobody saw me follow him down into the ditch, not even Lonnie.

Lonnie walked down that ditch into a round concrete pipe extending deep into the ground. It was huge to me, big enough so that even Lonnie could walk upright. I followed, hanging far back so that he couldn't see me. There was no light to guide me but Lonnie's flashlight, far ahead. In its way, the darkness was a blessing, because it hid me. Sliding my feet along the bottom of the big pipe, I made no sound, no splash that could reveal my presence.

Standing upright in the center with my arms outspread, I couldn't even reach the pipe's curved walls. If I leaned to the right, though,

I could drag a hand as I walked. The faraway flashlight, the pipe beneath my feet, and the pipe against my hand gave me three points to keep myself oriented in space. The sound of my breath oriented me, too, reminding me that I was alive, even though my brother was not.

At intervals, my hand lost contact with the wall for a few terrifying steps. The first time it happened, I groped silently until I realized that these empty spaces were the mouths of smaller pipes entering the larger one that enclosed me. I shuffled on, aware that the side wall was getting slowly closer to me as the pipe narrowed and curved to the left.

Eventually, even the very texture of my surroundings changed and my hand began to drag across rough brick. My foot landed awkwardly on a brick's edge, twisting my ankle. I almost went down in a splashing heap, but I was strong enough to hold myself upright and limp on. I was strong enough to do that, because I had to be. I had to know what he did with Orly. In my nightmares, I saw my brothers' bodies dumped in trash cans or consumed in flames. I had to know.

I remembered what Lonnie said to my weeping mother as she begged him to let her bury their son, so she'd have a place to mourn him.

"Are you as stupid as you look, woman? Don't you remember what happened at Waco and Ruby Ridge? The federal agents will come. We can't be letting 'em find graves and dead bodies. They'll use 'em to justify whatever awful thing they decide to do to us. I bet they're watching us now, so we can't be seen to be digging no graves. I'll find a place for the boy, just like I did with the other two."

As an adult with years of experience out in the world, I know now that this threadbare excuse for logic meant that Lonnie was either deceitful or stupid or delusional. If there were federal agents watching our pathetic little farm, then they would have noticed that three little boys had toddled around for a while and then disappeared. As a child, I was terrified of helicopters and people in uniforms, because Lonnie had convinced us all that such people would be firebombing us at any moment, but Lonnie had been the real bad guy.

All my life, Lonnie was the bad guy. Now that he's gone, I'm going to have to figure out how to live without him. He has always been my yardstick for right and wrong. Next to Lonnie and the things he did, nothing seems wrong to me. Certainly murder didn't, not when the victim was Lonnie. I feel not a shred of regret at what I did to him.

He is the reason I am still, after all these years, essentially alone. I have work colleagues and casual acquaintances, but friendship is hard when any conversation can go south in an instant. Even a casual reference to an insanely popular movie or pop song from my childhood years leaves me helpless. My go-to excuse for these memory gaps is "We didn't have cable," but what I really mean is "We didn't have electricity, running water, flush toilets, or any conception of what the outside world was like."

Well, that isn't fully true. As the firstborn, I lived with Lonnie and my first mother for five years before he acquired a second wife and lost his mind, moving his growing family far from the malicious government and from everything else. I and both my mothers remembered civilization, but the other children didn't have a clue. They only saw the outside world on Sundays from the crowded cab of Lonnie's pickup while on our way to the weekly service he held at The Sanctuary.

He never even rolled down the windows to let us smell free air. The children born after Lonnie fled the government didn't even have birth certificates. Only I do. Nobody outside the family ever knew my brothers and sisters were even born, so there were no repercussions for Lonnie when some of them died, not as long as nobody ever found the bodies. Hence this long slog down a dark pipe with a dead child in his arms, a slog that I was dead-sure he had taken twice before.

I dogged his steps the whole way and he never knew. When he stopped at last, he stopped so suddenly that I almost skidded into the flashlight's dim sidespill. I might have been discovered then, but his attention was diverted by a door set into the wall of the brick-and-mortar pipe.

I knew that door. I'd seen it before, from the other side, while I sat in The Sanctuary. For as long as my first mother worked at the Gershwin Hotel, we had easy access to the room where Lonnie liked to take his family for Sunday worship, the one that he pretentiously called The Sanctuary.

After my mother lost that job, we lost The Sanctuary, or so we all thought. When I saw Lonnie leave the storm sewer and crawl through the little door, I realized that he'd known how to get back in there the whole time, but he'd never told us. I had studied the door's battered contours every Sunday for years during the interminable church services that Lonnie had loved so much. They had given him a chance to expound on his heretical beliefs in front of an audience, and he had seized the chance with both hands.

Lonnie was always happiest when he had an audience. Never mind that the audience was small. Lonnie never stopped dreaming of an ever-growing congregation, but he'd never had one that didn't consist entirely of his wives and children. Only Orly was born after we lost The Sanctuary. The rest of us, the survivors, we will carry that place inside us always.

Orly. The name breaks my heart, even after all these years. All their names break my heart.

Gabe had been such a good boy during services, so sweet and quiet. Then Zeb had come along, also sweet and quiet, and then Orly.

Only now, as an adult, do I realize that babies aren't supposed to be sweet and quiet all the time. My brothers were sick. They needed the help of a doctor, but all they got was The Sanctuary, transformed by Lonnie into a crypt just for them.

Lonnie deserved the pain of losing his children, but Gabe, Zeb, and Orly didn't deserve to die. It would have helped me to believe that sickly sons were God's punishment for Lonnie, but I do not believe that God punishes children for their parents' evil. What kind of sense does that make?

After I saw my father tuck my brother under his arm and crawl through the little door into the Sanctuary, I crept slowly backwards and out of his sight. Without even the light from Lonnie's flashlight, I retraced my steps with only the feel of the pipe beneath my feet and against the fingers of one hand to guide me.

Because of the danger that he would soon turn around and walk back the way he came, I moved quickly until I was back in the bed of the pickup, hiding under the familiar tarp and waiting for Lonnie. Eventually, I heard him open the driver's door and start the engine.

I knew then that Orly, Gabe, and Zeb were in their final resting place, and it was The Sanctuary. No other explanation made any sense.

Years passed before I grew old enough to drive to the river, make my way down the storm sewer, force open the balky latch, and lay eyes on my baby brothers again.

From that moment forward, my entire life has pointed toward this day, my first day without Lonnie in the world. I should be so glad, but my mind keeps straying to the everyday evil that occupies the front page of every newspaper I ever saw, and the second page, and every page after that.

I was taught from a very young age that the way to righteousness was to obliterate evil. But how could anyone obliterate anything with so many faces?

Chapter Fifteen

The command center was already humming with activity when Faye arrived, despite the fact that the sun was barely up.

"Good morning, Madame Archaeologist," Ahua said, handing her a cup of coffee the size of a medieval tankard. "I'm glad you're here. I want to pick your brain about the paintings in that room we saw yesterday. Actually, I want to pick your brain about the room itself."

She took the humongous cup in both hands. "For coffee? No problem! My professional opinion can absolutely be bought with coffee."

"You don't have to work for coffee. I told you yesterday that I want to hire you as a consultant, like Bigbee did last summer. Just invoice me by the hour for your time spent. And that includes yesterday's underground adventure."

"A budget? With money in it? And coffee, too? You, sir, just hired an archaeologist."

"Okay, then. Today is the day you help me figure out what's been going on beneath this building for the past century."

"Well, we weren't exactly beneath this building—" she began.

"Agreed," he said. "We have no evidence of chambers directly beneath the Gershwin, except for a small portion of the staircase.

I put some of my graphics people on the night shift and I woke up to this. They do good work." He tapped the keyboard of a nearby computer and a map appeared on its very large display.

The person who made the map had considerately included an arrow pointing north, like any ordinary map, but Faye couldn't relate that to what she'd seen underground. North doesn't mean much when you can't see the sun or a city's street grid.

The map, though, was helpful in other ways. She could see that Ahua's mapmakers had outlined the staircase and the landing at its foot in black. The site of the explosion was marked with a big "X."

They had also marked the landing at the bottom of the staircase, where she knew that two doorways existed. One door led into a space labeled "Painted Room," and the location of the metal door into the sewer was marked on the far wall. The other doorway opened left into apparent nothingness. A graphic artist with a flair for history had labeled it "Terra Incognita."

Faye pointed at the upper portion of the stairway. "This is the only part that's underneath the Gershwin, right?"

"Right. If he thought he was carrying a bomb that would take down the building over it, then the hotel wasn't his target. Based on laser measurements, the downstairs room to the left of the stairs starts a few yards south of the Gershwin's lobby and extends toward the river. If there's a room beyond it, it goes under a street and a park. Eventually, it would go under the convention center, and wouldn't a convention hall full of oil executives be a great target?"

"Is that what's going on there now?"

"Yeah, but the bomb went off two hours before their first session."

He tapped a key and a second map, drawn in red, overlaid the first one. It was a regular, ordinary map of the surface. The north arrow pointed away from the river, and that helped because Faye knew where the river was.

"I don't know why else you'd want to set off a bomb down there." Ahua stared at the map like the answer was written on it.

"To destroy the children's bodies?"

"Why now? They've been down there more than twenty years. A bomb would only call attention to them, which suggests that the bomber wasn't involved with putting them there. Maybe he didn't know about them."

This was true, and Faye was disappointed. She'd hoped that there was a link between the bombing and the bodies. Otherwise, they represented a very cold case and cold cases were hard to solve.

"Okay," she said. "There's no reason to link the bodies to the bombing other than geography. We don't know why they're lying underneath downtown Oklahoma City and we don't know why the dead man took a bomb down there, either."

"Whatever his goal was, he died for it. Maybe he was hoping to take down a building, then got cold feet, came back upstairs, and accidentally detonated the bomb. Maybe he intended to take out a lot of people in the Gershwin lobby, terrorist-style, but the bomb went off before he got it into position."

"There weren't all that many people there."

"True. Maybe he was going to hide the bomb, wait until there was a bigger crowd, and detonate it remotely, but he screwed up. But if so, why go downstairs? There are plenty of ways to connect the dots on the facts we have, but none of them make sense."

Faye agreed. "So what do you want me to do for you?"

"I hired you because, as an archaeologist, you can help me get my mind around the underground structure itself. When was it built? How was it built? Is there anything in the past that's connected to the bombing or those bodies?"

"I'm on it. I'll do whatever it takes to help you put away anybody that helped the bomber. And if we find out that somebody murdered those children—" Faye flailed for the right words but there were none. "I'll do whatever you need to catch the person who did that."

"That, Dr. Longchamp-Mantooth, is the right answer."

Faye studied the layered map some more. It rekindled the claustrophobic feeling of being far underground with no light except the light they had brought with them. "If you wanted to make an anti-government political statement like McVeigh did, an industrial trade show just isn't sexy enough to fire up a bunch of malcontents. But check out this IRS office. It's just as close to the Gershwin as the convention center. For a political statement, that would be at the top of a lot of people's lists, but it's in the wrong direction." She pointed to a spot on the map. "The chambers don't go anywhere near it?"

"Not that we know of."

Ahua clicked another key and dark blue lines appeared on a map that was growing more confusing by the moment. "Here's the layout of the stormwater system. Some of those sewer lines are really old. The brick pipes we were in aren't the only ones under Oklahoma City. I think that's true in a lot of cities."

The computer screen looked like somebody had thrown a fistful of multicolored spaghetti at it. "That's...um...complicated."

"Well, yeah. You're looking at everything we know, from the surface all the way down. It's like we've stumbled onto an archaeological site where you don't even have to dig. You're the archaeologist. What do you think we've uncovered?"

"I don't see an obvious answer, but old maps aren't always reliable. Maybe he got down there and didn't see what he thought he'd see. That might have made him turn around and try to abort the mission. But the bomb had other ideas."

"We've got video that suggests you're right. Just minutes before the blast, the bomber came into the hotel lobby carrying a backpack."

"You've got video of his face? That's great!"

"Well, his hat was low and his collar was flipped up and he was wearing sunglasses. And he never looked directly at any of the cameras, so I think he'd done some reconnaissance on where they were. You or I might not recognize him if he passed us on the street, but the bureau has facial recognition software that may help with that."

She remembered a man in a cowboy hat spreading his arms and taking flight. "I think I remember him. I think I remember seeing him die. But that's all I remember. What did the video show?"

"He wandered around for a few minutes, then went into the alcove."

"It was right above the underground stairs, wasn't it?"

"You got it. The cameras weren't positioned for a clear view, but he touched the wall a couple of times and then disappeared. We think he opened a hidden panel. The Evidence Response Team is still sifting through the rubble, but they haven't found the latch to prove the secret panel theory. I believe it was there anyway."

Faye stared at the screen as if the answer was going to appear there in bold print. "So how much time passed between when the bomber opened the panel and when the bomb blew?"

"Not much. He only had time to go down the stairs, open the door to the painted room and walk through it, then turn around and climb back up the steps. The bomb went off just as he stepped back into the lobby. We ran the fingerprints. No criminal record. No identification. Nothing."

Faye remembered the condition of the body. She didn't even want to think about how it had been possible to recover his fingerprints.

Ahua answered the question she hadn't asked. "We got complete prints off the door downstairs. There was a good enough match on what was left of his hands to know they were his."

"Nobody's claimed responsibility?"

"Nope. Not even any fakers trying to ride on the dead guy's coattails. Oklahomans have very strong feelings about bombers since McVeigh. It seems that there are no radical groups of any stripe who want to be hated that bad."

"What do you know about the bomb?"

"My miraculous crime scene investigators actually found lots of pieces of the pressure cooker he used to make it. One of them carried the serial number."

"You can't be serious."

"Oh, but I am. They're that good."

Faye thought of her own pressure cooker, neatly stored in a kitchen cabinet, and tried to make herself believe that it was a deadly weapon. "How does that kind of bomb even work? My pressure cooker doesn't heat up by itself. Without a stove, it's just a really heavy pot. He wasn't carrying a stove."

"You just answered yourself. A pressure cooker is a really heavy pot *that's designed to withstand high pressure.* And its lid is sealed with a gasket that keeps steam from the cooking food from escaping until the pressure inside rises. When you're cooking, it's designed to release the pressure before it gets too high, so it's perfectly safe. But if you push it past its design parameters using something like gunpowder…"

"Boom."

"Exactly. They're very simple to make. Terrifyingly so, actually. You pack the pressure cooker with black powder for the blast. Add a heavy load of something small and deadly like nails or ball bearings for the shrapnel. Then you need something to light it up, which you can improvise with the guts of a cell phone. Or some Christmas lights."

"Christmas lights. You're kidding."

Ahua was describing something that you could build out of parts you bought at a yard sale. This creeped Faye out, almost more than the bomb itself.

"I wish I was kidding. You can use a timer, but the really slick operators use modified cell phones to generate the spark. They get total control over the timing of the blast, and they can set it off from a safe distance with a simple phone call. We can't assume that this guy intended to be a suicide bomber."

"If all you have to do is call a specific number, you could set it off from anywhere in the world."

"Exactly. We found mangled cell phone pieces in the rubble and a heavily damaged phone in his pocket. We think he intended to get away from the blast radius, then let his cell phone tell the thing to blow."

"But you don't know where his plan went wrong."

"Not a clue."

"What about the serial number Goldsby's people found? Will it tell you anything about the pressure cooker? Where it was bought? When?"

"When it was bought? That's the problem. According to the serial number, it's twenty years old. Even if we could trace it back to its purchase, the bomber could easily have bought it at a garage sale."

There was proof of Faye's garage sale theory.

"Or inherited it from his grandmother..." Ahua continued, "or stole it from a friend...or got custody of it in a divorce..."

"I get the point. Twenty years is too long for the serial number to help us trace the thing to a single person."

She thought of pressure cookers she'd used in her life. Sooner or later, they all started to leak. "You know what? Twenty years is too long to trust that the original gasket is still good. If I were gonna build a bomb, I'd want to know for sure that it was going to blow. Is there any way to find out whether somebody bought a gasket for that model recently?"

"*That* is an excellent angle. I've got people who love to do that kind of deep-dive research. Consider it done."

"So what do you really need me to do? Somebody in the FBI would have thought of the gasket angle eventually. It's just dumb luck that I like to keep my small appliances for a ridiculous period of time."

"I'm really interested in what you can tell me about the room we saw. It feels important."

Faye remembered the vivid paintings on the wall and the odd little door. Yes. It did feel important.

He fastened his eyes on her and gave her that FBI-approved "Now you're going to tell me everything you know" look. "Do you think it was built when the Chinese people built the other chambers, eighty or a hundred years ago? Or did somebody else built that room later—like maybe in the 1990s—and paint its walls and cut that door into the sewer?"

Faye had already suggested that he try to date the paint and she couldn't think of anything else useful. This could be the shortest consulting job ever. "Um...what if one of the pictures showed a television? Then we'd know it wasn't painted in 1920."

Now she was truly flailing for ideas.

"Well, yeah. That would be a big help. Why don't you wish for a miracle and hope the TV shows the World Series, complete with team names and score?"

This image made Faye laugh out loud.

"Well," he said, "we won't know if there's a painting of the 1994 World Series down there unless we look. Here are the pictures Goldsby took yesterday. They're preliminary, but they're all we've got for now. When the Evidence Response Team releases the room, he'll go back in with proper lighting and better equipment."

He called up a photo slide show and clicked through it, one photo at a time.

"We also have these." He clicked one more time and six images filled the computer screen, four walls, the ceiling, and the floor. "I asked my techs to piece together the photos Goldsby took from the bottom of the stairs with the ones we saw him take from the storm sewer. They're a little wonky, since they were pieced together from photos taken from two angles, but you can see the painted images pretty well."

He motioned for her to sit in front of the computer. "I want you to take a good long look at these photos while I go talk to Goldsby's crew about what they're finding. When I get back, please meet me at the door and tell me that you found a television screen painted on one of those walls, complete with the score of the 1994 World Series. Or even 1992 will do."

Chapter Sixteen

So the FBI has hired an archaeologist to help them poke around underground. Under ordinary circumstances, I would be intrigued. I have always been fascinated by history. Humanity has had so many years to get things right, and yet we just can't manage it. How hard is it, really, to be kind?

Too hard, apparently.

When Lonnie made the error of bringing the bomb topside, he opened me to exposure in a way that I never anticipated. How could I have guessed that the bomb would go off in the one and only place that could open the catacombs under this city to scrutiny?

The true catacombs, the ones inhabited by people too poor to better their lives in any other way, are no danger to me. It is The Sanctuary that puts my freedom on the line, and the freedom of those I love most in this world. The room is very old, but the paintings aren't, and they say too much. Or they did.

The paintings that addled, egotistical Lonnie left behind were a problem. They did not bear scrutiny, not by anyone and certainly not by someone trained to interpret them and, even worse, put a date on them. They needed to go and now they are gone.

And, unfortunately, Dr. Faye Longchamp-Mantooth needs to go, too. The FBI has done nothing but peek through the door, and this would not worry me, if they hadn't taken an archaeologist with them. Detailed photos of the paintings cannot possibly exist. I was in The Sanctuary mere hours ago, and there were no footprints in the dust on its floor but Lonnie's. Dr. Longchamp-Mantooth is the only expert who has seen them and she is the only expert who will ever see them.

She can estimate their age. She can interpret the history behind Lonnie's religious ravings. The risk that she can connect the paintings to my family is too great. This is regrettable, but once evil is obliterated, the second commandment emerges in full force. It tells me I must protect the ones I love. If I could do that and spare Dr. Longchamp-Mantooth, then I would. I cannot, so I will do what must be done.

This is what Lonnie taught me, and I am far stronger than Lonnie ever was. I keep the commandments he taught me, as I always have. He never suspected that those commandments would lead me to wipe him from existence.

Chapter Seventeen

Faye studied the photos of the painted walls, one at a time, expanding one interesting area after another. After maybe five minutes, she laughed and said, "Well, would you take a look at that?" but nobody was there to hear her, so she kept poring over the pictures.

When Ahua returned, she said, "I gotta say it. These paintings are interesting."

"Can you date them?" Ahua leaned over her shoulder to look. "Tell me you can."

"Don't I wish? Nope. There are a lot of nature scenes and those don't change much over time. And there's also a lot of religious stuff, some of it standard and some of it really not."

"What do you mean?"

Faye laughed. "You haven't looked at this at all, have you?"

"I've been a little busy."

"Yeah, I know. Look here. See? It's a cross on a hill, between two smaller crosses on smaller hills. That's definitely Christian imagery."

"Well, yeah."

"But this isn't." She zoomed in on the figure of a naked woman standing behind a cross, heavy breasted and large-bellied.

"Is that the Venus of Willendorf?"

"Yes, it is. You're good at art history for an FBI agent."

"Our training is very eclectic."

"I bet. Is it this eclectic?"

She zoomed in closer on the painting of a mosque, enlarging the grand staircase to its ornate door. Sprawled on those stairs was a naked woman in a pose more reminiscent of a Playboy centerfold than a priceless Stone Age sculpture.

"Well," Ahua said. "Would you look at that? My Muslim friends would call that Level One blasphemy."

"No joke. Whoever did this was a pretty good painter, but I don't think this is eighty years old. If I had to give a gut-level guess, I'd say very late twentieth century."

"Based on the style of pornography being published at that time."

"Yes," she said. "Based on 1990s pornography. Not that I'm an expert on that."

Faye zoomed out so that no FBI agent would walk up behind her and see a hand-painted centerfold on her screen. "So when do we go back down there?"

"Not sure. You'll know when I know."

"I'm on your payroll," she said, "so I'm ready when you are. But do you mind if I spend some time at the conference this morning? Off the clock, of course. Joe's giving a flintknapping demonstration in—" she looked at her watch, "—twenty minutes. I'd like to be there for him."

Ahua made a shooing motion with his hands. "Go. Enjoy your husband's talk. But keep your eyes open. Who's to say that Dr. Callahan's conference wasn't the bomber's target?"

"Who would want to bomb people who flintknap and make flutes and weave baskets?"

"People aren't always logical when they choose to hate other people."

Faye hadn't considered that someone might be angry that

Carson had brought in people from all over the country to cele-brate indigenous cultures built by brown people. How could she still be so naive after all this time?

The answer was obvious. Staying as naive as she could man-age was her personal survival mechanism as a brown person in America.

"Well, if he really was after a bunch of artists and archaeolo-gists, let's just hope he was working alone, because my husband's at the conference and I'm on my way."

———

As Faye walked from the command center toward the South Tower's, convention center, she heard two things. One of them was pleasant, and one of them was not.

Flute music seeped out of the building ahead of her when another guest opened the door to come out. It hung in the air, cool and pure. It made her smile. She was glad to know that she hadn't missed all of Cully's presentation.

The other sound was not so pleasant. It came from across the sidewalk to her right and it was the sound of a voice on a bullhorn addressing a heckling crowd.

"You don't have a permit, folks, and you're blocking the hotel entrance. You have a right to protest, but not to interfere with the operation of a law-abiding business. Not to mention people who are just trying to go about their lives. I need you to settle down and stop blocking the sidewalk."

Faye had woken up early and she'd been in too much of a hurry to check the news. She'd ridden an elevator down to Ahua's command center before seven, and the streets had still been deserted. She was only now getting her first inkling that a protest was going on.

Faye wasn't close enough to read the slogans on their hand-painted signs, so she was curious. What on earth was this protest about? She edged a bit closer. The group wasn't large but it sure was loud. Across the street was another cluster of people, also holding signs, who seemed to be baiting the larger group.

Great. The last thing Faye wanted was to be caught between protesters and counterprotesters, especially when she wasn't sure she agreed with the grievances of either group. Nor did she even know what those grievances were.

She tried to plot out a path to the South Tower, but the man holding the bullhorn had not been kidding when he said that the protesters were blocking the sidewalk. Faye needed to move quickly or she would miss Joe's talk.

Were they protesting the bombing? To what purpose? The bomber was dead. If they were protesting the organization that had sponsored his crime, they knew more than the FBI did.

She didn't want to wade right into the ruckus, so she stepped onto another sidewalk. It led away from the street, but she knew it would eventually take her to the convention center. She was irritated to have to go such a roundabout way, but it seemed like a reasonable workaround.

The Gershwin Hotel's Tower Annex sat on a well-groomed lot that extended across a city block, less than a block down the street from the historic hotel. The property was a leafy oasis in an urban business district and Faye enjoyed the flowering hedges planted on either side of her detour. She knew that the path opened up into a quiet courtyard centered on a fountain and encircled by more hedges. It never crossed her mind to be nervous about setting off alone down a path that had never been frightening before, not until she heard heavy, fast footsteps behind her. Now the beautiful hedges looked like a place for an attacker to hide, and they blocked the view of anybody who might come to her rescue.

Faye turned to see a man, broad and tall, running at top speed. Based solely on leg length, there was no way she could outrun him, but she only had to stay ahead of him for a few seconds. Once she was through the lonely courtyard, she'd be within sight of the South Tower. Surely someone would see her there. Or maybe someone would at least hear her scream.

She broke into a sprint. Her large and practical purse, the size of a horse's saddlebag, slapped against her hip and thigh as she ran. The heavy boots that were her everyday footgear, tight-laced around the ankles, constrained her gait. The man was going to catch up with her, and he was going to do it while she was in the courtyard, hidden on all sides by the gnarled and leafy branches of sasanqua camellia hedges planted when her grandmother was a girl.

As the sidewalk beneath her feet passed through a narrow opening in those hedges, she was faced with something even more terrifying than a strange man twice her size. The courtyard was hiding still more strange men, four of them.

They were clearly protesters, judging by the signs they were carrying. Ordinarily, she would have thought, "Great! That man behind me won't hurt me when he's got this many witnesses," but the protesters were throwing hostile looks her way. She couldn't figure out why. She certainly hadn't bombed anybody.

As she stumbled closer, she got her first clear look at their signs, and the inscription on the nearest one explained everything.

If we had a White Culture convention, you'd be pissed!

Faye, a person who was inarguably not white, was running headlong into the arms of people who felt strongly enough about their white supremacist views to march in the streets. This was assuredly not a good thing.

The slapping footsteps behind her drew near. Unexpectedly, the sound passed her and then stopped. The big man stood between her and the sign-carrying men. All four faces were still hostile, but now they were trained on him.

From behind, all Faye could see of the big, thick-waisted man was a gray T-shirt and a pair of snug, well-worn blue jeans. A single black braid, longer even than Joe's, snaked down his back.

It was streaked with gray, but the man gave no other indication of age. His arms and fists, held in a relaxed position at his sides, were dark brown. If these men didn't like brown people, then they were predisposed to dislike both Faye and this nameless man standing between them and her.

One of them said, "We know where you live, Ben. Wouldn't take long to drive out there." His sign was graced with a crude drawing of a hand grenade. Wavy lines in red, yellow, and orange radiated from its black outline in what Faye judged was a reasonable way to suggest an explosion for someone with a box of Magic Markers and a limited imagination. Its caption said, "This is what happens when they live among us."

The ponytailed man who was apparently named Ben said, "Yeah? Listen here, Graham. You know that I own just as many guns as you do. What exactly do you think is going to happen when you idiots come driving up to my house?"

"You won't like it much." The man who said this seemed to be a man of few words, since his sign said nothing but "White Power."

Ben didn't seem worried. "I'll like it fine. I'll meet you at the door with my daddy's old double-barrel. My wife will be behind me, live-streaming everything you do on her cell phone. Just like she's doing right now."

Faye was afraid to move much, but she turned ever so slightly. Behind her was a stout woman of about fifty, with two black and silver braids that hung over her large breasts and stopped at her waist. She held a smartphone in front of her face, making a video that Graham and his friends wouldn't want the world to see.

Graham slapped his left hand against his broad haunch. At this signal, the four of them retreated without a word, backing down the path that led to the convention center until they disappeared around a corner. Faye hadn't realized that she was holding her breath, but she took a deep one now.

"Thank you. Your name is Ben?"

"Yes, Ben McGilveray. And this is my wife, Gloria. Wherever

those idiot supremacists and their stupid signs are, we're there. Us and our friends."

"You were following me."

"When we saw you walking right into them," Gloria said, "we knew things could go bad for you pretty fast. Following you seemed advisable."

"And I thank you. But why are they here? Was the bomber a person of color, somebody that would draw out the white supremacists? Or was he one of them?"

"Oh, honey," Gloria said, as if she thought Faye and her misguided ideas were just so cute.

"You're the reason they're here," Ben said, as if that would explain everything.

"Me?"

Gloria stepped in to explain what her husband really meant. "Not you, personally. Your convention. What's it called?" She peered at the name tag hanging from a lanyard around Faye's neck. "The Oklahoma Conference for the Study and Celebration of the Indigenous Arts? Well, that's a mouthful, but it sounds just awesome. I'm a beader, myself."

Gloria held up an arm encircled by an intricately beaded bracelet and gestured at the beaded bands wrapping the ends of Ben's braids. "And Ben's a potter. But don't you know that those guys we just saw spend their time wishing they had girlfriends and griping about how they hate seeing brown people on the front page of the newspaper?"

And Carson had been so proud and happy about the press coverage of his conference. He'd worked like a devil to land that front page article. It had been below the fold, but still. There had been a picture of Cully and everything. And there had been photos of most of the faculty inside, on the "Arts" page.

Damn these people's hate. It tainted everything it touched. Ahua had been right that the conference might have been the bomber's target.

Gloria looked closer at Faye's name tag. "Longchamp-Mantooth?" She paused for a moment as if to wonder where she'd heard the name before. "I saw in the paper that a couple of the speakers were named Mantooth."

"They would be my husband Joe and his very distant cousin Cully."

"Take my advice," said Ben. "Do not look at the signs those people are carrying. And for God's sake, don't read the comments on the newspaper's website. You won't like what they say about your husband and his cousin and the rest of the faculty for your conference."

"The faculty?" Faye said, as if she didn't understand what he was saying, but she did. Joe and Cully were Creek. Even blond Carson was Creek, because his platinum-haired mother's ancestry could be traced back to the Dawes Rolls. Sadie Raincrow was Cherokee. Stacy was Chinese. Dr. Jackson was African-American.

It made no difference that Dr. Althorp and Dr. Dell were as white as the sign-carrying supremacists they had just seen. They were outnumbered, and racists are terrified of being outnumbered. Faye could absolutely see how news coverage of the conference had brought out people who were only happy when their group possessed a comfortable majority.

This made Faye angry and more than a little scared. The fear must have shown on her face, because Gloria reached out and patted her on the hand. "Don't worry, pretty one. We're here and we brought friends. And we're armed. See?" She held up her cell phone and snapped Faye's photo. "I'm dangerous with this thing. We'll keep the peace."

"Where are you trying to go?" Ben asked.

"To the South Tower. That way." She pointed toward the path on the far side of the courtyard.

"We'll get you there," he said, starting to walk without looking to see if she was following.

As they emerged from the thick hedges surrounding the

courtyard, Faye saw that she had a clear path. Maybe the path had already been clear, or maybe everybody had left when they saw Ben coming. When they reached the sidewalk, there was some hooting that was hard to ignore, but she could avoid the protesters' eyes if she kept her own eyes straight ahead.

Once they had run the gauntlet, Gloria held up a hand of farewell and Ben said, "Enjoy your day. If they spoil it for you, then they have won." And then they were gone.

Chapter Eighteen

Kaayla sat in her temporary office on the first floor of the South Tower, trying not to think. She had saved the Indigenous Arts conference, but it had required her to work into the night, finding hotel rooms for displaced guests and rearranging the schedule for every meeting room in both towers.

Her entire staff had clocked a massive amount of overtime, but if somebody from headquarters tried to bark at her about that, she would calmly say, "Bomb. In my lobby. What would you have done differently?" It wasn't like they were going to fire her. And it wasn't like she was going to let management do something to hurt her staff, like cut their hours later to make up for all the overtime they were working now.

Kaayla didn't have a husband and she didn't have children, but she had assembled a group of hardworking people and she respected them. Loved them, even. Most of them had led hard lives before they came to the Gershwin—before they came to her—and she took her role as their protector seriously.

Red-haired Jason was seventeen and supporting himself on the salary of hotel desk clerk. Gray-haired Karen had a diabetic husband whose life depended on Karen's health insurance. Even Julia, with her long golden curls and the unfurrowed brow of a princess, used her salary to pay the mortgage of the home she shared with her parents. These people were Kaayla's family.

And Grace and Lucia? They had worked the longest and hardest of all. They deserved raises and they deserved to be promoted into jobs that wouldn't wear them out before they were forty, but Kaayla was no fool. She knew that the American passports they had presented as proof of citizenship when she hired them were questionable at best, and so would Kaayla's bosses if they ever had reason to look closely at them. For one thing, people applying to be hotel maids were a lot more likely to have driver's licenses and social security cards on hand than they were to have passports. To what foreign country could Grace or Lucia afford to go?

If anybody ever looked too closely at those documents, Kaayla could say, "How could I have known? They gave me counterfeit documents." Nothing would happen to her, with her shiny plastic Oklahoma driver's license and her birth certificate with its government-made raised seal, but Grace and Lucia would be ripped from everything they knew and loved. They would be deported to…somewhere. Kaayla didn't know and she didn't want to know.

For their sakes, they needed to stay out of sight and nobody was as invisible as a hotel maid. If the day came when she could safely promote them to a better position that might still keep them under the radar of corporate management—housekeeping manager for the night shift, maybe, or pantry chef—then she would do it. For now, they wielded mops and her workers with noncounterfeited documents held down the more visible positions.

Kaayla knew that she was capable enough to move up in the company. The leadership training program would send her to work at a sequence of hotels in quick succession, some of them in glamorous foreign locations that she would love to see, but she could never leave the Gershwin. She knew her calling in life, and it was to take care of people who needed her.

The next time she needed to make a hire, she would tell Grace and Lucia to ask around and find someone who needed a job, no questions asked.

———

In front of Faye, people were wandering out of the South Tower, all of them chatting and some of them lighting cigarettes. She supposed that Cully had finished his session and they were on break.

As she moved toward the door, Cully himself came out and lit up his own cigarette. Glad to see a friendly and familiar face, she called out to him and he looked up with a smile. Then he looked over her shoulder and gave someone behind her a bigger smile.

She turned and saw that he was responding to the mob gathered across the street behind her. Based on a lifetime of dealing with crowds that had gathered just for him, it was natural for Cully to presume that this one was for him, too. He patted Faye on the shoulder and moved past her, ready to greet a group of strangers that he presumed loved him because so many other strangers did.

This was dangerous. If his aging eyes missed the protesters' signs, he could get way too close to a crowd that wasn't friendly to a brown man, not even a famous one.

Faye hurried to stop him but he was moving fast for a man his age, especially one who smoked. His eyes were indeed showing their age, though, because he was much too close to the protesters before he saw the signs and stopped abruptly.

As much as she hated the idea of approaching that hostile crowd, even feared it, she couldn't let Cully walk alone into that kind of danger. She rushed to catch up with him. "We need to go."

She didn't have to say, "We are both obviously not white. We may not be safe here." She just tugged his sleeve and started backing up, hoping he came with her. No luck.

"Are these people seriously protesting Carson's conference? I've seen assholes like this all of my life and I've never understood why they're so angry." He shook his head. "It bothers them that people want to come and hear my flute and watch my Cousin Joe flintknap? They feel threatened because people think Sadie Raincrow's baskets are beautiful?"

"Apparently so. We should go, Cully. The police will take care of things out here."

Faye looked around for Ben and Gloria and their counter-protesting friends, but they were nowhere in sight. She and Cully stood alone, with nothing but a few feet of open sidewalk separating them from an angry crowd.

One of the protesters raised an arm and swung it hard, lobbing a soda can at them. To Faye, the can looked like it was moving in slow motion, soaring to the top of its parabolic flight path before plummeting to the ground at her feet. It hit hard, opening a crack in its side, and Faye could tell by the thunk that the can had been full and unopened. Root beer spewed out of the crack and drenched her pants from the thighs down.

Cully reflexively wheeled around, eyes scanning the crowd. "What if that had hit you? Who threw that? Who threw it?"

Fists ready, he started to advance on the protesters, as if he were about to avenge a wronged buddy in an old Western, but there was no stunt double here to take Cully's punches for him.

Faye grabbed the back of his shirt with both hands. "No, Cully. You might get hurt. These people aren't worth it."

"You're worth it. I'm not going to stand here and watch people like that treat a woman like you this way. Besides, there aren't that many of them. Maybe eight or ten, don't you think?"

Faye was thinking that the headcount was upwards of twenty.

"They look at me and see an old man. What they don't know is that the best stuntmen in Hollywood taught me to fight. And they fight dirty, so that's how I fight. I could take 'em."

Faye wasn't so sure. Maybe Cully could have taken them in 1978, and Little Girl Faye would have happily munched popcorn while she watched him do it, but not now. And that was leaving aside the likelihood that some of the protesters were carrying guns and knives.

"Please," she said, succeeding in getting him to turn his head her way and away from the crowd. She thought maybe his hearing wasn't what it once was, and she was glad. If Cully were to hear and understand the terrible names they were being called, her fight to keep him from walking into danger, both aging fists swinging, would be over.

The policeman was nowhere to be seen. She saw Ben and Gloria approaching, flanked by two people that she presumed were their friends. The four of them, plus Cully and Faye, against twenty people did not sound good to Faye. If more of their counterprotesting friends joined them, the odds would be better but the brawl would be bigger. Being arrested for starting a brawl didn't appeal to her, but it sounded better than being beaten to a pulp.

"Please, Cully," she whispered, succeeding in getting him to keep his eyes on her. She wanted him to focus on her quiet voice. "Getting yourself hurt will not get the root beer out of my pants. Why don't you help me find a place to clean myself up?"

His eyes drifted toward the jeering crowd. She was losing him.

"Listen, Cully. Joe will be talking in five minutes and I want to hear him. It's important to me to be there. I don't want either of us to miss his talk because we're in handcuffs. Because you do know that I would never let you fight those cretins alone."

He turned his head away and took one more look across the barricade. "Joe said that you were scary."

"Joe's right."

His fists uncurled. He gave the protesters one more look, flashing them the grin that he used at the end of a shootout on the silver screen, when his character had emerged victorious. He pulled himself to his full height, working some magic of charisma that made him suddenly impossible to ignore. The crowd quieted, despite itself.

Ben and Gloria and their friends stopped in their tracks, watching and waiting.

Cully waited for a beat to be sure everybody was looking at him. Since he was so totally sure that all eyes would turn to him, they did.

When he finally spoke, his voice had changed, settling into a timbre that punched through any remaining ambient noise. Faye had heard radio people call this vocal trick "presence." The protesters quieted at the sound of his full and resonant voice, so they heard Cully's farewell to them loud and clear.

"This face has made me millions. I'm not risking it for these losers."

Chapter Nineteen

Faye ducked into the meeting room seconds before Joe's session was due to start. She hated to be late, because she knew it would stress him out if he thought she wasn't coming. Nevertheless, it would stress him out worse if she had to explain how the dark, wet stains splashed across her pant legs got there and why she smelled like root beer.

The room was full, with only a few open seats in the back. She grabbed one. Faye was ecstatic to see Joe's talk get this kind of reception, but she had known it would. There were a lot of people in the world who would be fascinated by the things Joe could do, if they only knew he existed. Nobody ever imagined a stone tool that Joe couldn't make.

Cully settled into the chair beside her just before Joe started to speak, and Jakob flopped into the one next to Cully. Most of the other faculty had done the collegial thing and come to hear Joe. Faye saw Sadie Raincrow sitting right up front, next to Dr. Althorp. Dr. Dell was sitting directly in front of Faye. She smelled Dr. Dell before she saw her, because she had the aroma of someone who had spent the previous night binge-drinking. Faye guessed that the several drinks she saw the woman down during the party had been followed by a lot more when she was alone in her room afterward, and this made her feel sad.

Joe's chair was on a raised platform so that everybody in the room could get a good look at his gloved hands. He wore safety glasses, which he should really do all the time when he was making stone chips fly. Not that he listened when Faye nagged him about it.

Joe turned his face to the crowd but said nothing. They quieted immediately, and Faye realized that her husband had just exerted the same trick of charisma that she'd seen Cully use when faced with a mob of white supremacists. Maybe Cully and Joe were closer kin than they thought. And maybe Joe had gifts that he didn't know about yet, because he'd never had the chance to tap them.

He gestured toward the tarp at his feet. "I'm going to be making a lot of rock chips here today, so please stay in your seats when I'm working. The chips are gonna fly farther than you expect."

Faye knew that this was true. She liked to go barefoot outside, and this meant that she'd stepped on Joe's rock chips more than a few times. They were like little tiny knives.

"I put this tarp down around my feet because it ain't fair to leave chips for the nice people who sweep up around here."

Faye thought of Grace and the rest of the hotel staff. They had more than enough to do without cleaning up Joe's tiny knives.

"Here's something you should know about those chips. My wife and I have a cultural resources firm and we do a lot of archaeology in places where people flintknapped their tools a long time ago. The chips they left behind look pretty much like the chips I'm making right now. If you're flintknapping outside, just throw a penny down near your feet and leave it there. That way, if Faye and I dig it up someday, we'll know we aren't looking at something left behind a thousand years ago or more."

Oh, joy. He was promoting their business right up front. Joe had been worried that he'd be too nervous to remember everything he needed to say, but he was doing great. He didn't have a lot of experience doing public speaking, but Joe was always relaxed when he had a rock in his hand.

A voice rose up from the front row. "This penny we're supposed to leave with our debitage…does it need to be a penny made the very same year when we're working?"

This question told Faye a lot about the asker. By his use of the word "debitage," Faye knew that his interest in flintknapping was serious and he had done a lot of reading on the subject. His concern about the date on the penny said that he probably didn't have an archaeologist's sense of the scale of time.

Joe grinned. "Could be. Wouldn't hurt. But I don't think it matters all that much. In the grand scheme of things, there ain't much difference between 2019 and 1968, do you think? Not when the people the archaeologists are studying lived in the 1500s or the 1100s or maybe even before that. For somebody living in the 1100s, people nowadays, and their stuff, would pretty much all look alike to them. Or at least they would look equally weird."

Everybody laughed and Joe took the opportunity to regain control of his topic. "I'm using flint here." He held up his left hand and showed them a chunk of rock. "You could use chert or jasper or a lot of other things, even glass. Some people like to use beer bottle bottoms, and I gotta say that they do turn out pretty, green and brown and blue and shiny. But we're here to talk about rocks."

He brandished the brown chunk of stone. "How do you pick a good rock for chipping? Here's one way. If you find a rock you might want to try, give it a sharp tap. The higher the pitch, the better the rock, when it comes to chipping stone."

He held up a different object in his left hand. "See this? You can make a knapping tool out of lots of different materials, but I like antler. Listen to the sound when I tap this rock with a chunk of antler."

He held the rock and the chipping tool next to the microphone and banged them together. A high-pitched clink sounded, and a murmur followed it as people turned to their neighbors and said things like "That's cool" and "I've gotta remember that one."

People were taking pictures and videos on their phones. Some of them were even taking notes on old-fashioned paper. Faye was so proud.

"If you're working with good material, you get about a hundred-degree angle from a solid strike. Like this." He held up both hands, forming an angle with his palms that was a bit more open than a right angle. Then he struck the piece of flint and held up the broken pieces. "That's what you call 'percussion flaking.'"

He leaned down and handed the pieces to a woman on the front row. "Here. Take a look, then pass them around." Picking up another piece of rock, he held it up to show the crowd.

"Other times, like when you're shaping an edge, you might want to use 'pressure flaking.' Like this."

He pressed the antler hard against the stone's edge and a sharp, slender flake broke off. Then, again, he passed the example rocks around for everybody to see and feel. Joe was a hands-on learner and he was apparently a hands-on teacher, too.

He was looking out at the audience now, making Faye acutely aware of her stained pant legs. She was sitting on the aisle and it was just barely possible that Joe would notice them from where he sat. If wondering what had happened to her made him too distracted to give a good talk, she would need to go outside and throttle a few protesters, and she didn't want to do that. She reached down and tucked her pant legs in her boots.

Cully was still deeply, silently angry. Faye felt his anger more than she saw it. His leg, pressed close to hers by the jammed-together chairs where they sat, tensed and trembled. She looked at the leg instead of Cully, because she worried that his temper might get the best of him if she looked into his eyes. Around the hem of his pale gray pants, she could see a faint spatter of brown stains. He hadn't been standing far enough away from her to completely miss the spray of root beer.

Jakob shifted uncomfortably in his seat on Cully's other side. She thought at first that he was just an older man with too many aches to enjoy sitting in a cheap folding chair. But then she looked at his eyes. They kept returning to Cully's glowering face. Jakob was worried about his friend, and Faye could see that he wanted to do something to help. In that moment, she understood Jakob. He felt like it was his job as Cully's friend to help him be the best he could be. Maybe that was his job as his director, too.

Sometimes, she felt that way about Joe. She felt like he needed her to smooth a path for him. Make things easier. Keep him from getting in his own way. Maybe this was the job of a person who loved an artist.

For reasons that she could have never explained, she thought that it was too much to ask some artists to return the favor. They weren't wired that way emotionally. They had other gifts to give.

Joe could do it. Joe looked out for Faye every day of their lives. But Cully? She wasn't sure about him. Jakob looked out for him, but Jakob might well be on his own.

Today, she wanted to give Joe the gift of her own independence. She didn't need him to be worried about her. She needed him to shine as only he could.

The white supremacist rabble-rouser had rattled her with his can of root beer, but she planned to hold herself together, for Joe's sake. She hoped Cully could do the same, too, at least well enough to sit through Joe's hour-long talk. She wished that she'd told him not to bother her husband about the root beer incident. There was no need for Joe to know that his wife had a problem that he couldn't help her fix.

———

Jakob would have known his friend was upset, even if they hadn't been squeezed into their chairs, thigh touching thigh. If there was one thing Jakob knew, it was actors. He'd directed too many films to be under any illusion about their mental stability. Or lack thereof.

As actors went, Cully was a model of mental health. Usually. He could be kind. He had called Jakob on every one of his last forty-eight birthdays.

He was unfailingly generous. Jakob didn't know how many flutes Cully had given away over the years, and he wagered that few of the recipients had any idea how long it took to craft the deceptively simple-looking instruments.

For an actor, he had a manageable ego. By this, Jakob meant that Cully knew exactly how handsome he was and he knew how to use his looks to his benefit, but he was, in the end, self-aware enough to know he was doing it. He could poke fun at himself, and Jakob knew precious few people who could do that, actor or not.

In Jakob's observation, Cully's mental health grew rocky when he had uninterrupted time to brood. This is a problem for a composer, whose job asks him to lock himself in a studio for weeks on end. It had been a bigger problem in recent years, since Cully lost his wife. Cully and Sue, alone in that house far from Los Angeles and its bustle, had enjoyed the comfortable lives of two homebodies in love.

For three years now, Cully had lived without her in that big house in a canyon far away from everything, with no place to put his energy except into his music and the long hikes that kept his body in fine working order for a man his age. His musical output had been astonishing, fresher and newer than anyone would expect from a man his age, but Jakob doubted that he'd enjoyed a truly happy moment in all that time. If Cully and Sue had been blessed with children instead of a long series of miscarriages, so many things would have been different.

Jakob was still able to coax Cully out of his canyon from time to time. He was glad for the time with his friend, but he wouldn't necessarily say that their visits were fun. Cully's sense of humor, always dark, was obsidian-black these days.

In their younger days, when their Saturday nights were spent careening from bar to bar, Jakob's job had been to stand between Cully and his temper. They both carried a few minor scars from the fights Jakob couldn't stave off, but he fully believed that there would be a career-ending scar on Cully's face right now if Jakob hadn't been there to reel him in.

For this reason, Jakob's habit was to keep an eye on his friend's emotional status at all times. Maybe that's why Cully had invited him on this trip, because he knew he would need somebody to monitor his mental state. Today, Jakob would describe that mental state as "twitchy." This was not a good thing.

Chapter Twenty

An enthusiastic crowd encircled Joe, and Faye was so happy. Some of them had brought their own flintknapping projects to show him. Sweet-natured Joe praised unidentifiable and misshapen chunks of stone with the same enthusiasm that he showed for exquisitely chipped Clovis-style points that could easily pass for the real thing.

Others in the crowd were fondling the points that Joe had brought for visual aids. The savviest among them would see from their precise, symmetrical detail exactly how skilled Faye's husband really was. Some of those savvy people would have the budget to hire him to give a talk like this in another city. Another state. Maybe someday another country.

Jakob and Cully had slipped away when they saw that they weren't going to be able to speak to Joe. Faye had lingered until she, too, saw that there was no way to fight her way through the crowd, which made her perversely glad. Now she had an excuse to skedaddle up to their hotel room and change pants. Joe would never have to know about her encounter with a root beer-throwing bigot.

According to Faye's wristwatch, the enthusiastic crowd was messing with Carson's carefully planned schedule. It was way past time for Stacy to do her talk on the history of tribal storytelling in Oklahoma in the years since the Trail of Tears.

Faye looked around for Stacy, so that she could wish her luck. She didn't see her, but Carson's big body and shaggy blond head were hard to miss. He saw her looking at him and hurried to her side.

Carson skipped hello. He didn't even start with, "Wasn't Joe great?" He went straight to "Have you seen Stacy?"

"Not this morning, no."

Carson's eyes never stopped scanning the faces around him as he spoke. "I don't understand it. She would never be late for this talk, but she's dang close to missing it altogether. When it comes to her career, Stacy is…"

"Intense?"

"Yeah. Intense. She's not answering her phone. I knocked on her door and nobody answered. I thought maybe she'd gone to breakfast and left her phone behind, but she's not here, and now I'm officially worried."

"Is it time to ask Kaayla about opening up Stacy's room to see if she's in there, sick or hurt?"

Carson scanned the room once more. "Yeah. It's time."

———

As it turned out, they could have bypassed Kaayla and just taken the elevator straight to Stacy's room. When the three of them— Carson, Kaayla, and Faye—reached Stacy's door, they found it open. There were two housekeeping carts in the hall. A stout blond woman was stacking towels on the far cart but nobody was standing with the one outside Stacy's room, where the noise of a vacuum wafted out into the hall.

When they entered, they found Grace busily vacuuming the room's elegant brown-and-gold-patterned carpet. She jumped like she'd been caught stealing, then she looked at Kaayla with a question on her face.

"Hello, Grace. We're looking for Dr. Wong. Have you seen her?"

"Is this her room? There wasn't anybody in it when I got here."

"Is her computer here?" Carson asked, and Grace's brow furrowed.

"I haven't touched any of her things, truly," she said quickly. "Everything is just as she left it."

Faye hurried to ease her concern. "Nobody's accusing you of anything, Grace. We're just worried about Dr. Wong."

"If Stacy left here to do her speech, she would have taken her computer with her," Carson said. "She said that she'd be bringing all of her audiovisuals on her computer."

"Her computer? It's right here," Kaayla said, standing at the room's small desk. "It's plugged into the electronics port. We've installed one in all the rooms."

Faye saw a white cord dangling from the port. "Here's her phone charger. I don't know why she's not answering her phone, but it looks like she has it with her. Does anything else look unusual?"

The bed was unmade, rumpled on just one side. There was nothing in the trash can but a coffee cup and a potato chip bag.

Faye didn't know what else to do but check the bathroom.

She found nothing in the bathroom more surprising than a towel on the floor and a makeup bag on the counter. The shower curtain was half-closed. Faye couldn't say why she felt like she'd entered a crime scene, but she did feel that. Or maybe she felt more like she'd stepped onto the set of *Psycho*.

Faye peered around the shower curtain without touching it, because she felt like she should keep her fingerprints to herself. She stuck her head out of the bathroom and said, "The tub is dry and the towel is almost dry. If Stacy showered this morning, it was very, very early. Unless you've already cleaned it, Grace."

Grace shook her head.

Faye checked the area around the sink. "Her toothbrush looks dry."

When she came out of the bathroom, Carson said, "Stacy is pretty finicky about how she looks. I'm gonna say that the dry shower and toothbrush tell us the same thing that the computer does. When she left, she thought she'd be coming back here before she gave her presentation."

"Yep, I agree. She was coming back. Or she thought she was," Faye said, her heart sinking.

She would have dropped, discouraged, onto the chair beside the bed, but a black wool suit, stylishly cut, was already there. The jacket was artfully spread across the chair's back, and the skirt and blouse were draped over one overstuffed arm. On the floor in front of the chair, Faye saw a pair of high-heeled pumps. A pair of pantyhose, still in their cardboard packaging, lay on a small table beside the chair. Beside it was a matching set of lingerie in petal-pink lace—bra, camisole, and panties.

Stacy's beautiful underwear communicated vulnerability in a way that her computer and her toothbrush had not. Faye's eyes burned with sudden tears. Her friend had put a lot of effort into making sure her clothes were perfect for her big presentation. The owner of this underwear had not walked away and forgotten to show up.

"I'm calling the police," Carson said.

"Good idea," Faye said as her hand went to her own phone, but not to call the police. She knew that local police usually handled missing persons cases. Just because Stacy had vanished the day after a deadly bomb blast in the same hotel complex, it didn't mean that investigating it was the job of the FBI. Still, Faye's gut said that there was a link. If she was right that Stacy's disappearance was somehow connected to the bombing, then she supposed that the FBI would eventually step in. Why not now?

As far as Faye was concerned, jurisdictional matters were something for the police and the federal agents to work out. She was more interested in seeing her friend come back safe, so to hell with jurisdiction. She wanted to talk to Ahua. Her fingers were dialing his number into her primitive loaner phone before that thought had fully formed in her mind. She trusted his calm intellect, and she was deeply worried about the welfare of Dr. Stacy Wong.

———

Faye sat in Ahua's command center and waited for him to say something to make her feel better about Stacy. If not that, she hoped he'd say something about the bombing investigation that would distract her from her fears for her friend. He did not.

Ahua's silence was unnerving. He was a quiet, deliberate, thoughtful man. But he was also a warm person who could communicate that warmth without a lot of words. Faye was not feeling that warmth this morning, and on this day when a woman seemed to have evaporated, she felt the lack deeply.

She also felt an undercurrent of fear stemming from the fact that Ahua was sitting across from her at all. He was a very high-ranking agent to be spending this much time with Faye. Faye suspected that this meant he had reason to believe that Stacy was in deep trouble. Either that, or something else terrible was prompting all of this face time. The last time Ahua had made a point to spend time with Faye, it was because his agents had discovered the dead bodies of three little children.

As Faye waited for Ahua to speak, Liu entered silently, sat down at a computer with her back to them, and began to type.

"You said to come as soon as I could," Faye said to Ahua. "Is it about Stacy?"

"No, I have no news on Dr. Wong. I wanted to talk to you about the last chamber."

"The painted one? I think I've done all I can do with the pictures. Are you ready for me to go down there and look at it?" Despite everything, she felt a thrill at the thought of exploring the old underground system of rooms.

"Yes, it's about the chamber and, no, I'm not ready for you to look at it. Not in person. I want you to look at this."

Ahua walked over to a computer with a large high-definition display, the same one he had used to show Faye the maps he'd made of the catacombs below Oklahoma City. He motioned for her to sit. With a few keystrokes, he called up the six thumbnail images that Faye recognized, one after another. They were the composite images of the four walls, ceiling, and floor, showing all of the room's colorfully painted scenes.

He expanded each of them to full size, clicking through them quickly—one, two, three, four, five, six—then surprised Faye by continuing to click. More photos clicked past—five, six, seven, eight—and she rose slowly to her feet and leaned close to the screen as if that would help her understand what she saw.

The walls in these photos were splashed with white paint, obscuring almost all the colors. Here and there, smears in the painted scenes showed through the white paint. The damage was extensive. Very few of the family scenes were still distinguishable. After Faye had studied the photos for a while, she sat down heavily.

"Vandalism? In a room that nobody has seen but us?"

"Yes. Vandalism. In a room that nobody has seen but FBI agents, a city engineer, and you. Please believe me when I say that Patricia Kura is now undergoing the interrogation of her life."

"Do you think she did this?"

"My people tell me that she doesn't have white paint under her fingernails. Other than that? I have no idea. Maybe she did."

"Surely you don't think I did this."

"You don't have white paint under your fingernails, but yeah. It could have been you, but I can't imagine you destroying something old—old-ish—and irreplaceable. But it could have been somebody you told about the paintings. Could have been Goldsby or any one of the agents on the Evidence Response Team. Could have been somebody they told. Could have been Liu. Could have been me, for that matter."

Faye was stuck on the "Could have been you" part of his little speech. She couldn't think of anything much to say in response, other than "Wasn't it guarded?" and she bit her tongue on that one. The agency had surely placed a guard at the top of the stairs leading down to the painted chamber. Placing one at the bottom of the stairs would have risked contaminating the crime scene, but there was no reason that someone couldn't have been stationed in the storm sewer outside the metal door.

Ahua's failure to send someone to guard the storm sewer had allowed this to happen. It would naturally more piss him off if she pointed out how much that oversight had cost the investigation, and pissing him off was not in her best interests. She held her tongue.

"Tell me the truth," he said. "Did you tell anybody what you saw?"

"Not a soul."

"Not even your husband?"

"Not even my husband. You told me not to say anything to anybody, and I didn't."

Ahua's eyes held hers for an uncomfortable moment. "I don't think you did it. I think you'd put yourself between a bullet and something you thought was historically valuable. And I think you can keep a secret, probably better than any of my agents. There's something wary about you, Faye."

He turned back to the computer and pulled up one more photo, taken of the room's floor. It was decorated with multicolored dust and random splashes of white paint. "I'm pretty sure the vandal used three things—paint remover to wipe away as much of the paintings as possible, sandpaper to sand away what the paint remover didn't get, and white paint to obscure anything that was left."

Faye considered the white blotches and the smears. "Somebody really didn't want us to get a good look at those paintings."

"Seems obvious."

"We have Goldsby's photos. Anything else?"

"Nope. And they're not the high-quality work he would have done with the right light and enough time. But he got what he got, and it's all we'll ever have. The person who went to all of this trouble probably thinks we don't even have that much."

She clicked through the photos slowly. After her second pass through the post-vandalism photos, she felt regret and sadness shift into despair. "The bodies. They're gone. The vandal took the children's bodies."

"No. After we came up out of the sewer yesterday, I gave the Evidence Response Team orders to get those bodies, one way or another. They were only a few feet to the right of the door. Somebody my size could almost have leaned in and reached them, but it would have been too risky. One slip while you're that off-balance, and you go splat on the floor, obliterating who knows how much evidence. I told them to find the tallest agent that they could, with the longest arms, and get those babies."

Faye was glad the children weren't still lying there underground, alone.

"Somebody was already doing an autopsy on what's left of the bomber, but I told him to bring in more people, or work all night, or do whatever it took to find out what happened to those children."

"Any results?"

"We know they're all three boys, and we know that they were older than they looked. Toddlers rather than babies. Which isn't a single bit less sad."

"No kidding. When will you know more?"

"Soon. It has to be soon. We cannot have a long-term unsolved bombing with an unidentified bomber, not here in Oklahoma City and not with three dead children. People here remember McVeigh and that bombed-out day-care center. They will lose their minds over this, and I don't blame them."

Faye wondered whether there was a brutal streak running

through humanity that was beyond help from anyone, even the Almighty. Her mamaw would have made her tell God she was sorry for thinking such a thing, so she did.

"There are too many people walking the Earth with scars from that day," Ahua said. "They are not going to rest until we solve this thing."

"I'll do all I can to help," Faye said, "and it looks like my best chance of doing that is to find something important in these pictures."

He gave a short nod. "Study those photos. Don't look at what the vandal left behind. Look at what's missing and tell me why it's gone."

"Certainly. But we haven't talked about the reason I called you."

"Dr. Wong?"

"Yes. Do you have any idea what might have happened to her?"

"I haven't got a clue, but I do have a hunch." He paused like a man waiting to see what she was going to say.

Before she had time to think, Faye's eyes turned toward the computer display showing the vandalized paintings. "Do you think she had something to do with that?"

"I do, but I'm not sure how."

"Stacy would never have done something like that," Faye said, surprised that she felt so certain about someone she knew mostly by email. "She's been dreaming of finding the Chinese underground community for years. It isn't possible that she would set out to destroy anything about it, no more than I would."

"Yet she's missing. She made it clear yesterday that she would do anything to explore those chambers. Don't you think that maybe that's just what she did?"

Faye couldn't say that this hadn't occurred to her, because it had. "Trying to sneak down there is one thing. Destroying something that may have had historical value and definitely was important evidence is another."

"But what if she wasn't the vandal? What if she found a way

down there and crossed paths with someone who obviously has something to hide?"

Faye heard a soft noise behind her, like someone's breath catching. She turned to see Agent Liu's shoulders shaking. Ahua was at her side instantly.

"Cathy, what is it?"

Faye had never seen an FBI agent weep before, and she hoped to never see it again. She didn't think that FBI agents knew how to weep, but Liu did. Her mouth was screwed tight, trying to shut in the sobs. When Ahua put his hand on her shoulder, she broke down completely.

"It's my fault. I'm the one who always says, 'We have regulations for a reason,' but I failed the first time I was tested."

"How did you fail?" Ahua asked.

She shook her head, lips still pressed tight.

"Cathy, what did you do?"

"I told Stacy about the room. I told her about the room where we found the children."

Chapter Twenty-One

Faye was pretty sure that civilians weren't supposed to stand around and watch FBI agents have breakdowns that could involve spilling the bureau's secrets. She rose to leave.

Ahua was so upset that he kept talking like she wasn't even there. A command center full of agents bent over their computers and pretended to be deaf.

"I don't understand why you'd tell Stacy anything, Liu. You just met her."

Soft-spoken Ahua had turned up the volume a few decibels. Now Faye really needed to get out of there, except the two arguing agents stood between her and the door. The command center was impressively outfitted with state-of-the art technological doodads, and it was filled with a formidable staff of bureau personnel who all looked like they wished they could be anywhere else. Nevertheless, the command center was still nothing more than a gloriously repurposed semi, and it was crowded.

Faye was hemmed in on all sides by equipment and by people who didn't want to be where they were. Her only option was to lean over a random computer display and stare at it as if it were utterly fascinating.

"No, that's not true," Liu said. "I didn't just meet Stacy. I've known her for a long time. I didn't say so, because I didn't think it was pertinent to the investigation. Remember how I told you that the Chinese community in Oklahoma City is really small? Well, it's really tight, too. Our parents know each other. We go to the same churches. We shop at the same stores. Our mothers send us to the supermarket to buy oxtail, because they think maybe we might want to marry the nice-looking butcher."

Ahua's voice was gentle. "How did your mother feel about you choosing to be an FBI agent instead of marrying the butcher?"

"She got over it. But she would never have gotten over it if I'd married Stacy Wong." She turned away from him and covered her face with her hands. Faye took the opportunity to slip past her and get a few steps closer to the door. At least now her back was to the FBI agent who was decompensating in full sight of her colleagues.

"Are you and Stacy dating, Liu?"

"Oh, no. No. I've had a crush on her since we were in high school, but she has no idea. Oh, hell. I should just say what I mean. I've loved Stacy since we were fifteen, but she has no idea. She says hello when she sees me. She asks about my family. I ask about hers. We say, 'Gee, it's been a long time since high school.' That's the extent of our relationship."

"You said more than that to her yesterday."

Liu squared her shoulders, took her hands away from her face, and turned to face Ahua. "I did. She asked me to have a cup of coffee after I got off work and I said yes. I knew what she wanted and I knew it would be hard not to give it to her. I went anyway. No, I didn't just go. I went home, showered, and put on a pretty red blouse. Put in some earrings. Put on some perfume. It wasn't a date for Stacy, but it was for me."

"She wanted you to tell her what you knew about the underground chambers."

A woman swiveled her chair away from the argument, opening an exit route between Faye and the door.

"Stacy sure did ask me what I saw underground. And I told her everything I knew. I had planned to tell her just a few harmless tidbits, like maybe about the religious paintings, but I just couldn't make myself stop talking. As long as I've been an agent, I've never been tempted to reveal that kind of information. Now? Boom. I make up for years of excellent behavior with a blunder that may tank the investigation. Not to mention that the woman I love is missing and it's all my fault. Go ahead and say what you're thinking."

"I'm not going to say it, Cathy."

She gave a brittle laugh. "I'll do the honors. It's my line, isn't it? I've said it a hundred times over the years. 'We have regulations for a reason.'"

Faye got past the woman sitting in her swivel chair, and the door was in sight.

"Tell me everything. Do you know where Stacy is?"

"Promise me that she won't be in any trouble when we find her."

And now Faye learned exactly how far one had to push Ahua to get him to raise his voice. His deafening response would have been audible even if she'd made it through the door.

"I'M NOT PROMISING ANYTHING. Answer the question. Do you know that Stacy Wong was in the painted room last night?"

"I don't know it in the way that you know something you've seen with your own eyes. It's not like I ushered her to the hotel lobby and escorted her down the stairs. But I know Stacy and I know what she did with the information I gave her. She walked from the hotel to the river, and she walked into that storm sewer. I absolutely told her enough that she could find her way to the door we found yesterday."

"You what?"

"I think she went very, very early this morning. She would have wanted to be back by seven or so, when the city starts to wake up.

She'd have had to leave by about five to make the twenty-minute walk to the river, not to mention the hour it would take to get through the sewer to the painted room and back, plus some time there looking at it, plus the twenty minute-walk back to the hotel. Also, getting back at seven would give her plenty of time to get cleaned up for her presentation."

"Just when did you do this, Cathy?"

"Last night, maybe eight or nine. After that, I was up all night, worrying over what I'd done. It came home to me how much danger I might have put Stacy in, so I started texting and calling her before dawn. After an hour with no answer, on a day when I knew that she'd be up to rehearse her presentation, I got worried. I knocked on her door. I looked in the hotel garage for her car, and it's still there. I walked to the river, looking for Stacy. And then I went into the storm drains to see if I could find her."

Ahua had failed to regain his temper and now he had lost the ability to speak. Faye gave up on trying to get out of the command center and tried to help him. "Have you been down there looking for her all this time?" she asked.

Liu nodded. "I even went down some of those lateral pipes as far as I could go before they got too narrow. Stacy is smaller than I am, so she might have been able to go a little further, but I really don't think that's what she did. She had no reason to care about exploring those."

"Unless she thought there might be another entrance into what's left of the Chinese underground community," Faye said.

Liu's face crumpled. "I hadn't thought of that. What if she found one? She could be lost down there somewhere. In the sewer pipes. In a room dug out of the ground a hundred years ago. I have no idea where to start looking for her."

Ahua had found some words. From what Faye knew of him, he wasn't being intentionally cruel, but those words must have cut straight through to Liu's soul, nonetheless. "This is why we have regulations."

For the first time since Liu had made her startling confession, Faye really looked at her. Her pants were slightly damp all the way to the hips, and there was a smear of dirt on the back of her hand. Faye also noticed that Liu's hair was different. She had combed it back into a pretty barrette on top of her head, but now hair that had slipped out of the barrette hung lank around her face.

Liu had left the house that morning looking for the woman she loved, and she had made herself pretty before she went. The hours since she clipped that barrette in her hair had been hard ones.

"I'm sure Stacy is okay," Faye said, even though she wasn't sure.

Liu nodded, tears slipping out of the corners of her eyes. Faye could see that she had wept more than once this morning. She wasn't much past thirty, but today she looked jowly and worn.

"I was down there so long, looking for something. Anything. A wet handprint on the wall. A shoe in the water. Anything. I opened the door into that painted room, wondering if I was going to have to make my mistakes even worse by crawling in there to look for her. When I saw that," she pointed at the computer display showing the vandalized walls, "I knew that I couldn't go in there. Somebody did that, and it wasn't Stacy. Maybe the person who did that has kidnapped Stacy. If I went in there, I might accidentally destroy evidence that might save her. Maybe I already did destroy that evidence by going down there to look for her."

The blotches of white stared back at them from the photos, like blank pages telling them nothing about what had happened to Stacy Wong.

Ahua was still too angry to hide it. When he said, "Why didn't you call and tell me what you did as soon as you were above-ground?" His voice began quiet and slow, but every word came louder and faster than the one before.

"I wanted to tell you face-to-face. It cost us twenty minutes that I hope I don't regret."

Faye remembered raindrops pelting the expansive windows of Cully's penthouse during the party the night before. "It's rained since we were down there yesterday. Was the water deeper in the storm sewer today?"

"Maybe a little. Do you think Stacy got caught in a rush of stormwater after it rained?"

"It rained right after dark for just a few minutes, but I don't think it rained again," Ahua said. "There should have been plenty of time for the water to make its way to the river."

Faye hoped he was right. She tried not to imagine the rushing water knocking Stacy off her feet, bashing her head into the sewer's concrete wall, and dumping her unconscious into the river.

"I walked along the river but I didn't see any other outfalls where Stacy might have gotten out," Liu said.

Ahua pulled up the map he'd gotten from the city's engineers and tapped at the screen. "There are a few. Here's the closest outfall, but it's pretty far upstream from the one we explored yesterday. It's worth checking, but I'd say that outfall drains another area of the city."

Liu didn't look hopeful. "But if she'd crawled out of another pipe, she'd have beaten me back here, right? I was underground a really long time. The whole time I was walking back, I was hoping to find Stacy waiting for me but knowing that I was going to have to face you, Micah. I knew it was time to come back and tell you what I did."

The expression on Ahua's face would have frozen a summer day. Faye was glad she wasn't the one who had put that look on his peaceful face.

All he said was "Go home, Liu."

"You know I'm not going to do that. I'll be driving upstream and crawling in that other outfall inside of fifteen minutes, looking for Stacy."

"I say this with all the love and respect in the world, Liu. You are an FBI agent and you have been a good one, but if I see you anywhere below street level, I will have you in custody before you take another breath. And then I will waste no more time on taking care of you, because finding that missing woman and finding out who blew up the Gershwin Hotel and finding out who left three dead kids underneath it are the most important things in my life right now."

Liu's tears had dried. "Finding Stacy isn't as important to you as it is to me."

They stood there a moment, like two people who knew how to work together but had no clue how to be adversaries.

"Before I go," she said, "I need to tell you something Stacy told me last night. It's got nothing to do with her disappearance, not that I can tell, but the bombing? Yeah. I think this is important to that investigation. It's about Cully Mantooth and his Chinese mother. Stacy told me that Cully's mother lived underground with her family when she was a little girl. I asked if she was sure, and she said that it was common knowledge in her mother's generation. I bet he hasn't breathed a word to you or any other agent about that, has he?"

———

It had taken him a while, but Ahua had finally booted Faye out of the command center. He might be willing to argue with a rebellious agent in front of her, but he wasn't willing to talk in front of Faye about her brand-new cousin-in-law, Cully, who seemed to be keeping secrets from the FBI.

Faye wondered why she felt so immediately defensive about this man whom she had just met. He had been kind and genial, but even Hitler had managed to be kind and genial to his dog... until the day he decided to use her to test the effectiveness of his cyanide capsule supply. Who, really, was Cully Mantooth, other than a handsome and charismatic movie star who was talented enough to show her any face he chose?

She thought hard about what Liu had said. Was Cully's mother Chinese? She had thought his whole family was Creek. As she considered it, though, she realized that there wouldn't exactly have been a guard at the top of the stairs in 1920-whatever, checking people's bloodlines before they moved their stuff underground. Cully's mother could have been Creek and still lived underground, but Faye doubted it precisely because Liu had said that Stacy was so sure.

If Cully had really had a Chinese mother, people in a small, poor, marginalized community in a not-large city like Oklahoma City would have been pretty sure. They would have made a big deal about knowing Cully, because he was famous.

But did any of this really matter? Even if Cully didn't tell the FBI everything he knew about the history of Chinese people in Oklahoma City, Faye saw no straight line that led from that omission to suspecting that he was guilty of the bombing or Stacy's kidnapping or both.

If Cully had been keeping his past to himself, then Hollywood had been flat-out lying about their Native American star. But then, isn't that what Hollywood always did? Its directors had cast Mickey Rooney as a Japanese man and John Wayne as Genghis Khan. People who believed anything that Hollywood told them were fools.

Maybe Cully had his reasons for keeping his family history to himself but, as far as Faye was concerned, finding a bomber and a missing professor trumped those reasons. Cully was a generation or more older than Ahua or Liu or anyone else working on the case. When he was born, people may still have been living underground. He could turn out to be a critical resource for cracking these cases.

Even if his mother had kept her earlier life a secret from her son—and why would she?—plenty of other people could have told him about it. Faye was pretty sure he knew a lot more than he was telling, and she planned to find out what it was.

Chapter Twenty-Two

Cully had been expecting the call from Ahua ever since the bomb cracked open a hole in his past. Fifty years had passed since he left Oklahoma City, but that didn't mean nobody in the city remembered him.

Of course, they remembered him. He'd worked his whole life to be memorable.

In his case, the likelihood that he would be remembered was doubled, because he was spawned from two communities that had surely burst with pride as they watched his rise to fame. When Cully had been born in the 1940s, hardly a hundred years had passed since a big portion of the Muscogee tribe was uprooted by people who called them Creeks, driven from their homes in America's Southeast and dragged to Oklahoma. A generation later, his Chinese ancestors came to North America to help build the railroad that spanned it. When it was finished, they came to know that they were in a place where they weren't wanted.

He guessed that his people had stayed in Oklahoma because being hated in one place is as good as being hated in any other place. Everybody needs a home, and the Muscogee Creeks and the Oklahoma Chinese had made theirs here, for better or worse.

For both communities, Cully was the ultimate hometown

boy who had done good. Every time one of his movies hit the theaters, he had known what was happening at home, as surely as if he'd been there to see it. He had known that there were people in Oklahoma paying money that they couldn't spare to buy tickets, just so they could see Yu Yan and Wayman's boy on the silver screen.

Never mind that he hadn't spoken to anybody in either community since he was a seventeen-year-old runaway. And never mind that people in both communities knew something about why he'd left and why he had stayed away. Or they suspected.

As Cully rode the elevator down from his penthouse, he had time to think about how much of his story he wanted to tell Agent Ahua.

He knew he should probably tell him all of it. He'd told Jakob the highlights on the plane from California. He'd told him about the boarding school and the beatings. He'd even told him about the car wreck that took both his parents in an instant, leaving him with no place to go. After they were gone, he had stood on the horns of a dilemma: He could choose to endure the beatings or he could choose to run. He had run.

Telling the story in this way gave it a certain nobility. No, it gave *him* a certain nobility, but it left out a crucial detail. And that detail was Angela.

———

Ahua had launched his game of psychological chess. He had called Cully and set up an interview, establishing himself in a position of power by naming the time without asking if it was convenient. That time was forty-five minutes in the future. After the briefest possible conversation, he had broken the connection, staring at his phone for a moment.

He'd learned the news about Cully's connection to the underground Chinese community while surrounded by top-notch agents who were already seated at their workstations. Minutes after he sent Liu home and asked them to ferret out all of Cully Mantooth's old secrets, they had found the 1962 newspaper articles reporting on two Creek runaways, both of them seventeen. One of them was Cully and the other was a girl named Angela Bond. The world knew what had happened to Cully since then, but it didn't know what had happened to Angela. His researchers hadn't found any newspaper report of her being found yet, nor had they found any evidence that she'd ever had a credit card, driver's license, or any other marker of a modern human's existence. Given time, they might find more, but he knew enough now to question Cully closely on the subject of Angela Bond.

If Cully had any secrets about this Angela person, he'd had fifty years to come up with a story. Giving him long enough to prepare for an interview would not be in Ahua's favor, but giving him forty-five minutes to get nervous? That was more Ahua's style.

He wanted to give Cully time to wonder what he knew. And he wanted to give himself a chance to meditate on the matter, so he closed himself up in his mobile office and did that. In forty-five minutes, the time would come to peel back an actor's mask and see who Cully Mantooth really was, but that time had not come yet.

———

Faye knew that Joe had called and told his father she was safe, but she also knew that Sly would want to hear it directly from her. She owed him a call, but she'd truthfully been pretty upset and pretty busy and, for a time, pretty spaced out on tranquilizers. Now, though, she was ready to make that call, and it was only partly because Sly knew more about Cully's early life than anyone else she knew. Maybe he knew more than anybody else still alive.

She enjoyed talking to Sly. He sounded like Joe, but he didn't. His voice had a graveled edge earned from uncountable cigarettes and uncountable miles spent in the cab of an eighteen-wheeler.

It was nothing like soft-spoken Joe's mellow speech. Yet there was something in his measured delivery and stealthy humor that was very like her husband. Or, since Sly had been on the earth longer than his son, she guessed the truth was that Joe sometimes sounded very like Sly.

She and Sly exchanged hellos and she embarked on an effort to convince him that she was really and truly okay.

"That bomb was no joke, Daughter. You might wake up tomorrow with some little ache or pain you don't have today. If you do, I want you to promise to go get it checked."

She promised. And then she hesitated.

"Sounds to me like there's a reason for this phone call. Not that I don't enjoy seeing your name on my phone's screen when it's ringing, whether you've got a reason or not."

"Yes, I have a reason. I want to talk to you about Cully. What do you know about his past?"

"Well…"

Faye waited. She didn't often hear Sly hesitate before speaking, not like this. His conversational style was usually more like a congenial steamroller.

"Well, I don't know much. He's a lot older than me, so I was maybe in first grade when he left. Not sure. I know it was before my brother, Joseph, caught the pneumonia and died, and I was ten then. I only remember seeing Cully in the summertime at the family reunions. Relatives would come to Sylacauga from far and wide, and they'd stay for a week. My grandmama's house would fill up. People that couldn't get a bed there would either pitch tents in her yard or they'd find someplace else to sleep. Usually, Cully's family stayed with us. His parents would sleep in our room, mine and Joseph's. Cully, Joseph, and me, we'd throw some blankets down on the hallway floor and sleep there."

"I had no idea you knew Cully at all."

"I haven't seen him since I had most of my baby teeth. Well, except in the movies. I've seen a lot of Cully there. Plenty of water's gone under the bridge. I had some hard years since Cully left, and he wasn't part of them."

Faye wondered if there was any end to the trouble Sly had survived. She'd known about his time in the penitentiary. She'd known he lost his wife Patricia, Joe's mother, when she was under fifty. But she had never once heard anyone mention his brother, Joseph, whose death was a loss so hard that Sly had named his only child after him.

Sly was warmed up now, so Faye felt certain that she was about to hear everything about Cully that her father-in-law ever knew.

"Lots of teenaged boys wouldn't have wanted to be stuck with two little kids like me and Joseph, but Cully was always good to us. He made us flutes and taught us how to play 'em. My grandmama thought he couldn't do no wrong, so she made sure his pockets was always full of cookies. We ate most of 'em for him, and he'd just laugh at us making pigs out of ourselves. Whenever he saw us getting rambunctious, he'd sneak us away from the boring old folks and take us to the creek. Come to think of it, Cully taught me to swim. And to fish. I'd forgot that until this very minute."

Faye remembered Cully's fatherly arm across her back as they were knocked off their feet by the bomb. "Sounds like he was really good with children, even when he was just a kid himself."

"He was. I remember one time when I'd done something I really shouldn't oughta done. I hid in the pantry and listened while he asked my Daddy to go easy on me. He said, 'Sly's a good boy, sir. He's just a little too smart for his own good. You gotta be smart to think up the kind of mischief Sly makes.'"

Faye laughed. "He had you pegged."

"Yeah. He did. The family lost touch with him when he took off from school. I remember it was Eastertime, just a year before he was due to graduate. Woulda been the first one in the family to manage that, too, so you know he wanted to get out of there bad. It nearly killed my grandmama. As far as I know from the movie magazines, him and his wife never had any young'uns. Always thought that was sad, myself. There he was, sixteen years old, and telling Daddy how to raise me. And he was right, too. I heard him say in as many words, 'Please, sir, don't ever send them boys to that school.'"

"The boarding school? The one he ran away from?"

"Yep. The very same one that my daddy sent me to, right after Joseph passed. He said I was smart and he wanted me to learn things. He said maybe it wouldn't be fun, but school wasn't sup- posed to be fun. Daddy always meant well, but I'm here to tell you that Cully was right. Children shouldn't oughta be treated that way. And they belong with their parents. Cully's the kind of person to just take hisself away from a situation like that. I ain't. Know how I got away? I behaved like the devil's own son until they done me a favor and kicked me out."

Faye wondered what kind of devilishness it could possibly take to get kicked out of an abusive boarding school. Knowing Sly, his transgressions were probably entertaining.

"I remember the grownups doing a lot of talking when Cully took off, but I didn't understand what they was saying. Not at the time. When I got older, I come to understand what they meant when their voices got real quiet and they said, 'You know he didn't go alone.'"

This had to be the answer to the question that Faye didn't know to ask.

"One of the other students ran away with him?" she asked. "Do you know who it was?"

"Her name was Angela. I remember thinking her name suited her, because she was pretty like an angel. So you know what the grownups must have been talking about when a young man and a young woman run away together." Sly's voice lowered, as if to echo the hushed voices he'd heard when he was too young to understand the gossip of adults.

"You don't know her last name?"

"Nope. All I remember is the name Angela. Then, eight or ten years later, everybody was talking about Cully again."

"What happened? Did he call home?"

"Nope, never did that. But 'bout ten years after he left, that's when he got real famous, famous enough to get his picture in the movie magazines. Remember them? Before the internet, that's how regular people kept track of famous people. My aunt was a beautician and she always had a big stack of movie magazines in her beauty shop."

"I remember them," Faye said.

"Everybody came to the beauty shop to see that first article about Cully. I remember there was a picture of him and his wife." When my mama saw it, she said, "I always wondered about that, and there's my answer. If you can call it an answer."

"What are you saying? Was the picture of Cully and Angela?"

"That's the thing. They all took a look at his wife's picture, but nobody had a bit of doubt. It wasn't her. All those years, everybody in Sylacauga had been wondering what happened to Cully and Angela, and Cully had finally showed up without her. Now we knew what happened to him. But what happened to Angela?"

Chapter Twenty-Three

Ahua sat face-to-face with Cully and started strong.

"I understand that your mother was familiar with the subterranean rooms that were uncovered by the bomb. I'm told that she lived down there for quite some time, possibly years."

Cully leaned back in the chair and crossed his legs. "I see that Oklahomans gossip as efficiently as always."

"You might call it gossip. I call it cooperating with the ongoing investigation of a very serious crime. You honestly weren't going to tell us what you knew about the Chinese community that lived underground here for most of the early twentieth century?"

"I don't remember anybody asking me."

"An agent spoke with you immediately after the bombing, before we found the stairway. Even then, we wouldn't have known to go back and talk to you, because you didn't tell us that your mother was Chinese."

Cully uncrossed his legs. Still leaning back in his chair, he placed both palms flat on his thighs. "Nobody asked me that, either, which is a real good thing. I don't think it's appropriate for law enforcement to pry into people's racial or ethnic backgrounds. Bad things happen when they take those things into account."

When it came to revealing his emotions, Ahua only had one

tell that he knew about. When he was angry, he talked a little faster and a little louder than his usual quiet and reasonable speech patterns. He was angry now, so he was fighting that tell. "Look at me, Mantooth. I am black and I am Nigerian. Are you seriously suggesting that I would discriminate against you for being a minority? Or a double-minority? Or a quintuple minority? Don't you understand that I know what it's like?"

"I'm older than you. If you'll pardon my French, I've seen some shit. I keep my personal business to myself. Always have. I don't break any laws. If you or any other officer of the law asks me questions, I will answer them honestly, but I am not going to come to you and spill my guts. I'm just not. Why don't we move on past what I didn't tell you, because you didn't ask me to tell you? Then we can get to the part where I answer the questions you do ask. Because I have a real nice penthouse up there waiting for me and I'd like to get back to it."

Ahua drew a deep breath between his pursed lips. "Let's start with your mother's experience living down there. What did she tell you about it?"

"She said that it was dark and cold, but she also said that it wasn't so bad, most of the time. She didn't mind sleeping in a little room along with her parents and her sisters, with just a curtain for the front wall and dirt for the back wall and thin wallboard for the other two, because she didn't know any other way to live. I do remember her saying that there weren't many children down there nor women. Most Chinese immigrants in the early days were men who came here planning to earn some money and go back home to get married. When the money didn't pan out, they were stuck in this country, alone with no money. Nobody to marry, either."

"Yet your grandfather somehow beat the odds and found a wife. Presumably. He found a mother for his children, at the very least," Ahua said.

"I like to think he beat those odds with his extreme charm and good looks, and I like to think that those things are hereditary."

And now Cully was trying to use his undeniable charm to divert their attention from the family history he clearly didn't want to discuss.

Ahua wasn't having it. He kept pushing. "Do you know what brought your Chinese grandmother here? Your mother's mother? It would have taken an extraordinarily brave woman to cross the Pacific from China in those days."

"Ah, but I think you're assuming something that might not be true. I never knew my grandmother, but I'm thinking maybe she wasn't Chinese. I've got good reason to believe that my grandfather was Chinese, because his last name was Chen and my mother considered herself Chinese. Her first language was Cantonese and she never shifted to Creek, like my aunts and uncles did when they got tired of talking English. But her mother? My grandfather's wife? She could've been white or black for all I know but, looking at me, wouldn't you guess that maybe my Chinese grandfather married a Native American woman? Most people, when they look at me, they just assume I'm all Creek. So maybe I'm three-quarters. If my grandfather did marry a Native American woman, then he must've been some kind of man to get her to move underground just to be with him."

Cully's voice grew soft. "My mother said that she felt safe underground in a way that she never had, before or since."

Ahua knew that he should just let him talk, but he found himself speaking anyway. "Because everybody looked like her down there?"

"Pretty much. And they spoke her language. I think her family was happy in their snug little hole, until the diphtheria came."

Ahua thought of hundreds of people living underground, packed into small spaces. A disease like diphtheria, spread by coughing and sneezing, would rip through them like a wildfire.

"My mother said that she and her parents survived, but her sisters didn't. She didn't like to think about them, so we only talked about their deaths once. I couldn't even bring myself to ask her how many sisters she lost. Or how old they were. Or how sick she was. I don't like to talk about it, either, so I hope this is the only time we have to do that. All the old stories say that there was a cemetery somewhere underground, three levels below the surface. That's a long way, so maybe not or maybe so, but I have to wonder whether my aunts' graves are down there still."

Ahua was trying to figure out when this epidemic would have happened. If Cully was born in the mid-forties, his mother had probably been born around 1920 and her sisters were probably dead by 1930 or so. He was pretty sure that the diphtheria vaccine was developed about that time. It made him physically ill to think of all those people in their tiny living quarters, dying of a disease that could have been prevented and filling up that mythical cemetery, three levels down.

"I'm very sorry for your family's loss," Ahua said with his usual kindness. Any reasonable person could understand why Cully might not want to talk about something so painful, and Ahua was eminently reasonable.

"Do you know where exactly your mother lived? Is it possible that we're going to be able to access that area from the staircase leading under the Gershwin?"

Cully looked a little more relaxed, too, so his next words could have been confrontational, but they didn't feel that way to Ahua. They just felt matter-of-fact. "Agent, you know a lot more than I do about what you've seen down there. Doesn't matter, though, because I'm not going to be any help. My mother told me there were several entrances, but she only showed me one. It was in the basement of a building near the corner of Robinson and Sheridan, and the building's not there now. I walked over and checked it myself this morning. Maybe that entrance originally connected with the area you've explored, but I just can't say."

"Did your mother ever tell you about anything like this?"

He called up a photo of the painted room that was taken before it was vandalized. Cully's face made a single tell-tale twitch, but he was an actor. He regained control.

"No, but it's lovely. It does remind me of some drawings of my grandfather's that I saw when I was a kid. They're gone now. Everything from my childhood is gone." He looked at it more closely. "Lots of people draw trees and people. This could have been my grandfather's work or it could have been done by somebody he knew. Or they could have both been imitating art that was famous where they came from. There's no way to know, is there?"

Ahua looked at him closely, hoping to see that momentary reaction again, but he saw nothing. And he said nothing but, "Guess not." He clicked the mouse and another photo appeared, then another, all of them showing the colorful work of a talented but untrained artist. He was careful to avoid the photo that showed the three bodies.

This time, Cully's reaction was just as momentary, but it was even more obvious to Ahua that he wasn't playing it straight when he said, "Nope. My mother never mentioned a room like that. And she would've, if she'd ever seen it. Like I said, her father was an artist, and I think she would have been one, too, if she hadn't spent her short life taking care of my father and me. She just loved color. If my mother knew about this room, she would have told me."

Ahua let the silence hang. An accomplished actor like Cully surely knew that the agent was making an opening for him to speak and, hopefully, say more than he intended. Cully took the bait anyway.

"I'll tell you something else," he continued. "It's a big thing to buy that much paint. And in so many colors. It doesn't make sense to me that people who were living in holes because they couldn't afford anything else would spend that kind of money on painting pictures."

"You make a good point," Ahua said.

Cully's eyes hadn't left the computer screen. "Here's what

I think. I think the place where my mother lived is ninety or a hundred years gone, and I think it should stay that way. Somebody crawled down there sometime later and painted those pictures. From where I sit, that person is as bad as a vandal disturbing graves. The past is dead, Agent Ahua, and I think you should let it rest."

He rose. "I've told you what my mother told me about the Chinese underground and how people lived down there. Am I free to go?"

"Not yet. Does the name Angela mean anything to you?"

Cully was prepared for this question, because his response was almost too calm. He didn't flinch. His eyes didn't blink. His voice stayed even. He just said, "We were two unhappy boarding school kids. We had that in common, and we mistook our shared misery for love. We ran away together but we didn't make it a week before she left me."

"What happened when you split? Did you argue?"

"Agent Ahua, we argued every day that we were together. I couldn't abide her drug-taking, and she couldn't abide me nagging her about it. I hung around for a few days after she took off, because I felt bad about leaving a young woman alone in the world. When I was sure she wasn't coming back, I moved on."

"Did you file a missing persons report?"

"I was on the run and underage. I did not. If, in the course of this investigation, you are able to find out what happened to her, I would appreciate it if you'd let me know. It would ease my mind after many years of worry. Am I free to go now?"

Ahua nodded and watched silently as Cully left. The older man still moved with a practiced grace, but the swagger was gone. Time creeps up on everybody, even movie stars. The man knew something.

Cully knew something about poor people living in terrible conditions sometime around the Great Depression. And he knew something about some paintings that were probably made a long time after that. He knew something about a woman named Angela who had been missing for fifty or so years. But what those things had to do with a missing professor and a fatal bombing, Ahua couldn't say.

Chapter Twenty-Four

After saying goodbye to Sly, Faye found a pair of pants and a pair of socks with no root beer stains. Her boots wiped pretty clean, leaving her smelling only a little bit like sassafras. Shortly after she gave up on getting them any cleaner, Ahua called her with an assignment that was, to be honest, pretty tedious.

She knew the reason why she was stuck at a computer and not out looking for bad guys or finding Stacy. She didn't like Ahua's reasoning, but she understood it. The reason was that she was not an FBI agent, but she was a darned good archaeologist. And some-times, archaeologists get stuck doing tedious computer work. Or library work. Archaeology was only exciting in the movies or on those once-in-a-lifetime occasions when something really cool emerged from the earth. When Ahua hired an archaeologist to consult on this case, this was exactly the kind of problem that he'd had in mind for her to solve.

She was facing two computer monitors. On one, she had a selection of the photos Goldsby took before the vandalism. On the other, she was paging through the shots taken since the paint-ings had been defaced. Ahua wanted her to continue with her original task of trying to determine the age of the paintings and the rooms, but now he wanted her to take it a step further.

"There is a reason somebody wanted specific scenes gone, and they wanted them gone bad enough to obliterate them with sandpaper, paint thinner, and paint. Your job is to figure out what that reason is."

It had taken her a while, but she'd selected all the photos that included areas that were later sanded away. They were now arranged on her left display. Then she'd selected photos taken after the vandalism that centered on the sanded-away areas, arranging them on her right display. Now her job was simple: she needed to figure out which images were so important that the vandal had needed them obliterated.

One image of people happily enjoying each other's company caught her eye. She knew that the painter, whose style was primitive but still graceful and fluid, wanted her to know that the people were happy, because beatific smiles shone on all of their faces. A bearded man, smiling, held an infant in his arms. A child leaned against his leg and smiled down at the baby. Beside him was a large-breasted woman with long dark hair, also smiling down at the baby. The child wore a long smock-like garment over pants. So did the man and woman, so she couldn't be sure if the child was a boy or a girl.

Nearby, another woman, also with long, dark hair, reclined beneath a tree. Faye couldn't tell if she was supposed to be part of this group. If not, this might even be another image of the same woman at another time in her life. She was hugely pregnant, perhaps with one of the children in the other picture. The painting celebrated her fertility, giving her the heavy belly, breasts, rump, and thighs seen on so many prehistoric fertility figures.

The walls were covered with scenes like this one. On every wall, three trees were painted from floor to ceiling, separating each of the walls' rectangular spaces into four parts that were further divided by clusters of flowers or strands of ivy that served as frames for the paintings of people. And everywhere there was color. Magenta flowers, emerald leaves, aquamarine streams, a big yellow sun-ball in the sky.

On the trees, she saw fruit of every color, apples, pears, blush-bellied peaches. Between the trees grew rows of tall corn capped by golden tassels, separating rows of fat tomatoes, round cabbages, and chartreuse broccoli. The benches pushed up against three of the walls were painted to disappear into the scene, but the door in the wall was painted to draw attention. Its metallic surface was enhanced with sparkly silver paint, and it was ringed with a garland of ivy with every leaf carefully painted to convey the texture of its rib and veins. The ivy sprawled out onto the surrounding walls, tying all the scenes together with its vegetal ropes. Carmine red handprints were scattered everywhere.

Religious imagery, too, was everywhere, sharing space with magical symbols like pentagrams. If asked to describe the scene, Faye would have called it an effervescent celebration of magic and fertility. Or maybe it celebrated the magic *of* fertility.

Did these paintings date to the 1920s, when she knew for a fact that the underground community was occupied? The fantastical gardens and forests of the artist's world had a hippie vibe to them, which would suggest the 1960s or later, but pastoral images were timeless scenes.

How could she give these pictures the date that Ahua needed? A garden planted in the early 1900s, when the Chinese underground city was built, would look pretty much like a garden planted in the 1940s, when the catacombs were thought to have emptied. It would also look like a garden planted in the 1990s, when three little bodies had been placed on one of the benches in the pictures. And it would look pretty much like the garden growing right now behind her house on Joyeuse Island.

Except...hmm. She zoomed in on the rows of vegetables. If her memory could be trusted, broccoli didn't have a long history in the Americas.

She pulled out her phone to check how long Americans had been growing broccoli. The answer was ambiguous. The vegetable originated in Italy, but it didn't catch on in the United States until Italian Americans began growing it commercially in the 1920s. Wide-scale availability came after World War II and the Chinese community was back aboveground by then. More to the point, those people were living underground for the entire early period of broccoli in America, from the 1920s until World War II. They likely never saw it growing and thus wouldn't have been able to paint it.

Besides, even if they'd seen it when they were living topside, Faye didn't think that people living on the economic edge would look at a strange, new, and probably expensive food on their grocery store shelves and think, "Hey! A new vegetable that we've never eaten. Let's give it a whirl. What do we have to risk? Starvation?"

If asked to bet cold, hard cash that a poor person living underground before 1940 had painted broccoli into their idealized memory of a vegetable garden, Faye would have said, "Heck, no."

Something else bothered her about the broccoli. The plants were a beautiful shade of yellow-green, it was true, but healthy broccoli plants were supposed to be dark green. And they weren't usually shaped like squat, pointy pyramids.

She zoomed in on the chartreuse plants. Then, interest piqued, she zoomed in some more. The masses of meticulously painted buds on each broccoli plant resolved themselves into spiraling geometric patterns that Faye recognized as fractals, and this wasn't just a mathematical oddity.

The painter hadn't been portraying just any old broccoli growing in Eden. This was Romanesco broccoli and the miraculous internet that lived in her phone told her that it wasn't commercially available in the U.S. until the 1980s. She would bet serious money that these paintings were from the approximate time that the bodies were left behind. But who were those three children?

She turned her attention to the people painted among the plants. She was certain Ahua would prefer for her to spend her time on them, instead of on garden vegetables.

There were faces everywhere, all of them in varying shades of light tan. She didn't see any black people here, but she couldn't say for sure that the people were all white. They peered out between leafy branches. They breached the water, their skin wet and their mouths laughing.

As she studied one face after another, it struck her that there was only one adult man. He had a receding hairline and wore a short brown beard, and he was recognizable in every single scene that contained more than one person. She remained confused by the woman or women. They all had long dark hair, and they were all dressed alike. Perhaps there was one of them and perhaps there were two or three. Perhaps there were more. They were uncountable.

As for the children, her first instinct was to say that they were all girls, because their hair was long and the smocks they wore were a bit like dresses, but that was a dangerous assumption. The brown-bearded man wore his hair long. He and the women (woman?) wore clothes identical to the children's. Faye could assign an apparent gender to the adults by secondary sexual characteristics—a beard, breasts, swelling hips, a receding hairline—but not so for the children. She could be looking at multiple images of one child growing up, or she could be looking at a group of children the size of a kindergarten class.

The presence of babies was variable. Sometimes there were only older children in a scene. Sometimes the man was holding a baby. Sometimes a baby was in the arms of a black-haired woman. Sometimes there were two babies being held by two adults. There were no pictures including three babies. This was the only thing that kept Faye from leaping straight to the conclusion that there was a link between the pictures and the bodies they'd found. Still, all three babies could be there, with different ones being shown in different scenes.

The photos taken after the paintings were damaged were much harder to interpret. More than an hour passed while Faye looked from one screen to another, comparing the scarred, blurred, paint-splashed images to their original versions. It was painstaking work that required her to make a rough sketch of the room, locating and numbering each scar and penciling in the details of the images that had been obliterated.

Eventually, she put her pencil down and tried to make sense of what she'd learned.

First, the vandal had carefully wiped out every trace of the man. His face was gone from every scene where he had appeared.

Second, the children were gone, and so were the babies. The woman or women remained.

And third, random stretches of ivy had been sanded away, just a few inches here and there. Faye studied her sketch obsessively, looking for patterns. Sometimes she thought that obsession was her best quality.

It took time, but her obsessive attention to detail paid off. It became clear that there was a single damaged area in each scene that didn't involve a person. None of those areas were large, and they inevitably included just a few inches of painted ivy. Zooming in on a spot of ivy in a "before" photo, she saw what she had been missing. The ivy's ground-away stems had formed a single word. A name.

Faye wished with all of her heart that the artist had been self-aggrandizing enough to use his full name, but having his first name was better than nothing. Ahua should be pleased.

While she waited for him to return, she studied the letters. The L had a sweeping curve that made it far larger than the lowercase letters that followed it. Still, he—and she thought that this name usually belonged to a man—had carefully formed each of those smaller letters, showing the self-esteem of someone who insisted that his signature be readable.

Faye knew nothing of handwriting analysis, so she could draw no more conclusions from a simple signature. She could only look at the flowing script spelling out "Lonnie," wondering who he was and what had happened to the people he'd painted so lovingly.

Chapter Twenty-Five

Ahua looked tired. He looked like a man who needed to walk away from this case until he'd had a chance to get over the sight of three little blanket-wrapped bodies. Judging by the sick feeling in the pit of Faye's stomach, she estimated that a couple of years of rest and recuperation might do it for her. Ahua was a trained and hardened FBI agent, so maybe he could manage it in a year.

"We just got some lab results back. Autopsy, too," he said, scrolling through pages of data on his phone.

"On the bomber?"

"No. Well, yeah, that came in an hour ago. This is about the children."

No wonder he looked too tired to go on. "What did you learn?"

"There was a reason they were all older than they looked. They were sick."

"What do you mean by 'sick'? Are you saying that they died of natural causes?"

"Yeah. The lab manager called me up to explain it to me. She said that all three looked like young toddlers, but their growth had stalled. The medical term for that is 'failure to thrive.'"

Faye had a hard time voicing her question, but she toughed it out. "Is that a nice way of saying they were starved?"

"No, no, nothing like that. At least I don't think so. It's hard to tell much after all these years, but she said that they were neatly dressed. They were wrapped up carefully, and each of them had a well-worn toy in the blanket with them. And flowers. She got the sense that these children had been well taken care of. Loved, even. It was just that they had an inherited condition that eventually killed them all."

"And they all coincidentally inherited the same condition? Were they related? Did they all die at the same time?"

"We can't be sure about the time of death, but we do know that they were brothers. And they were hemophiliacs."

Faye's knowledge of hemophilia wasn't medical. It was historical.

"Hemophilia? That's the disease that Queen Victoria passed on to her children. And because she was Queen Victoria, those children married into most of the royal houses of Europe. There were a lot of sick princes in the next couple of generations. It's an X-linked recessive disease, so women carrying the gene don't ordinarily get sick. Men only have one X-chromosome, though, so if that one X-chromosome has the defective gene, then they've got the disease. In Victorian times, this usually meant that they didn't live long."

"Correct. And wow. When you need to remember something historical, you really remember it."

Faye waved off the compliment. "But hemophilia's treatable these days, isn't it? Why would three brothers with hemophilia born in the late 1980s or early 1990s all die so young?"

Faye tried to imagine losing three children, together or one after another. The thought hurt, so she quit trying.

"Lack of money, maybe," Ahua suggested. "Everybody doesn't have Queen Victoria's fortune. Although one would hope that they would have qualified for some kind of medical care if they were too poor to take a kid with a life-threatening illness to the doctor. Or it could've been a religious thing. There are people who don't believe in doctors. They'd rather pray. If it was one of my kids, I'd do both."

Faye did her best praying when one of her children had a fever—her mamaw would have been proud—but she gave them acetaminophen between prayers. "You haven't found any records of three missing brothers in the 1990s?"

"Nope. It's like these kids' bodies miraculously appeared underneath Oklahoma City sometime during the Clinton administration."

"And I don't think you ever told me how you zeroed in on that time frame."

"One of the boys was wearing a T-shirt celebrating the Dallas Cowboys' 1994 Super Bowl win. Size 3T."

Faye's son, Michael, had only just outgrown that size. "What kind of religion asks people to watch their children die of treatable diseases?"

"Well, for one thing, it's the kind of religion that keeps a low profile. That's probably why there are no missing person reports and no death certificates. My best guess is that there weren't any birth certificates, either. If they'd tried to have those children buried in the normal way, they'd have opened a serious can of worms, legally speaking. Disposing of the bodies was a real problem."

"You wouldn't want to bury them in your backyard," Faye said, "not even if your backyard was twenty acres. There's too much risk that somebody, someday, will uncover three little graves and want to know who put three children in them."

Ahua nodded. "But if you somehow knew about the deserted chambers under downtown Oklahoma City and if you knew how to get into them, you'd have a safe place to leave your dead children."

"Hold on a minute. You just said something that gave me an idea. You said, 'And if you knew how to get into them.' We know of one person who knew how to get into those chambers."

"The bomber," Ahua said. "You're onto something, Faye. Let me think. Would their father have hemophilia? Or be a carrier? Could we ask the lab to look for that?"

Faye shook her head. "The gene is on the X-chromosome. And

men get their X-chromosomes from their mother. But he'll have other genetic markers that he would have passed on to his children. If he's the father, the genetics lab will be able to find them. But I haven't shown you what I found in these photographs."

She turned to the computer and slid its mouse around to wake it up. The before-and-after photos of the painted room returned to the two screens.

"Look here." She used the mouse to point out the key photographs. "The person who vandalized the paintings sanded off the faces of the adult man and all of the children. The women were sometimes sanded away, sometimes splashed with paint, and sometimes left alone. I think this is a sign that the vandal found the women to be immaterial."

"Now, look at the ivy. If you look closely—and I mean really closely, because the painter was trying hard to camouflage this— you can read words hidden among the vines. In four places, I found the sentence, "Evil must be obliterated." Other sentences appear, like "Set yourself apart from the world" and "A leader has been chosen and you must follow," but "Evil must be obliterated" was a very important directive to somebody."

"When a man tells other people that they have to follow one particular leader," Ahua said, "he's usually convinced that he's the chosen leader."

"You sure this person is a man?"

"Not necessarily, but the bomber is. If we're lucky, we'll find out they're the same person. Guess I'm banking on being lucky."

"I think you're lucky. Because I believe I've found the artist's signature, and it's usually a man's name. The vandal left the inspirational phrases alone, but almost all of the artist's many signatures are sanded away."

She enlarged a photo that showed the signature of somebody named Lonnie hidden in a garland of ivy. "I don't know who painted this, but his name is Lonnie."

Ahua was so excited that he pummeled Faye's shoulder and

held out his fist for her to bump. "Oh, yes. He's a man. As soon as you pointed out that the bomber needed a brand-new pressure cooker gasket, I set some people to work tracking down that lead."

He looked down at the computer and scrolled for a moment, then moved aside so that Faye could see. On the screen were notes from another agent's conversation with an online hardware retailer in Texas.

Morris Elroy of Elroy Hardware says that he got an online order for a gasket for the model of pressure cooker that the bomber used, just three weeks ago. He said that he'd never sold a gasket for that particular model, which I guess doesn't prove anything but it is indicative. The buyer mailed him a money order.

This next part is key. The gasket was mailed to a Shirley Conroy in Yukon, Oklahoma. I sent some agents right over and they found a really big house owned by a really snobby woman in her seventies. She tried to shut the door in my agents' faces and then got the vapors when they told her that she just couldn't do that to the FBI. She says, and they believed her, that she's had a handyman until just recently. He had a lot of things delivered that she thought he should have gone out and picked up himself. She eventually fired him for, in her words, "stealing a few measly boxes of nails."

Faye looked up from her phone. "Did the bomber pack nails in the bomb for shrapnel?"

"Yep. Keep reading. She says that the handyman's name was Alonso Smith. Sounds like an assumed name to me, so the name may not mean a thing, but Yukon's a twenty-minute drive from the Gershwin Hotel. I think this is our guy. I've got a big team of people combing Shirley's house for clues and she's not happy about it."

"Smith might be an assumed name," Ahua said, "but Alonso's not. Not when the paintings were signed by somebody named

Lonnie. We've tied the paintings to the bomber. Good work, Faye." He pounded her shoulder again.

"So the paintings are tied to the bomber," she said. "The three bodies were brothers, so that ties them to each other. If the painted babies that were obliterated by the vandal represented those three brothers, then the paintings tie the dead children to the bomber."

"Yes. And if we have a vandal who's focused on eliminating Lonnie's name and the faces of an unidentified man and some children, then I'd say the vandal is linked to the bomber."

"Going a little fast there, aren't you?" Faye asked. "Considering that the bomber is dead. And so are the brothers."

"Yeah, but we don't know that all of the children are dead. They'd be adults now, if the paintings were done in the nineties. And then there's the dark-haired woman. Women? I can't tell. The vandal didn't bother to obliterate their faces."

"I'd say women. I think there's more than one of them. Maybe the vandal knows for sure."

"Or it might mean that there's no point in hiding the women's faces because they're dead," he said.

"Wow, Agent. Your job takes your mind into some dark places."

His face stilled, but he said only, "You got that right." His eyes traveled to the computer screen and studied the photos. "So you think this guy knew how to get underground as early as the 1990s? If you needed a place to hide the bodies of three little boys, you couldn't imagine a better place. It would seem like a gift from God."

Faye didn't have a lot of answers when it came to religion, but she had an answer to that. "God had nothing to do with this."

Chapter Twenty-Six

Stacy Wong never leaves my mind. I see Stacy wherever I look. I suppose I always will.

Stacy was never supposed to be caught in the fallout of Lonnie's wickedness. She had no part in the evil that must be obliterated. Anyone could see that. She just came a little too close to ferreting out some secrets that could not—must not—ever see the light of day again.

It was a hard slog through the storm sewer with a gallon of paint thinner, a gallon of white paint, and more sandpaper than I like to remember. And I did it while wearing Lonnie's old boots, making my footprints untraceable to me.

Everything needed to be perfect, and it almost was.

I rubbed away and sanded off every single mark on those brightly painted walls that would have pointed the FBI to the family. Then I sanded off some more stuff, just to confuse them, and I splashed a gallon of paint around to confuse them even more. I bagged up the sandpaper, the empty cans, the brush, and the rags, passing them through the metal door. Then I prepared to crawl through it myself and drop into the ankle-deep water.

That should have been the end of it. And it would have been if Stacy hadn't appeared at the open portal at just that moment, standing in the storm sewer and peering in. I will never forget the grief in the woman's voice as she looked at the defaced paintings and shrieked, "Did you do this? Why would anybody do such a thing?"

If Stacy had known what those paintings stood for, she would have helped me sand them away. Together, we would have dabbed gouts of white paint over every multicolored square inch that Lonnie had painted. If Stacy had known the truth, she wouldn't have seen them as history or art. She would have seen them as documentation of the misery of eight people. She would have seen them as an indictment of Lonnie for the premeditated murder of my brothers. She would have understood.

But there was no time to explain it to her. Stacy took one look at the paint on my hands and freaked out.

"You had no right. No right! This was history and you've destroyed it. It's gone. Obliterated."

The word "obliterated" triggered the violence that has been buried in my psyche since I was six years old, sitting on a hard bench in that cold room and listening to Lonnie justify the obliteration of anyone outside the family.

"Evil must be obliterated," he said, time and again. "Until that day, we must separate ourselves from evil in all its forms. We will look back on this hard time and know that we were purified here. Here, we achieved our metamorphosis."

I am the only living soul who remembers what Lonnie was like during the winter of our metamorphosis. My first mother is dead now, so she can't help remember. My other mother, Sandra, is dead, too. Lonnie was guilty in their deaths, as guilty as he was in my brothers' deaths, because people who don't get things like mammograms and routine cholesterol testing don't tend to live very long.

My first sister was barely toddling during the time we lived in this room, and my first brother was an infant. The others weren't born yet. Only I remember the terrible winter when we lived in The Sanctuary. It was the time of purification, when we passed from the real world into a world that existed only in Lonnie's head.

My mothers had spent the winter petrified of leaving The Sanctuary *without Lonnie's permission. His was a great talent for mind control. I give him that much credit. Even when he left to get groceries and paint—lots of paint that consumed money he could have used for jars of peanut butter and bags of bread—my mothers stayed underground voluntarily, buried until he decided it was time for our resurrection.*

My second mother, already heavily pregnant with Zeb, spent that winter begging little Gabe to live. The baby's illness hardly registered with Lonnie, busily daubing the walls with his hallucinations. He only put down his paintbrush to sleep and to dole out stingy portions of food.

"When we run out of money, it will be a sign that it's time to rise to the surface again." Lonnie said this on a daily basis, while opening a single can of beans to feed a man, a child, a toddler, and two women, one of them a nursing mother, but he had lied. Lonnie never opened his mouth without a lie coming out. We weren't waiting underground until God gave us a sign to leave by cutting off our food. We were waiting for Lonnie's father to finish dying so that we could have his house and his thirty acres.

Fortunately, my grandfather died early in the spring. Otherwise, we would never have gotten the garden planted, and this might well have killed us all. Our money was nearly gone, and Lonnie would have let us starve before he accepted help from the government. I was an adult before I escaped him. Only then did I learn that the government he hated so much might have given my brothers the medical care they needed to stay alive.

On the day I learned that my brothers didn't have to die, I became a ticking time bomb. Lonnie deserved to be caught in my blast radius. Stacy Wong did not.

Chapter Twenty-Seven

Lunch was awkward. This made Carson antsy.

Ordinarily, a room full of people eating tasty food had a happy, collegial feel, but this room felt a little off. It felt awkward. If Carson listened closely, he could hear certain words pop out of the buzz of voices.

Stacy.

Bomber.

Afraid.

All around him, people were saying "What happened to Stacy?" and "Where's Stacy?" and "They're saying that the bomber acted alone. What do you think?" and "Are you afraid?"

Knowing that there was nothing he could do about this, Carson stepped up to the podium and tried anyway. Unfortunately, he was too honest to pretend there was nothing wrong, so he only made it worse.

"I'm so glad you're all still here. There are about a million FBI agents crawling around this place, so if you have any dark secrets, you should keep them to yourself." In response he got a communal chuckle that felt cautious and stressed. He plunged on. "I feel strongly that we're safe. The FBI's Assistant Special Agent in Charge has told me that he will be in touch immediately if that should change, but he doesn't expect it to."

A hand shot up. "What's going on with Dr. Wong? We're worried about her here at Table E. It's not like her to skip out on an important talk."

"I'm worried about her, too. The most important thing for you all to know is that there is no sign of foul play. We believe that Dr. Wong left the hotel of her own accord early this morning, and this is something that adults are allowed to do. Nevertheless, law enforcement is concerned that she isn't back, so I am in touch with them about Dr. Wong's whereabouts at all times."

Just inside his peripheral vision, he saw a woman in a hotel uniform stop what she was doing. In the middle of replenishing trays of leftover sandwich meat, she paused, hands still in the air, and looked at him. He didn't blame anyone for being jumpy, not after recent events. The hotel staff had to be wondering whether it was even safe to come to work.

The woman pulled an old clamshell phone out of her pocket. Speaking quickly into it, she backed out the door, talking all the while.

Carson was sorry that he'd paused in the middle of an announcement that was supposed to be reassuring. Now he was hearing other words in the ambient buzz, words like "not safe" and "go home." Well, there was nothing he could do about that, other than remind them of what they were leaving.

"We have some new events for you. Mark your programs so you don't miss them. Joe Wolf Mantooth will be giving a free hands-on flintknapping workshop tonight at 7:30. He has rock for you, but if you have material you want to use, bring it. You can bring a project that's not going well, too, and Joe will help you make it into something beautiful."

He saw Faye give him a big thumbs-up for promoting Joe's work. The woman could be completely single-minded, but he found it rather sweet that she used that determination to help her husband shine.

Carson had known Joe since they were boys, and he fully

believed that Faye was the best thing that had ever happened to him. Carson's own mother had hoped that Faye would be the best thing that ever happened to him, until she spied the gold band on Faye's left ring finger. Since his mother had always had a soft spot for Joe, she couldn't wish him ill, so praying for Faye to divorce him wasn't an option. Carson's mom had been forced to settle for adding Faye to her list of grown-ups that she thought needed mothering. Faye didn't seem to mind.

Thanks to the great news about Joe's flintknapping workshop, the room's conversational buzz was distinctly changed for the better. Even the group's body language changed, as people sat up straighter or leaned over to a neighbor and said things like, "I'd pay a lot of money for that, but he's offering it for free," or simply, "I'm in!"

"Tomorrow evening's new activity is going to be just as artistic but a lot more relaxing. And with less chance of leaving here with a black-and-blue fingernail."

He was rewarded with a few laughs. Some of his listeners held out their hands, displaying their flintknapping wounds for their neighbors to admire.

"I'm also honored to announce that Cully Mantooth will give a concert of traditional Muscogee Creek songs, playing flutes that he made himself. He says that he learned the songs from his father and that his father learned them from *his* father at about the time of the First World War. The flutes, too, adhere to traditions established many years ago. To the best of his knowledge, the music and the flutes' design date to a lot earlier than World War I, going back to the Creek's ancestral homelands southeast of here, but he wanted you to know that they have a long heritage right here in Oklahoma."

The crowd was making an unmistakably happy buzz now. Carson looked around for Cully with no luck. It would have been far better for attendance at his concert if he'd been here to meet and greet his fans, but he supposed Cully knew his business. And perhaps Cully knew that he could fill a modest-sized convention venue without lifting a finger to promote it.

"Mr. Mantooth will do a Q&A after the concert. He says that he'll answer questions about any part of his career, from what it was like to work as an extra in John Wayne films to how he composes his soundtracks. I think you'll all want to stick around for that."

He overheard somebody saying, "Even if the FBI wasn't saying that we're perfectly safe, I'd stay to see that man play the flute."

Carson said, "You people go back to your food, but remember. We have a lot of excitement in store for you."

Then he dropped into his chair, exhausted from nerves but fairly sure that there would be butts in the chairs for the duration of his conference. This gathering of artists, would-be artists, and people who appreciated indigenous art had been Carson's brainchild. He felt very strongly that indigenous art should be valued and that the techniques should be preserved. This conference was a way he could use his abilities and his connections to do something that needed doing. He was not in the mood to let the bomber or the protesters outside stop him. Maybe the protesters were working against themselves, calling attention to the art of people they did not respect. Carson liked that idea.

He scanned the room for his faculty. Stacy was missing, obviously, but almost everybody else was there. Dr. Dell was missing, too, but he had called to check on her barely five minutes after lunch started. According to her, she was nursing a stomach virus. Carson thought it was probably a hangover, but it wasn't his job to police the behavior of his faculty.

As the host, it worried him that the ham and turkey were getting low, but the woman who left never returned and the remaining workers seemed way more focused on refilling water glasses than on keeping the sandwich bar stocked. Carson kept an eye on the cold cuts, and when he saw that they were nearly gone, he called out, "Don't forget! We have an ice-cream sundae bar!"

His guests shifted their attention from sandwiches to dessert, and all was well, except for the uneaten slices of ham and turkey that grew less attractive with every minute they approached room temperature. The missing worker never returned, but the ones who had stayed behind cheerfully scooped everybody's ice cream into individual blue china bowls, and ice cream has the power to make people focus on the lusciousness in front of them.

Nobody seemed to notice the unappetizing leftover cold cuts. Except, of course for Carson.

———

Faye had just filled her mouth with a big spoonful of chocolate ice cream when Sadie Raincrow elbowed her.

"Have you been keeping an eye on the internet?" she asked, placing her phone on the crisp, smooth tablecloth and pulling up *The Oklahoman*'s website. The lead story's headline was printed in huge type.

NO SUSPECT YET IN DOWNTOWN BOMBING

"Not that one," Sadie said. "There's nothing new in that story. But take a look at this one." She scrolled down to the next headline.

LEGENDARY UNDERGROUND CHINESE CITY UNCOVERED BY BOMB

Faye picked up the phone and read the story, which began with a rehash of the 1969 newspaper article detailing the last time the underground chambers had been uncovered. When she reached the third paragraph, she reached into her purse and scrabbled around for her reading glasses. With her readers perched firmly on her nose, she read the part of the story that was news to Sadie but not to her, then she read it again.

The doors at the bottom of the staircase conform closely to the description of a heavy wooden door seen in 1969. Behind one of the doors is a modest-sized room with all surfaces—door, walls, and ceiling—covered with colorful paintings, and in that room were the bodies of three little boys.

Faye's eyebrows climbed to her hairline. Somebody had leaked a description of the painted room to the media.

"Three children. Can you imagine? And did you know about that room?" Sadie asked. "I thought I'd heard all the rumors about underground Chinese that there was to hear."

Faye shook her head, which was a lie. Yes, she knew about the room, but she doubted that Ahua had mentioned it to the press yet. He seemed like a man who kept his cards very close to the vest. But if he didn't tell anyone and she didn't tell anyone, then the investigation had a leak.

Who talked?

Goldsby? The engineer, Patricia Kura? It was possible, but Faye would need to know a lot more about them before she could think of a reason they might leak information from a critical investigation. Her money was on Liu. She would do whatever it took to find Stacy Wong.

She kept reading.

The paintings and an unusual metal door high on one wall set this room apart from surviving descriptions of the underground community's living space. Recorded eyewitness accounts from the 1920s do not mention this room, nor does the 1969 newspaper article, although oral history does describe a wall decorated by an artist who used a sharp implement to draw a landscape scene on an earthen wall.

Faye shoveled the last few bites of her ice cream into her mouth. She needed to find Ahua.

"I'm worried about Stacy," Sadie said.

"Because of this article?" Faye handed Sadie's phone back to her.

"No. Well, yes, it worries me. If Stacy weren't already missing, she would have read this article and found a way to get down there, even if it meant hijacking an oil rig and drilling herself a hole."

"I'm not sure that's how oil rigs work."

Sadie waved a dismissive hand. "It was just a metaphor. An Oklahoma metaphor. I'm just saying that, with every second that passes without Stacy in this room, I'm more sure that she's down there under our feet."

Sadie didn't say whether she thought Stacy was alive down there under their feet, and Faye didn't ask her. She didn't want to know.

Chapter Twenty-Eight

Faye, intent on getting to Ahua, wouldn't have noticed the scene in Kaayla's office, if it hadn't been for the sound of a woman weeping. The hotel manager's temporary office was near the elevator bank, so it was impossible to miss the quiet sobs.

As she neared Kaayla's office, she saw the door swinging shut. Nothing of Kaayla was visible but her hand, pale against the rubbed bronze doorknob. She was silent, but Faye heard voices coming from further inside the room. One of the speakers was weeping.

Faye got a single glance through the closing door, but she only saw one of Kaayla's guests, a woman who sat in a chair opposite her desk. It was Lucia.

Faye had noticed Lucia's quick exit from the lunch buffet, right after a quick phone conversation. She hoped the young woman hadn't gotten bad news. At least Kaayla's personal kindness made Faye feel like this incident wasn't going to be a mark against Lucia with the boss. Faye admired the way that Kaayla interacted with her staff. Her demeanor was unfailingly professional, but still very warm. People who worked in jobs like hotel housekeeping and maintenance had to put up with a lot of dehumanizing treatment from the people they served. At least the employees of the Gershwin Hotel didn't have to take that kind of treatment.

As she power walked out of the South Tower, Faye tried to focus on the question of where the reporter learned about the painted chamber, but the scene in Kaayla's office kept popping back into her head. Lucia's tears could stem from something unrelated to the bombing or her job, and they probably did, but seeing her with Kaayla reminded Faye that the hotel staff had access to parts of the Gershwin Hotel that most people wouldn't even know existed. Was it possible that someone associated with the hotel had been down the hidden stairs into the underground network of rooms?

If anybody was likely to stumble onto the hidden door and get a look at the painted room, it would be someone like Lucia who could have dusted the right panel in the right way and accidentally opened the door. Or perhaps a handyman. Or perhaps Kaayla had stumbled on it somehow during her work as the hotel's assistant manager.

But why would they pretend ignorance? The FBI had surely interviewed everybody associated with the hotel, and they would have asked questions designed to find out who knew about the secret door. It made no sense not to tell the FBI if they'd been down the hidden staircase. Exploring a strange place was no crime and Faye had no inkling that they were suspects.

Deep down, Faye could not make herself suspect any hotel employee she'd met, especially not the devastated Lucia. She suspected that Lucia's breakdown didn't come from a dark, secretive place. Anybody could fall apart after a trauma like the explosion and delayed responses were perfectly normal.

When Faye reached the sidewalk, she saw that the protesters and counterprotesters had all gone home. The world outside the towers looked completely normal. Nothing stood between her and the site of the bombing but a few hundred feet of sidewalk and the FBI's barricades, but it somehow seemed very far away.

As she entered the mobile command center, Ahua met her eyes with a cold stare, prompting her to say "It wasn't me!" in her best imitation of a guilty person.

He didn't say anything, so she tried to channel innocence as she said, "Seriously. I didn't tell a soul. Who do you think spilled the beans about the painted room? Is it the same person who talked about the children's bodies?"

"Could've been you both times, but it wasn't. It was me. Why do you think I trusted you so easily last time?"

"But why?"

"I thought surely somebody would remember three missing children. And I thought that spilling the beans about the painted room might stir up some people who've been listening to family stories about the Chinese underground for their whole lives."

"Did it work?"

"So far, no."

"Remind me never to believe anything you say."

"I have a lot of FBI mind tricks up my sleeve."

Now Faye felt like she was face-to-face with a master manipulator, and she very probably was. This made her unaccountably eager to talk.

"I've been thinking that it's possible that someone in the hotel knew about those stairs. They may even have been down them, although I guess it's been years, considering the dust. Are Kaayla, Grace, and Lucia old enough to have gone down there in the nineties? I'm not sure about the redheaded desk clerk, but the gray-haired woman who works with him is certainly old enough. They're the only hotel employees I know on sight, but I've seen plenty of others because it's a big hotel and Kaayla's got them all on overtime. Frankly, they all need to go home and sleep before one of them cracks."

"We've spoken with Kaayla and all of her employees, so their ages are on file, but the ones you mentioned by name look thirty-ish. Maybe a little older, maybe a little younger. So does the red-head. The gray-haired woman? I'd say fifties, don't you think?"

Faye, who was terrible at guessing ages, nodded like she agreed with him when she, in fact, had no clue.

"You're wrong about one thing," he said. "Yes, the dust was thick on the floor of the painted room. Goldsby and his people have made enough progress at the foot of the stairs to know that the room to the left is blanketed with dust, too. But the stairs? They weren't nearly so dusty."

"Are you saying somebody swept them?" Faye pictured Kaayla ordering her housekeeping staff to sweep this space that no hotel guest would ever see.

"No, not at all. It's just that the stairwell seems to have had a very slow water leak. Or maybe the water condensed off those cool plaster walls and collected on the floor over a period of years. The brick stair treads were covered with a light skim of dust that had been wetted and dried over and over. Goldsby says that people could have walked up and down those stairs without leaving evidence, easy."

Faye wasn't sure whether she thought that this was significant, but she mentally filed it away for later.

"I suppose you have agents working in the newspaper archives?" she asked.

"Yes. Because, despite what a lot of people want to think, the FBI is not stupid."

"I didn't think you were. But do you mind if I take a look in those archives, too? They may have historical photographs of downtown Oklahoma City from the years when those underground rooms were occupied. I would dearly love to find another entrance."

"You and me both, but people have been looking for years."

"None of them were the FBI. And none of them were me."

He laughed out loud and said, "Well, that's true. I'll pay for a few hours of your library time. You may already know this, but you don't have to go work in *The Oklahoman's* archives. Their back issues are digitized all the way back to 1901. You can access what you need from a computer in the comfort of your own hotel room, and I want you to. There are just too many people in this command center so, and I mean this kindly, please get out."

Faye rose to leave.

"Go find something that a lot of people have been trying to find for years. Something about you makes me think you can do it. That's why I hired you."

———

True to Ahua's word, Faye's computer took her straight to 1969 while she was sitting in the comfort of her own hotel room. There, on the front page of the April 9 edition of *The Daily Oklahoman,* was a headline saying:

HIDDEN CHINESE CITY?
MAYBE SO, MAYBE NO.

Accompanying the article was the picture she'd already seen on her phone, showing a man in a suit shining a flashlight on an old oil cookstove.

The discovery of a world beneath downtown Oklahoma City had been front-page-and-above-the-fold news, and coverage had continued for more than a week. Older residents had shared their memories of the underground community, some of them confirmed observations and some of them rumors. One reporter, skeptical about their oral histories, said that if every rumored entrance had been real, it would have been impossible to walk down the street without falling into the catacombs below.

Faye learned cool details, like the fact that the ceiling sockets in some of the newly uncovered rooms had still held light bulbs. One writer said that explorers had found a map of the United States on one wall. She imagined immigrants studying it to learn the shape of their new home.

None of the few published pictures depicted the room that Alonso Smith would eventually fill with color. Faye looked carefully for the small metal door, but failed to find it. No matter how many times she reread the 1969 articles, she wasn't able to find a useful clue that she could tie to the bombing.

She clicked back to the first article about the discovery of the underground chambers, published on April 9, 1969. At the very top of the front page, above the headline about the hidden Chinese city, was a headline reading:

OTHER INDIAN SCHOOLS NO BETTER THAN CHILOCCO

It detailed an investigation by the Bureau of Indian Affairs into the conditions at the schools that Sly, Cully, and many other indigenous people had attended. Investigators had found abuse at some schools, as well as a widespread lack of the most basic tools of education—paper, books, and chalk.

Faye thought of Joe's grandfather sending Sly away to boarding school because he thought his intelligent son deserved an education, and she burned with anger. What could he have accomplished if someone had helped him reach his potential? How different would her husband's growing-up years have been?

Cully, too, had left his family for a promise that was never kept. Both he and Sly had made their way in the world without even a high school diploma to open a few doors for them.

The thought of Cully's high school diploma made her think of the reason he'd lost it. Sly had said that he ran away from boarding school a year before he would have graduated. Cully had consistently avoided speaking of this past. Maybe Angela was the reason.

This reticence on the subject of Angela had been risky, because it had kept Cully from being straight with the FBI. This made him look bad.

Would Cully and Angela's escape from boarding school have made the papers? Maybe. Two missing teenagers would have been noteworthy, or so it seemed to Faye. She didn't know the name of his school, but she knew that his extended family still lived well east of Oklahoma City. She wasn't at all sure if *The Oklahoman* would have covered their disappearance, but it was the newspaper of record for the state. She might as well start there, then branch out to the *Tulsa World* and then to smaller newspapers to the east, if need be.

What year would Cully have graduated? Faye didn't even know how old he was.

But the internet did. In the twenty-first century, celebrities were entitled to no privacy whatsoever. A quick web search for "Cully Mantooth birthday" brought her the date she needed—March 11, 1945. Presuming he would have graduated at eighteen, as most Americans do, he would have been a seventeen-year-old runaway at Eastertime in 1962.

She typed "runaway" into the search box and chose a time window from March 1, 1962 to April 30, 1962, planning to refine the search with Cully's name, but there was no need. Six articles popped up and all of them were about Cully and Angela, whose last name was given as Bond.

The first headline said, "Teenage pair runs away from tribal boarding school," and it asked for help in finding them. Two photos, obviously taken for the school yearbook, accompanied the article.

Angela had been heartbreakingly thin, with huge dark eyes and a tight-lipped smile. Black hair, parted in the center, framed her heart-shaped face. She wasn't beautiful but she looked easy to love.

Joe had been a part of Faye's life for so long that she had forgotten how young he had been when they met, how very young they had both been. Joe had left Oklahoma at about this age. When she met him at twenty-five, he had looked startlingly like his distant cousin Cully at seventeen. He looked more like Cully than he looked like his own father, and Faye had always thought that Joe took after Sly. Looking at Cully's photo felt like time travel. One moment, some part of her believed that she was looking at her husband's square jaw, soft eyes, and broad shoulders. Then in the next moment, she recognized the age of the photo and knew that she couldn't be looking at Joe.

What had happened to this boy and girl when they disappeared in 1962?

She scrolled forward through the later articles. There were a few mentions, very brief, saying that there had been no news on the disappearances. As the articles' dates proceeded through April, she found more of the same. Until she didn't.

On the last day of April in 1962, the body of a young woman washed ashore on the banks of the North Canadian River. In the years since then, the stretch of the North Canadian that rolled through downtown Oklahoma City had been renamed the Oklahoma River, a name that the city's boosters thought more appropriate, considering that it lay a thousand miles south of the Canadian border. But in 1962, it was still called the North Canadian from its source in New Mexico to the point where it merged with the Canadian River in east Oklahoma.

The North Canadian was, and still is, a shallow stream that winds through sandbars and, in parts of Oklahoma, brilliant red clay. During the dry summers, a very old joke circulates, with the punch line being that Oklahoma was the home of the only river that needed to be mowed.

The stretch through Oklahoma City, however, is deeper than it used to be. It has been altered over the years, time and again. It has been deepened and straightened. The water that falls on the city's mostly paved urban area is now diverted to the river through an underground network of storm sewers, one of which Faye knew intimately. The water that discharges from those sewers converts the urban stretch of the river into a rampage after Oklahoma's notoriously violent thunderstorms.

The woman's body was found in 1962 on a sandbar in a river that was still shallow and sandy. She was found east of the city, caught in twiggy undergrowth that hung down from its banks into its shallow water. It was hard to say how long she had been there, given the limits of 1960s forensic science, but her flesh was largely decomposed. Her fingerprints were a thing of the past and her facial features were obliterated.

The article reporting the discovery of the corpse mentioned the two runaways, Cully Mantooth and Angela Bond, speculating whether Angela had been found and whether Cully's corpse might be nearby. Or whether Cully might have had a hand in her death.

Faye's hand went to her phone and dialed Ahua's number by feel. There was a lot about the disappearance of Cully and Angela that she didn't know, but now she knew one critical fact. She knew why Cully might be so reluctant to tell the FBI much of anything.

Chapter Twenty-Nine

Faye sat in the command center with Ahua, who was shaking his head. "Why haven't my people already brought me this information?"

"Why would they be focusing on Cully? Is he a suspect in the bombing? Seriously? A major suspect? I can't imagine that he is. Yeah, his mother lived in the underground community and he didn't tell you about it, but what does that really have to do with anything? Why would he come back from Hollywood after all these years to blow up a hotel sitting on top of the community where his mother lived?"

Ahua shrugged, which she supposed was as close to saying, "Yeah, your cousin's probably not a homicidal bomber," as she was going to get. She figured that advocating for the innocence of her distant relative had put her about five minutes away from being fired from this consulting job, so she kept talking while she still could.

"I think your agents missed this information on Cully because they have more important things to do than snoop into the history of a man *who did not set off that bomb.* Besides, I knew something they didn't when I sat down to do my research. My father-in-law told me details about exactly when Cully ran away that helped me narrow the search."

"And you didn't tell me?"

"I figured out that the things he told me were really important about five minutes ago, and here I am. Look what happens when I search *The Oklahoman* for Cully's name."

She typed in a search string—"Cully Mantooth"—but left the date open. Then she hit the enter key. A list of articles filled the screen. Faye pressed the down arrow key and held it down while fifty years of movie notices, reviews, and feature articles scrolled by.

Gesturing at a half century of press coverage rolling over her screen, she said, "It would take a team of persistent agents a very long time to sift through all that information and find Cully's name in an article about a woman's body being found downriver from Oklahoma City."

"Yeah, maybe," Ahua said. "But I have felt all along that there was something off about that man. I still do. And there's something I don't understand. Maybe the people investigating that woman's death hit a dead end in 1962, because nobody knew where Cully was. But why didn't they go after him five years later when he became a star? Everybody knew where he was then."

"Because they knew by then that the dead woman wasn't Angela."

Faye pulled up an article from May 1962.

DEAD WOMAN FOUND IN RIVER
STILL UNIDENTIFIED

The text of the article stated that Angela Bond's stepfather had viewed the body and confirmed that it was not his missing daughter. Though badly decomposed, the skin on its upper back was sufficiently intact to show a large birthmark. The article included a photo of Angela in a bathing suit that confirmed her stepfather's statement that she had no birthmark on her left shoulder blade.

"I called the police department and asked if that body was ever identified," Faye said. "The answer was no."

"Did Angela ever show up?"

"No. But that doesn't mean that she didn't have a happy life somewhere. Maybe she's still living that long, happy life. If Cully hadn't gone on to be famous, we wouldn't know what had happened to him, either. Sometimes, runaways disappear. Sometimes, they're leaving a life so terrible that nobody would want to go back to it."

Ahua scanned the last article again, the one where Angela Bond's stepfather denied that the unidentified body was hers. "I get it that they were unhappy at boarding school, but why didn't they just go home?"

Faye scrolled back to the first article about the runaways. "Cully's parents were dead. This article says that they died in a car crash a few months before he took off. From what I know about his extended family, I feel sure they would have taken him in, but maybe he didn't believe it. As for Angela's mother and stepfather, it's hard to say. Maybe they just didn't get along."

"I hear what you're saying. You think it's unlikely that he bombed that hotel, and maybe you're right, but there's still something that man isn't telling me. I can tell. I want to find out what it is."

"You do that. But first let's talk about Alonso Smith."

"My people did a much better job of getting information on Smith out of the newspaper archives than they did on running down what Cully Mantooth was doing in 1962. Smith does actually appear to be his last name. It's a good thing that Alonso isn't so common."

"What about Lonnie Smith? Did you find anything under that name?"

"Nothing useful. There was a minor league baseball player here in the eighties named Lonnie Smith. He showed up in the sports pages quite a lot until he got traded away, but he's not the same guy who turns up under the name Alonso. And, trust me, the ball player's not the guy we're looking for. It's gotta be the yo-yo that sometimes went by Alonso, because he's a real piece of work. Or he was, if we presume he was the bomber and I think we should."

Faye was disappointed. She was really liking the idea of tracking down the bomber by following the career of a late-twentieth century minor league baseball player. She imagined him being traded from one team to another, moving from city to city as he aged and his skills declined…

Ahua snapped her out of that fantasy by saying, "We know where Lonnie-Smith-the-baseball-player is. He's alive, so he's not our bomber. Alonso Smith, however, disappears from the public record in the mid-1990s. And he does some nutty things before he goes."

He pulled up an article in a small-town newspaper detailing a 1995 encounter between Alonso Smith and an attendance officer for the Cashion Public Schools in Kingfisher County. The officer was following up on a report that Smith had one or more children of school age who were not in school and who had no letter on file certifying that they were being homeschooled. Witnesses had reported four or more children living with Smith, but the school system had no records on any of them.

The article also mentioned previous altercations at Smith's property. He had threatened trespassers. His wife, Sandra Smith, had called for help more than once, citing domestic violence, each time changing her mind before help arrived, saying something like, "Never mind. Everything's fine now." None of those reports had mentioned children on the property.

The attendance officer looking for truant students had reported that Smith was confrontational, denying that he had any children, then launching into what the article called a 'ten-minute lecture on the evils of bringing children into this misbegotten world,' delivered while his wife stood silently by his side. More concerning to Faye was his statement that if he did ever have children, he wouldn't "trust the Satan-followers running the county schools to come near them."

"Do you think he had children that he was hiding?" she asked Ahua.

"The attendance officer said that there were six chairs and a table on the house's front porch, plus a porch swing, which seemed like a lot of places to sit if Smith and his wife were the only two people living there. He said that they didn't seem like people who had a lot of money for extra furniture. The reporter rendered her opinion that they also didn't seem like the kind of folks who entertained a lot of company."

"You gotta love small-town reporters. They call it like they see it." Faye scanned the article. "It doesn't say where these people lived. Were they so far out in the country that they could really hide their children?"

"Kingfisher County has fifteen thousand people spread out over about a thousand square miles, and that's including some towns. You could hide a lot of children in the spaces between those towns, if you were so inclined."

"Do you think he did?" Faye said, thinking of the bodies of three boys, found in a room with walls covered with the signature of Alonso "Lonnie" Smith.

"Cashion is half an hour east of here. I've got people on the scene looking for that attendance officer and the house where he saw Alonso and Sandra Smith. Let me show you something else interesting. It was in the bomber's hip pocket, so my brilliant and patient evidence technicians had to piece it together."

He pulled up a series of photographs that showed several small scraps of paper. Their edges were frayed and singed, and they were stained with something brown that was almost certainly Alonso Smith's blood, but some of the words written on the fragments could be read.

The first fragment clearly showed the beginning of a letter.

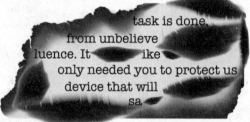

Father,
so happy to have found you again.
erjoyed to finally be able to work with you
toward the goal you set for us as children—
Evil must be obliterated. And
can all be tog

"It's typed," she said. "That's too bad."

"Well, we won't be able to tie it to anybody through their handwriting, but we might be able to tie it to a particular printer."

The second fragment was harder for Faye to wrap her head around, but it seemed to refer to a goal or task he had set for his children.

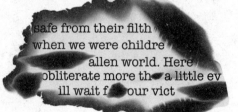

task is done
from unbelieve
luence. It   ike
only needed you to protect us
device that will
sa

The third fragment was the most damaged of all.

safe from their filth
when we were childre
allen world. Here
obliterate more th   a little ev
ill wait f   our vict

The fragments jumped off the screen at Faye with their direct references to the commandment that she had seen on so many of the photographs of the painted room. The third one used the word "obliterate" that she'd seen painted again and again on the wall of the underground room.

"This is what you get when you piece them together," Ahua said, "plus an educated guess as to what the damaged areas said. They put the guesswork in bold type."

Dear Father,

I am so happy to have found you again. **I am ov**erjoyed to finally be able to work with you toward the **g**oal you set for us as children— Evil must be obliterated. And **when the** task is done, **we** can all be tog**ether, away** from unbelieve**rs and** safe from their filth**y inf**luence. It **will be l**ike when we were childre**n. We** only needed you to protect us **from a f**allen world. Here **is a** device that will obliterate more th**an** a little ev**il.** **I w**ill wait **for** our vict**ory.**

"I guess it would be too much to hope for a signature?" Faye asked.

"Apparently so. The bottom of the page was burned away. Even the FBI's geniuses can't reassemble a piece of paper that no longer exists. So what do you think this tells us?"

"That's a pretty broad question to be asking me when you only hired me to do archaeology work. I wouldn't know where to start." Faye put the lie to this statement by immediately leaning close to the screen, flipping back and forth to study the photos of the paper fragments and the FBI's interpretation of what they said.

"What if you dug up an old stone tablet?" he asked. "Wouldn't you try to reconstruct what it had said? Or even better, a papyrus scroll that had been through a fire."

"I've never worked outside the continental US. Archaeologists in my field don't see a lot of papyrus. Stone and pottery? Yes."

She used the mouse to magnify the image and get a closer look at one of the fragments.

"Still, is this so different from archaeology?"

She finally looked up at him. "No, not so much. Okay, I'll play this guessing game. I'm going to presume that the letter was written to the bomber, since it was found on him. We have good reason to believe that he was Alonso Smith. The letter writer addresses him as 'Father.' Unless she was born after 1995, he lied to the school attendance officer about at least one child."

"That is all very well-reasoned, but why do you presume that the letter writer is a woman?"

"Well, we can't know for sure, but if you're going to bet on the gender of an adult child of Alonso Smith, you'd be smart to guess female."

"Because the three sons we found died of hemophilia?"

"Exactly. Their mother must have been a carrier." As Ahua spoke, his eyes never left the screen displaying an image of the letter's fragments. "Hemophiliacs can live to adulthood with modern medical treatment, but Alonso didn't seem to be into taking his kids to the doctor. If he had adult sons, they were either born to a different woman, one who didn't carry the gene for hemophilia, or they got lucky in the coin flip of which of his mother's X-chromosomes they got."

"Whoever wrote it used a phrase straight off the walls of the painted room: 'Evil must be obliterated.' So there's a link," Faye said. "But the most important thing I get from this letter is that it was written by someone who seems to have been an accomplice in the bombing."

Ahua gave a satisfied nod. "We can stop wondering whether Alonso Smith was working alone."

"Exactly. There's still somebody out there for the Bureau to chase. And not just as an accessory. The letter says, 'Here is a device.' The writer provided the bomb to Smith. That's the work of an equal party to the crime, maybe even the person who masterminded it. Although this letter reads like it was written by a mastermind who wanted Alonso Smith to believe that *he* was the mastermind."

"But why arrange for a bombing? If somebody wanted that bomb to send a message, nobody knows what it was. That's not the way terrorists usually work."

"I think it was a family matter. What if this letter was written by a child who wanted to follow in Alonso Smith's antisocial footsteps? Smith never managed to cause much trouble, but if his ideas took root in the mind of someone more capable, you could be looking at big trouble."

"We need to find Alonso Smith's child, the one that wrote this. Or any of his children might know what this note means."

Faye rose as if to run out into the world and find the mysterious letter writer, but Ahua stopped her.

"One more thing. We know that Alonso Smith was causing trouble in Oklahoma City long before he tangled with a truant officer in Kingfisher County."

"We do?" Faye asked. "How?"

Ahua pulled up another article, this time from *The Oklahoman* instead of the small-town paper that had reported Smith's Kingfisher County woes. It detailed a 1986 clash between Native American activists who wanted fair funding for their schools and an anarchist group who wanted government schools abolished. Two men dominated the article's photo. According to the caption, one of them was Alonso Smith.

Faye was not surprised to see Smith carrying a sign reading "I'LL TEACH MY OWN CHILDREN, THANK YOU VERY MUCH!" but she was stunned by the identity of the man he was staring down. Smith's adversary's long braids weren't yet threaded with gray, but they were familiar. He may even have been wearing the same hat she'd seen just that day.

It was Ben McGilveray.

Chapter Thirty

Faye studied the photo of Alonso Smith and Ben McGilveray for a long moment, until it suddenly occurred to her that she knew someone else who had been an activist in 1980s Oklahoma. She poked in Carson's number, one digit at a time.

He answered with his usual jolly "Hey, Faye! How ya doing?" but she went straight to the point.

"Carson, I've got a question for your mom but I don't have her number in this loaner phone."

"Lucky you. She's sitting next to me. Want me to hand her the phone or are you brave enough to come talk to her face-to-face? She's as scary as ever."

Faye heard Alba Callahan say something that sounded like, "I had to be scary to raise you. It probably kept you out of the penitentiary."

Faye had a hard time imagining Carson in prison, but she could absolutely imagine Alba as the terrifyingly stern single mother of a teenaged boy. Whether wearing jeans or a tailored dress suitable for arguing a court case, she was always impeccably dressed for the situation at hand. Faye had never seen a single one of her sleek blond hairs out of place.

Faye suspected that Alba had demanded that sort of perfection from her only child without ever quite getting it. Carson was intelligent, accomplished, and big-hearted, but asking him to be perfect would be about like asking a bison to spend a day working in the Library of Congress. It wouldn't end well.

Alba was a committed political activist who had lived in Oklahoma all her life. Despite the sleek blond hair, she was an enrolled member of the Muscogee (Creek) Nation, so much— though by no means all—of her activism was centered on indigenous people's issues. Faye knew for a fact that Carson had spent his growing-up years attending political rallies and protests with her. It beggared belief that Alba wouldn't know Ben McGilveray, who would have been protesting on the same side as Alba, at least on tribal issues. Likely, she knew Alonso Smith, as well, as an opponent.

"I want to talk to Alba in person. Is she here in your hotel room, or are you at her house?"

"She's here. She wants to see Joe's talk tonight."

Faye took her leave of Ahua and hustled toward Carson's hotel room.

———

Alba greeted Faye at the door with a hug and a kiss on the cheek. Her jeans, neatly pressed and fashionably torn at the knee, said, "I'm an attorney because I have to make a living and I'm sixty-something because nobody can stop time from passing, but I'm still a radical at heart."

"What can I do for you, Faye? Carson said that it sounded urgent."

"It is. What can you tell me about Ben McGilveray?"

"Oh, nothing much, except I probably would have married him if we'd met when I was single and if I hadn't had ten years on him. Or thereabouts."

Carson was looking at her like a forty-something-year-old

man who would prefer not to be reminded that his mother had a history that didn't involve him.

"So he's a good guy?"

"The best. I still see him and Gloria around town. Gloria works here, you know."

"Here?"

"At the Gershwin Hotel. I think she works in the financial office."

Faye did not know that. She needed to make sure that Ahua knew that the wife of the man facing down Alonso Smith in that 1986 photo was a Gershwin employee.

Alba was still talking about the McGilverays. "They're at every protest, and they're always on the right side. I'm sure you've seen them over the years, Carson. They're both Creek, but we're not kin."

Carson was still speechless.

Faye took advantage of his silence. "What about Alonso Smith?"

"Lonnie? Good Lord. I haven't thought of him in years. Decades, probably. He seemed to just drop off the face of the earth, and good riddance. You stay away from him. You too, Carson, but especially Faye. I never heard a good thing about the way he treated his wife. Janet was her name, I think."

Faye showed Alba the 1986 picture of Alonso and Ben. "Is there any chance you were there when this photo was taken?"

"Oh, honey. There's hardly a chance that I wasn't. Tribal education has been a favorite cause of mine for forever."

"They're all favorite causes, Mom."

"But education is my *favorite* favorite." Alba peered at the photo. "Don't see myself in the background, but that doesn't mean I'm not there. Look, there's Janet." She pointed at a freckled young woman with shoulder-length brunette hair who stood a pace behind Alonso, holding a baby.

Faye remembered the dark-haired woman that Lonnie had painted all over the walls of an underground room. Did he paint freckles? Would they have shown at the resolution of the photos she'd examined? And what about the police report that gave his wife's name as Sandra?

"They stopped coming around not long after that. He'd been threatening to take Janet and the baby out in the woods to live, far away from the government that wanted to…I don't know what he thought the government wanted to do. Educate his children, maybe? I've spent my life yelling at the government to do its job, because I've never thought people were meant to make their way in this world all alone. If Lonnie hadn't been such an idiot about doctors, their first daughter might not have died. It was a breech birth. Nearly killed Janet. This baby, their second one…she was a beautiful thing. Like a little doll."

Faye thought of the painted scenes where both Lonnie and the dark-haired woman were holding babies. Was Alba talking about one of the children left in the painted room? No. It wasn't possible. The girl baby that Lonnie and Janet lost in the eighties couldn't have turned into a boy baby, especially not one wearing a shirt dating from the nineties. If Faye was counting them properly, Lonnie's aversion to doctors had cost him four children, and at least one of them was Janet's newborn daughter. Faye ached for this woman she had never known.

"Did they have more children after the little girl in the picture and the baby that died?"

"I don't know. Later on, I heard that he had married a woman named Sandra. Funny thing, though. I never heard anything else about Janet. Don't know if she died or what. I'd like to think she got smart and divorced him, but I just don't know what happened to her or to that little girl."

Now Faye was counting children. According to the attendance officer, Lonnie was rumored to have had at least four children in 1995. DNA testing on the three boys' bodies had proven that he was their father. Alba said that the baby in the 1986 photo was his daughter and that there had been another daughter who died.

Was that all of them? There was no way to know, but he could certainly have had more children by Janet or by his second wife.

Did it matter? The note in Lonnie's pocket indicated that he had a surviving child who could be the key to solving the bombing. One of his other children could, at the very least, be able to shed some light on why he wanted to bomb something in the first place. Most important of all, finding one of Lonnie's children might tell the FBI whether there were surviving accomplices planning to bomb something else.

In any case, Faye imagined that any child of Alonso Smith would be a very angry individual.

———

As soon as Faye left to talk to Alba Callahan, Ahua picked up the phone. Faye might have just met Cully Mantooth a day before, but he was still her distant relative and she didn't need to be part of this conversation.

This time, he didn't mess with the older man's mind by giving him forty-five minutes to get antsy before the interview. This time, he messed with his mind by saying, "I want to speak with you. Now."

Then he hung up on Cully and called the number of the man who knew more about Cully than anybody. He asked Jakob Zalisky a single question, then he ended the call and waited for Cully.

Cully might cultivate a relaxed, affable image, but he wasn't so relaxed that he didn't know when it was time to do exactly as he was told. In the space of time it took him to hustle himself onto an elevator and walk to the command center, he was sitting in a chair across from Ahua.

The man had to be nervous. His very speed in arriving showed that, but he had been projecting quiet, manly confidence for a long time. Cully looked comfortable in his T-shirt and jeans, not at all like a man who was about to talk to the FBI about a missing woman last seen in his company.

Ahua led from strength. "So you weren't alone when you left for California."

"Correct. Like I told you, Angela Bond and I ran away from school together."

"But, according to your buddy Jakob, you were in California within a year, alone."

Cully took in a breath and let it out. If it bothered him that his friend had spoken of him to the FBI, Ahua couldn't see it. "Like I told you, she left me. Angela was my first love. How many people do you know who are still with their first love? It broke my heart to lose her, but just about everybody gets their heart broke sometime."

"Getting your heart broken is one thing," Ahua said, "but abandoning a seventeen-year-old high school student who's far from home? That's quite another. We don't know of anyone who has heard from Angela Bond since you two left school, so it's altogether possible that she came to harm. Maybe you could have prevented it."

Ahua didn't say, "Or maybe you're the one who harmed her," but those words hung in the air.

Cully answered the words that Ahua hadn't spoken. "I didn't hurt Angela. God. The very idea of hurting her rips me up inside. She left me. We hadn't gone far. We hadn't even got out of the state when she stopped loving me. I don't know why. She literally ran away from me, with me running after her, begging her to stop. I waited for days, but she never came back. When I ran out of food, I had to move on."

Ever the actor, Cully's voice had stayed smooth, reasonable, well-modulated, but now he lost the ability to control it. It rose in pitch until it could have been mistaken for the voice of a seventeen-year-old suffering the loss of his first love. "I never saw her again."

"We know she didn't go home," Ahua said.

"Of course, she didn't go home." Muscles knotted in Cully's forearms, moving beneath weathered brown skin. "Nobody in their right mind would go back to her bastard of a stepfather. I had aunts and uncles who would have taken us in, but they wouldn't have stopped him when he come to take her home. They thought he was a good man. He was a deacon in the church, right? So he had to be a good man. When we ran away, we knew we had to go far from him and never come home."

"But why did you keep going after she left?" Ahua asked.

Cully's face was puzzled. "Go home? Without Angela? When she left me, I thought no place would ever feel like home again. Going west seemed about as good as going back east toward where I lived when we were together. Better, even, because there wouldn't be nothing to remind me of her. I felt that way for years, until I met Sue. I married Sue as quick as I could before she could run away, too. And now she's dead and I feel just as empty as I did when I lost Angela. Have I told you everything you need to know, Agent Ahua? This conversation has left me feeling old and tired, and I'd like some rest."

Chapter Thirty-One

Ahua watched the door close behind Cully. He believed the man had just told the truth. He just didn't believe that he had told all of it.

Cully was holding something back. Maybe it was something that he thought would incriminate him or somebody he cared about. Or maybe he thought it wasn't pertinent to the case and therefore it was none of the FBI's business. But there were times when the things he wasn't saying were louder than the things he was.

This was the art of Ahua's work that someone like Faye would never understand. She was a scientist, always looking for inarguable evidence. This was what made her such a useful consultant and it was the reason that Bigbee had urged him to hire her, which was not an obvious thing to do when he had a small army of trained FBI agents at his disposal. As it turned out, Bigbee was right. Faye would have made an excellent agent.

Ahua doubted that she'd consider dropping the archaeology and the business she'd spent years building to join the agency. Still, he doubted she would balk at the chance to do more work along the lines of what she was doing now. Maybe he would recommend that the bureau train her for that. Ahua would dearly love to be a fly on the wall, watching the people at Quantico put Dr. Longchamp-Mantooth through her paces.

And now here she was, bringing her own special energy into the command center and well-nigh burbling with excitement over what she had to share.

"Alba Callahan knew Alonso Smith. You need to get a trained interviewer over there to talk to her, but here's what we have now. The man was married to a woman named Janet. Alba heard about a later wife named Sandra, which tracks with the newspaper article from Kingfisher County, but she doesn't know whether there was a divorce or whether Janet died. Janet and a baby—Alba says she was a girl—are in the picture from 1986 and Alba knew of one more child who died at birth before that time, also a girl. She says that Alonso and Janet Smith and their baby girl dropped out of sight in the late 1980s, and she hasn't heard anything about them since."

"Good to know," Ahua said, neglecting to mention that he had successfully hustled Cully in and out while she was gone. "Progress on finding out about Alonso Smith is progress on finding his accomplice in the bombing. I wish I could say that we knew anything at all about why Stacy Wong is still missing, but I've got nothing. I'm sure you can imagine how many agents we have at our disposal, and a lot of them are looking for Stacy Wong. She's disappeared without a trace."

"Do you think that Liu is right that Stacy left the hotel because she wanted to get a look at the underground rooms by way of the storm sewer?"

"It's conjecture, but yes. I do think that Liu may be right. She's the one who gave Stacy the information to find that back door in the storm sewer, and she knows her pretty well."

———

Faye agreed with Ahua, but there was another option and she felt compelled to put it on the table. "It's always possible that she got sick of her life and walked away. It happens."

"Yes, it does."

Faye was a scientist, so she was uncomfortable with squishy data and conjecture. Faye liked to prove things with numbers and photographs and, when absolutely necessary, with eyewitness reports that were confirmed by multiple people. Preferably crowds. She steered the conversation to data that was incontrovertible because it came with the blessing of a laboratory scientist.

"What about the bombing? You've got lab data there, and your evidence people are still working."

"Yes. They could crack it open tomorrow. But now? Objective evidence? We haven't got much. We have DNA results that tell us that the children left in the painted room are the bomber's sons. They also tell us that the boys had hemophilia, which the bomber did not have, meaning that their mother was a carrier."

"That's almost always the way it works."

"True. Footprints found in that room match the boots on bomber's body. A gasket for a pressure cooker like the one used for the bomb was shipped to an address where Alonso Smith was known to work and to receive mail. The signature on the walls reads 'Lonnie,' which is often a nickname for Alonso, so we believe the bomber and the painter are the same person, but this takes us out of the land of hard evidence and into a soft circumstantial place."

"And there's no evidence to tell us who defaced the paintings? No footprints, no fingerprints, no anything?"

"None. The room was accessed from the storm sewer and the vandal splashed paint on the floor on the way out to cover any footprints."

Faye's head was full of images—the painted psychedelia of the room that connected to the storm sewer, the memory of a tremendous blast that turned her world inside-out, and the heartbreaking sight of three blanket-wrapped bodies.

"We're getting nowhere," she said, "and I can think of no reason for you to be paying me to sit here while we chase our tails."

"I can."

Puzzled, she said, "What do you need me to do?"

"I want you to look at the photos of the paintings again, now that we have a photo of Alonso Smith and his first wife, Janet."

Ahua pulled up the photos on the workstation in front of him, rose, and gave Faye his chair. "Now I need to go light a fire under some forensics people. They just might be able to get me some evidence that's not based on conjecture."

"Even better—maybe they can get you some evidence that isn't squishy."

———

Faye was beginning to appreciate the artistry of "Lonnie," and she was now pretty sure that he also went by "Alonso." The portraits that he had painted appeared to be hardly more than cartoons until she looked closer. Now that she'd seen a photo of Alonso and Janet Smith, she saw that Alonso Smith had painted the people in his murals as individuals.

In just a few brushstrokes, he had captured his own image, time and again. Every man's painted face was framed by a distinctive receding hairline. Beneath each wispy brown beard was a similarly receding jawline. The gray eyes of every male face were set deeply into their sockets. All of those faces looked like the newspaper photograph of Alonso Smith.

Faye could see now that he had painted the women as two distinct individuals, and only two. Janet and Sandra resembled each other, to be sure, but only superficially. Lonnie/Alonso had a type, and that type was women with long, dark hair and swelling hips. When magnified as far as possible, Faye could distinguish the individual brushstrokes that made up their faces and bodies. It was almost like reading the artist's intent.

A straight line along one woman's jawline made her look younger and thinner than the soft curve of the other's jaw. The younger woman's breasts sat higher on her chest and her waist was narrower. After all, a man knew the shape of his wife's body. No, make that his wives' bodies.

The older woman's eyes were a lighter shade of brown and her lips were thinner. Stippled shading over her cheekbones suggested the freckles that she'd seen in Janet's photograph. Her skin was more pale than Sandra's, paler even than Lonnie's. It was possible that Sandra was Asian or Latina or Native American, but not Janet.

Now that she could distinguish the adults, she understood the groupings of the family scenes better. In two of the scenes, she counted five children. Lonnie held a baby and a young child leaned against his leg. Another child sat on Sandra's lap. Janet held a second baby, and an older child stood to the side, leaning against a tree.

But these couldn't be all of Lonnie's children, because three swaddled bodies had been left in the painted room and the three older children were bigger than those little boys ever got. The list of Lonnie's children included these five, plus at least one more baby boy and the baby girl who had died at birth. This scene must have been painted before the boy was born or after the missing boy died.

That made seven children total. There could have been more, but not fewer. Faye wanted to believe that some of them had survived to adulthood. If any of them were girls, they had a reasonable shot at survival. Any boys would have had a fifty-fifty shot at avoiding hemophilia, which would make them far more likely to survive. Their mothers, too, could still be alive.

It seemed critical to Faye that at least one of the people in the paintings be found. All of the women and children had dark hair, but how many brunette men and women between the ages of about twenty-five and seventy could there be in Oklahoma? And who was to say that they were still in the state?

In just a few days, Faye had met so many people who fit that description. Ben McGilveray and his wife, Gloria, were brunettes. So was Cully. Stacy. Kaayla. Sadie. Dr. Dell. Dr. Althorp. Grace.

Lucia. Agent Goldsby. Even Agent Liu. There was no reason to expect that she was looking at painted images of any of these people, but Faye's intuition—which she would never admit that she trusted—was telling her that the answer she sought was nearby.

A quarter-century or more had passed since the artist named Lonnie captured two dark-haired women and their dark-haired children on four blank walls. He had walked away from those paintings so long ago that a mat of dust had collected on the floor beneath them. During that time, he had gone underground.

While she stared at the photos, Ahua called to say that Alonso Smith had never been legally married, despite telling people that Janet and Sandra were his wives. Only one of the children existed on paper, a little girl born in 1985 and named Lonna, because of course Alonso Smith would name his daughter after himself.

Other than the lucky strike of finding the man who had sold him a pressure cooker gasket and the woman whose lawn he had cut, they'd found no trace of Lonnie/Alonso Smith since the 1990s. He had filed no tax returns since then and he'd held no job traceable by the IRS. He had no credit history at all. They knew that he had let his driver's license lapse in 1996 and had owned no registered car since then. He'd never been arrested. And that is all that they knew.

The answer to the mystery of Alonso Smith would not be found by computers. It lay in long-held human memory.

Her hand went to her phone and pressed speed dial.

"You want me to do what?" Carson asked.

"Get your mother to look at the pictures on your conference website. Ask her if she recognizes any of the faculty. Then take her walking through the hotel but don't act like you're looking for anything special. Just walk around and let her look at the employees and guests. Heck, tell her to look at all of the FBI agents running around. Bonus points if you can find Agent Goldsby and Agent Liu." She almost said, "Try to find Cully, Ben, and Gloria," but that would have been silly. Alba knew

Ben and Gloria, and everybody knew what Cully Mantooth looked like.

"And if we find them, then what?"

"Ask her if she recognizes any of them from a long time ago. That's all. If she recognizes them well enough to know their names, even better. But don't tell her why."

Carson laughed for a long time. "You want me to tell my mother I won't answer her questions? That's funny."

"Tell her you're doing a favor for me and I didn't tell you why I needed it done. Because I'm not going to tell you, so don't ask me."

———

Faye's second attempt at tapping long-held cultural memory came up dry. A phone call to her father-in-law Sly was as entertaining as usual, full of snide political commentary and sparked with filthy jokes, but Sly knew nothing about Alonso Smith and his family or separatist cult or commune or whatever it was.

It made sense that Alba Callahan had been more tapped into Smith's world in her younger days than Sly. She, like Alonso Smith, had been a fervid political activist. Even opponents know each other. Sometimes they understand each other better than their friends do.

Sly, like Alba, had been born in Sylacauga but he had never lived anywhere else. He had married young and started driving trucks right afterward. Joe had been born right after that. Sly had no reason to know Alonso Smith. From what Faye knew of Smith, not knowing him was a very good thing.

As she said goodbye to Sly, she cast about for other people with long histories in Oklahoma who might be able to help. It hurt her heart to think that the next person she would have called was Stacy, whose life work was Oklahoma history.

Joe had been a kid when Alonso Smith and Alba Callahan had been raising hell, and so had Carson. The only other people she knew in Oklahoma City were associated with the conference and, among them, only Cully was a native Oklahoman. But how could he be any help when he left the state while Alonso Smith was just a child?

But maybe Angela Bond didn't. She, too, fit the too-broad-to-be-useful profile of an adult between twenty-five and seventy-five with dark hair.

If her stepfather was telling the truth when he said that the body found in the Oklahoma River in 1962 wasn't hers, she would have been about the right age to be Alonso Smith's older wife, the one whom Alba knew as Janet.

Faye's loaner phone wasn't capable of downloading the photos of Alonso Smith's paintings, so she went old-school and printed some of them on the command center's printer. She put the one that gave the best view of the older woman right on top and folded the printouts before putting them in her back pocket. She placed a call to Cully and, when it went unanswered, she decided to corner him in his palatial suite. It was time to go to Cully and get some answers.

Chapter Thirty-Two

Faye only glimpsed Cully for an instant, walking across the grounds of the Gershwin Annex. So he wasn't in his palatial suite.

She set out after him, but the conference attendees were on break and it was hard to make her way through the crowd. If she didn't hustle, she was going to be outrun by an old man, and she was damned if she'd let that happen.

Cully was fumbling with a pack of cigarettes, which was normal for him when he was outdoors. The strange thing was that he was leaning forward a bit, which was not ordinary for a movie star with perfect posture. Dodging a cluster of gossipers, she got a better look at him and saw that the forward lean was compensating for a backpack, which seemed even less in keeping with Cully's public persona. Why was Cully carrying a backpack?

And why was he wearing a black T-shirt? This wouldn't have been notable for anybody else, except for the fact that Cully had been wearing a sport coat and collared shirt when she met him and on every occasion when she'd seen him since. Musing on his wardrobe took her to his pants. He was wearing jeans, which in no way fit his carefully cultivated casual-but-not-too-casual image.

A movie star was letting himself be seen wearing jeans and carrying a backpack. Where was he going and what was in that pack?

A nervous-looking woman approached, and when Faye tried to step around her, the woman put her hand on her shoulder and said, "I hear Cully Mantooth is a relative of yours. I've always loved him in the movies. Can you tell me what he's really like?"

Ignoring her went against everything Faye's mother had taught her about how to treat people, but there was a time when using good manners was the wrong thing to do. Faye shook off the hand, bolted to the left, and ignored the nice lady asking questions.

And now Cully was out of sight.

She stood in the space between the hotel's two towers, knowing that he must be somewhere near. Spinning in a circle, she searched for an older man who looked like he wasn't quite comfortable in his casual clothes.

Other people walked past, blocking her view, and she dodged and weaved between them. He wasn't to her right, between her and the street that the Tower Annex faced. She didn't see him straight ahead, entering the other tower. Scanning the sidewalk to her left, she found Cully walking away, his long black-and-silver ponytail swinging free of the dun-brown pack on his back. A flash of white on the bottom of his foot told her that he was wearing sneakers, meaning that his clothes were out of character from neck to sole.

These clothes were so far from his everyday image that Faye thought he must have shopped specifically for them. Cully must have had a reason to go out and buy some down-market clothing, and he'd done it in a hurry. He was heading for a place where he needed to be comfortable, to move freely, to get dirty. Cully was going to a place where he needed shoes with traction. She ran after him, wondering what on earth was in the backpack.

The first time he looked back over his shoulder, she was sure that he'd seen her, but no. He kept moving forward without turning to ask why she was following him. She ducked behind a dumpster at the rear of the North Tower, pressing herself close to its warm metal sides as she watched him walk.

A few fat raindrops fell, leaving star-shaped wet marks on the pavement beneath Faye's feet. Cully looked back again, but her hiding place did its job and he didn't see that he was being followed. He turned left and she watched to see where he would go next. Cully obviously didn't want to be followed and this made her sure that following him was the right thing to do.

He was moving fast, maybe because he was in a hurry and maybe just because the rain was starting to come down harder. When she gauged that he was far enough away, she eased out from behind the dumpster.

At that moment, Cully was moving surreptitiously around the corner of the building next door to the South Tower, a nondescript Depression-era storefront building. When Faye reached the corner, she paused to flatten herself against its bricks. Taking a quick peek around the corner, she saw a blind alley that ran between the building where she stood and a still-shabbier building made of concrete blocks ending at a brick wall.

The alley was a problem. Faye couldn't follow Cully, because the alleyway was as devoid of hiding spots as a wind tunnel, so she was trapped where she stood. She wished hard for her binoculars.

Far down the alley, Cully stepped behind a lean-to shed that projected from the back of the concrete building. It was so small that Cully's entire head and one of his shoulders was visible above the sloping roof. He reached down and did something with his hands. It looked to Faye like he was manipulating something small, mechanical, and balky, like a lock or a latch that was rusted shut. Making it work was a strain for him—Faye could tell by the tension in his shoulders—but he must have accomplished whatever it was he had set out to do, because he stood up straight again. Shaking the tension out of his neck, he reached into his backpack again. A flicker of light on his face told her that he had flicked on a flashlight.

Next, Cully took a deep breath and bent down so low that Faye couldn't see him over the shed's low roof. He disappeared and, though she waited for more than a full minute for him to stand back up, he never did.

———

Joe was one of those men who truly enjoyed the company of women. He sought their opinions and he laughed at their jokes. He also enjoyed the company of older people, which was only to be expected of a man who loved fishing, gardening, flintknapping, cooking, and hunting, all of them activities that were usually learned through the patient instruction of an elder. Therefore, when Joe saw that Carson had brought his mother to the conference, he headed straight for Alba, who greeted him with a hello hug.

Then two more people charged up from behind him, also intent on hugging Alba.

"Ben McGilveray!" she cried. "And Gloria! It has been just eons. Do you know Joe Wolf Mantooth?"

Four eyes swiveled toward Joe. He felt his lifelong shyness with strangers kick in, but he'd learned to cover it. He shook their hands and said he was pleased to make their acquaintance but they kept looking at him. He really would have preferred that they go back to looking at their old friend Alba. After a long moment that Joe spent wearing an awkward smile, Gloria said, "Mantooth? Do you know Cully Mantooth? Because we're looking for him."

"Do you know Cully?" Carson asked. "I'm the conference organizer. I can find him for you. I don't know where he is right now, but I'll see him eventually."

When they said they'd never actually met him, Joe watched his old buddy shift into protect-the-celebrity mode. "I can't get you face time with him. If I did, everybody would expect it. But you're welcome to come to his talk tomorrow night."

Ben and Gloria leaned their heads together and whispered for a moment. Then Ben said, "We'll do that, but there will be a lot of people there and we might not get a chance to speak to him personally. Will you give him this?"

Gloria pulled a sealed envelope out of her purse and held it out. It was the kind of envelope that came with stationery or a birthday card, a squat and almost square rectangle, and it was yellow.

Carson hesitated. Given what had just happened, Joe figured he was trying to decide if the slim, flat envelope could possibly hold a bomb. He eyeballed Gloria and Ben, but he must have decided they were safe, because he took the envelope.

"Thank you," Ben said. "This means a lot." He turned to Joe and said, "It's very nice to meet you. We'll see you again tonight, because we wouldn't miss your flintknapping demonstration. And we'll be at Mr. Mantooth's concert tomorrow night, too." And then they took their leave and walked away.

Alba turned her attention to Joe. "It's so good to see you. Maybe you can help me with this weird scavenger hunt of Carson's."

Joe raised his eyebrows at his old friend, but Carson said nothing to explain his mother's comment.

Alba waved her phone at Joe and said, "First, he made me look at pictures of some people who I'm sure are very nice but I don't know them. Now we're wandering around the hotel looking for people with dark hair, which is a lot of people. Oh, and we're also looking for an Agent Liu. And an Agent Goldsby."

"This sounds like one of Faye's wild goose chases," Joe said.

Carson still didn't answer him, so Joe knew that he was right.

"I wouldn't doubt that your wife is involved, Joe," Alba said. "All her wild goose chases are for a good reason, so I guess I'll keep humoring my son," Alba said. "Where is Faye, anyway? We've been all over the grounds and all through the public areas of both towers but we haven't seen her."

Joe hadn't seen Faye in hours, not since he finished his talk that morning, but he had figured she was chumming around with the FBI. Now she had moved on to involving Carson and Alba in some kind of skullduggery and that worried him. He decided it was time to lay eyes on his wife. He said goodbye to his friends, then found a quiet spot to loiter while he texted Faye.

He got no answer, which worried him. Even without her real phone, Faye would have taken the time to text him back with the dinosaur of a loaner phone she'd gotten from the repair shop. True, Faye was capable of being so focused on a task that she didn't hear the phone buzzing in her purse, but she was more than a little rattled by the bombing and by Stacy's disappearance. She had been so rattled that she asked for an extra goodbye kiss that morning. For Faye, that was clingy behavior. It was weird that she wasn't answering him.

Joe thought it seemed like a good time to wander around the Gershwin's Tower Annex and try to find his wife.

———

Faye made her way down the alleyway, alternately attracted to and frightened by the lean-to where Cully had disappeared. Every time she took a step, it seemed like her foot banged on the pavement with a sound that echoed off the alley walls. Her breathing sounded almost as loud, and so did the heartbeat that sounded in her ears.

A drizzle of rain dampened her hair and it was only getting worse. The pavement under her feet, greasy with a century of engine exhaust and oil leaks, worried her. If she needed to run, she might slip and fall.

Why was she afraid that Cully might hear her? She had started out looking for him, so she could ask him questions about Angela, and the pictures that she'd wanted to show him still rustled in her back pocket. But then she'd seen him walk away in his weirdly practical clothes and somehow this meant that she didn't want him to know she was behind him? That made no sense. Why the change?

The answer was that her goal had changed. Now she wanted

to know where Cully was going and, based on his skulking movements, she was pretty sure he wouldn't tell her. To get that answer, she needed to trail him until he reached his mysterious destination. This need for secrecy made sense, but her fear didn't. Cully had never been anything but kind to her.

She supposed the fear had kicked in when she saw his stealth. She was trailing a man who was obviously protecting a secret. Cully himself might or might not be a danger to her, but Faye knew from hard experience that secrets could be dangerous indeed.

Chapter Thirty-Three

Faye opened the door of the lean-to where Cully had disappeared and looked into a darkness that didn't surprise her. The lean-to concealed a stairway leading down, just as she had known that it would.

Of course it did. Cully had said that his mother lived underground as a child. It only made sense that she would have told him how to get down there.

The narrow brick staircase looked as old as the one uncovered by the bomb. Cully was nowhere to be seen. More importantly, the beam of his flashlight was nowhere to be seen. There was nothing but darkness at the foot of the stairs. Maybe he'd moved further into the underground warren and hadn't seen her open this door, flooding the upper half of the stairwell with light. She had no way to know.

Sunshine lit each stair tread, inviting her to explore. Unfortunately, the sunlight could only penetrate so far. By the time she reached the bottom step, she would be in utter darkness.

Stepping into the unknown would be so tempting, and so stupid. Faye took a step back from the open door and reached for the phone in her pocket so that she could text Ahua about what she'd found.

Before her fingers closed on the phone, she heard the sound of a clicking latch behind her. She turned to see Cully coming out of an abandoned building. How stupid of her not to realize that if Cully knew one secret way to get in and out of his mother's old home, then he probably knew two.

On his back was a pack and in his hand was a gun. If he'd been wearing a cowboy hat and boots, he could have walked out of one of the old Western movies that her Mamaw had loved. Faye didn't know if he looked comfortable holding a gun because he knew how to use it or because he'd been acting like he knew how to use it for years and years. Or maybe he had spent the past two days acting like a kindly old gentleman. Was anything in an actor's world real?

"Give me the phone, Faye. There's no reason to let the rest of the world know about this place. They'd only mess it up, like they mess up everything."

"Would you really hurt me, Cully?"

"I just want a chance to explain things to you."

"You need a gun to do that?"

He looked flustered. "Please. Let's not have this conversation up here where someone might hear us. Come downstairs with me and I'll tell you everything."

Faye looked around. There was no one else in the alley. Who would hear this conversation that he wanted to have? More to the point, who would hear her if she screamed?

Faye was not stupid. She knew how foolish it would be to let a man with a gun lead her to a place where he could shoot her with a reasonable hope that her body might never be found. She knew she must be in shock, because she started to give him a rational explanation of why she didn't want to do this, but he interrupted her as he was taking her phone out of her hand.

"Please, Faye. Just listen to me. I think I know how to find Stacy, but I will not let you go until you understand how important it is that you keep my secret. Secrets, actually."

"Will you put down the gun?"

"When we're downstairs."

———

Joe had gone beyond searching the places where hotel guests were supposed to be. He'd explored the lobbies, the meeting rooms, the stairwells, and the restaurants of both towers. Now he was going to look in places where the guests weren't supposed to be. He figured he'd start with the laundry.

———

When Faye reached the bottom step, she paused. Cully was behind her, a gun in one hand. With the other, he used his flashlight to illuminate the steps as he followed her. There was no other light to illuminate the space. Some prehistoric corner of her brain remembered the sound and feel of a cave, and it used the echoes of his footsteps to give her a sense of the chamber's substantial size. This room was big, much bigger than the painted room. When she reached the bottom, she stepped out into something that she knew intuitively was a place where people had lived. In the darkness, she felt like she was stepping out into nothing.

Cully joined her in the nothingness. Still standing just behind her, almost close enough to touch his rib cage to her spine, Cully swung the flashlight's beam around to illuminate the room's walls. The narrow beam only lit a few square feet at a time, making a spot of brightness that was painful to her dark-adapted eyes.

She guessed that the side walls were ten feet away from her on both sides with the wall in front of her being much farther away than that. As the light slipped down the long wall to her right, it revealed a scene that correlated precisely with all of the eyewitness accounts of the underground community. One open doorway after another pierced the wall. Presuming those eyewitness accounts were correct—and why shouldn't they be when they'd been right about everything so far?—the doorways marked the entrances of the small sleeping rooms where entire families had passed their nights. Cully raked the light over the wall to her left, and it looked identical to the one on the right, door after door after door.

At the far end of the room, the light beam made a bright circle on the far wall. The wall looked like a blank white-plastered rectangle with a closed door in its very center. Cully flicked his wrist upward and the flashlight lit metallic conduit pipe running down the center of the ceiling. The pipe served three empty light receptacles. Then he flicked his wrist down and she saw a heavy layer of dust, scuffed in the middle by a long row of footprints.

"Have you been down here?" Faye asked.

"Not since 1962."

"Then somebody else has been, recently. And more than once."

Cully took a step forward. Since Faye was still in front of him, she reflexively did the same. She supposed she could balk and refuse to walk in the direction he wanted to go, but he did still have a gun.

"I thought you were going to put that thing away when we got down here."

"You're in no danger from me, Faye. This gun isn't for you. It's for the person who took Stacy."

"Where do you think she is?"

He used the gun to point to the door in the middle of the big room's far wall.

"Probably that way. But I want to check every last one of the sleeping chambers opening into this room, just in case."

———

In a stroke of luck, Joe bumped into Agent Ahua on the sidewalk in front of the South Tower. He'd been afraid that the agent was holed up in his command center where civilians might not be allowed to go.

He got straight to the point. "Have you seen Faye?"

Ahua stopped to think. "I've seen her since lunch but not lately. You checked your hotel room?"

"Yep. And most every place in the Annex, inside and outside."

To Joe's relief, Ahua didn't blow him off. Or maybe not to Joe's relief. As he thought of it, he would prefer for an FBI agent to tell him that there was nothing to worry about and his wife was perfectly safe.

Instead, Ahua said, "Stacy just dropped out of sight this morning. If Faye has disappeared, too, I'm concerned."

Great. Now Joe had confirmation that he needed to be worrying. This was just as well, because he already was. "Can you ask your people to look for her?"

"Yes, and I have a lot of them. I'll start by ordering a search of the grounds of the Tower Annex. If she's here, my people will find her quickly. If she's not, I'll expand the search."

As he spoke, Joe saw Jakob hustling in their direction, traveling quickly for a man of his age and size. Before he had even reached them, he called out, "Have either of you seen Cully?"

Ahua met Joe's eyes. Joe saw frustration there. Maybe even fear, if FBI agents can be said to show fear. Ahua turned to Jakob and said, "I'm sorry, but I don't know where your friend is."

Then, maybe to Joe and maybe to himself, he said, "Too many people are missing. Or maybe they're just hiding from their friends and family. I don't know. But I do know that three missing people is three too many."

Jakob's eyes stayed on Ahua's for just a second too long, like a man who was counting to three.

Stacy.

Cully.

His eyes flicked back toward Joe, and it was as if he'd said his thoughts out loud. *Oh, crap. Faye's missing, too.* He'd moved close enough to reach out and grab Joe's hand. The way he squeezed it made Joe simultaneously feel comforted and wish for his dad. Ahua said, "My people are on it. We'll find them. All of them."

Not being a trained FBI agent, Joe now felt a little useless. And he was also acutely aware that Ahua's people were having trouble finding Stacy, so he couldn't count on them to find his wife any more easily. He knew he was supposed to get out of the way and let Ahua's people search for Faye, but no. That wasn't happening. Joe was a natural hunter and he knew Faye's habits. He needed to be part of this search. More than that, he needed to find his wife.

Chapter Thirty-Four

Motes of dust, kicked up by Faye and Cully on their slow passage along the side walls of the long room, danced in the flashlight beam. One by one, they searched the sleeping rooms, but they found nothing in any of them. It was time to pass through the door on the far wall and see what was on the far side. Cully held his flashlight beam on the door while Faye pushed it open.

The wooden door was coated with paint that was crumbling with age. It was held shut by a latch made of hand-wrought iron. The latch resisted her efforts to open it, offering up a metal-on-metal squeal that sliced open the silence, but Faye was able to work it open.

She put her hands flat on the door and pushed gently, feeling its substantial weight resist her muscles. After the first shove failed to open it, she took her hands away from the wooden surface and prepared to try again. For a moment, she stood fascinated by the ghostly glow of her dark palms, coated in powdery white pigment.

"Try again." He pressed the hand that was holding the flashlight against the door, preparing to help her.

Faye heard the muted brush of her own hands on wood as she looked for the best way to push.

"It'll open," Cully said. "The footprints go right under it, so somebody opened it not too long ago. Push hard."

She moved her feet apart, crouched into a more powerful position, and shoved.

He shoved, too, saying, "That'll do it."

Cully's words were still hanging in the air when Faye heard a tremendous percussive crack. Thinking it was a gunshot, she reflexively tried to drop flat on the ground but instead she just crumpled beneath something that was pinning her to the dusty floor.

"Are you okay? Faye? Tell me you're okay."

Cully tilted the heavy door so that Faye could crawl out from underneath it. She pushed herself to her knees, her eyes on Cully as he pulled the gun from his back waistband, where he had tucked it so that he could use both hands to lift. The door had hit her head hard, and her bones ached from their collision with the cold floor.

"You okay?"

Cully asked the question as if he cared about the answer. He said it as if he cared about her, and this made her feel safe. But was she? He had said that the gun wasn't for her, but he had also said that he had secrets. Well, if Cully's secret was that he had killed Angela or Stacy and if he was expecting her to keep quiet about it, he might as well shoot her now. That was never going to happen.

Still crouching by the door, she felt along the side of it nearest her. Cully had thrown the flashlight to the ground to pull the door off her and it was now pointed ineffectively at the wall. She could barely see her hands in the indirect light. "The hinges gave way. Well, they weren't hinges in the way we think of hinges. They were more like leather straps."

"Yeah. Leather," he said. "Thick straps of leather work fine for hanging doors, when that's all you've got, but you can't expect leather to last forever."

He helped her scrabble to her feet and she limped forward through the door opening. This was the second time in two days that she'd been knocked to the ground with no warning. In between, she had made the physically grueling trek through the storm sewer, and she'd endured emotionally grueling events like an encounter with white supremacists and the discovery of the bodies of three small children. Faye was sore and exhausted, and she wanted to sit down and quit.

When she heard the denim of Cully's jeans creak as he stepped forward, ready to press on, she thought of Stacy and knew that quitting wasn't an option. She kept going.

They passed into a second large room, longer than it was wide and lined on both sides by sleeping rooms. A single doorway, again, stood in the center of the far wall. Footprints crossed the center of this room, too, from door to door. Some of them were headed in the direction they were moving, and some of them came back.

The ceiling over their heads was lower than a standard eight-foot ceiling, but it wasn't oppressively low. Faye, at five-feet-nothing, didn't even have to stoop. Cully was already stooping to support the backpack, so the ceiling cleared his head easily, but she doubted that he would have been able to stand straight.

By reaching her hand overhead, Faye followed the electrical conduit pipe for the length of the room. Her fingertips found one old ceramic fitting after another. Each of these had held a single bulb needed to bring light underground. How much light had those bulbs been able to throw? Had the space been dimly lit, or could people see well enough to live comfortably? She couldn't say.

Again, they moved down the right side wall from door to door, looking into small sleeping chambers where Stacy wasn't. Faye's hope was fading.

———

"Is this where you hid when you ran away?"

They stood looking into one of the sleeping chambers. Cully

had led her to each of the others, saving this one for last. Or perhaps steeling his resolve to look into a portal into his difficult past.

"Yep."

"You and Angela?"

Cully didn't say a word to answer her. He had moved behind her like a shadow as they explored the sleeping chambers, creeping from doorway to doorway and hoping desperately that Stacy was alive in one of them.

Each room seemed barely large enough for a single sleeper or, at most, a couple, but Faye knew she was seeing them from the perspective of a middle-class person in the twenty-first century. The people who had built this amazing space had probably considered each compartment to be suitable for a family, big enough for two adults and several children to sleep in, with enough extra space for a few possessions. Faye felt along the sides and top of a door opening and found a hole on either side, probably to hang curtains for privacy.

The back wall of each room was dirt, and no one had bothered to face the dirt walls with brick or wood or plaster. The side walls were lightweight wooden partitions. These were handmade caves. Many of them featured several rectangular niches carved into the dirt wall, and Faye pictured people storing possessions there. Some dishes in this niche, perhaps, and a few carefully folded articles of clothing in the next one. Maybe even a book, rare and treasured.

Each sleeping room was clean of everything but dust. There were no blankets or beds, and no artifacts of daily life like plates and cups.

The absence of artifacts was not a surprise. In an odd way, it meshed perfectly with the oral history that she had heard. For a group of people so poor and so persecuted that it made sense to move to safe quarters underground, it would have been unforgivably wasteful to leave anything behind. People desperate enough to dig their own caves did not have spare blankets or spare plates or even spare chopsticks. When the time came to pack up and leave this place, they had packed up literally everything and moved on.

Except for an oil stove, cast iron and lonely, that had been seen by visitors in 1969 but not since, as far as Faye knew.

Faye looked into this last chamber, the one where Cully and Angela had hidden, trying to imagine the lively sounds of families filling this space as they lived their lives. She couldn't do it.

"I feel like I'm in a tomb," she said. "Or a womb."

Cully didn't answer. His flashlight was trained on the chamber's walls and he stared into the emptiness, so rapt that the hand holding the gun was drifting slowly where it would be no defense against the kidnapper they feared.

She glanced back. Cully looked like a gunfighter from a Western movie, old and washed-up but too afraid of old enemies to lay down his gun.

"Would you look at that?" he asked, waving the flashlight at the far wall. Instead of carved niches, this earthen wall had been devoted to beauty.

Someone had taken a sharp stick and scratched a picture on it, covering the entire area from floor to ceiling, six feet high and six feet wide. It was a landscape scene with mountains, trees, and a flowing stream, and it put Faye in the shoes of someone who wished very much for a view of the outdoors. No, not just the outdoors. This scene was made by someone who wanted to be home.

Faye didn't know what China looked like, but she thought that maybe this was it.

"Whoever did that was an artist," she said.

"My grandfather did it."

Faye turned her face to his, but he didn't look at her.

"My mother brought me here when I was a kid, so I could see where she lived. I knew he made this as soon as I saw it, even before she told me. Some of his drawings hung on our walls when I was a kid, and they looked a lot like this."

Faye leaned farther into the room and saw that another landscape was sketched in pencil on the wallboard that separated this chamber from the one on her right. It showed rolling hills flecked with wide-spaced trees and divided by a river. "This one's very different, but China's a big place. There's got to be a lot of different landscapes there."

"No, that's Oklahoma. I made that one, after Angela...after she was gone. While I was waiting for her, eating the last of my food and deciding what to do next."

He turned without another word and led her toward the big room's far door. As Faye neared it, she felt herself shrinking from it reflexively. Was it going to fall on her like the last one did?

She felt its hinges and found that they were made of roughly wrought iron, perhaps made by someone who never wanted a door to fall on him again. She turned her attention to the latch and found that it was locked. The lock felt oddly slick and shiny. It felt new.

"Put some light on this."

He did, and the modern padlock gleamed silver in her hand. The hand holding the flashlight was trembling. "See, Faye? I told you I knew where Stacy was." Cully eased his backpack to the floor and pulled out something with two long, metallic handles.

He tossed the gun at her and she caught it in both hands. Then she laughed out loud, because it was plastic. He grinned sheepishly, then he elbowed her aside and set to work with a pair of bolt cutters that might just be large enough to cut through the padlock's shank.

———

The padlock put up quite a fight, since the bolt cutters were undersized for the job, but Cully insisted that he could handle it.

"I bought the biggest backpack I could find, and then I bought the biggest bolt cutters that would fit in it. The bigger the bolt cutters, the easier they cut. Not to mention that little ones can only get their blades around a skinny piece of metal. It's not like I could get a forty-two-incher down here, but I did the best I could in the little bit of time I had."

Faye busied herself by talking to Stacy, who she believed must be on the other side of the old door. There might be other reasons for it to be padlocked, but she couldn't think of any of them.

"Stacy! Can you hear me? It's Faye. I'm here with Cully Mantooth and we've come to get you out." Faye repeated this reassuring message time and again, but she never heard a sound on the other side of the door. All the while, Cully was working the blades of the bolt cutters around the padlock's shank and grunting as he strained to squeeze the handles together.

At last, she heard the sound of tortured metal being sheared in two. Soon, the same sound came again and she saw the padlock come away from the door in two pieces. Panting, Cully held the pieces on his palm and glowered at them until Faye gently edged him aside and shoved the door open.

Faye braced herself for what she might find on the other side of the door, then she and Cully walked into a bottled-up past.

The room was a near-twin of the painted room that Faye had studied so closely. She had enough of a sense of Lonnie's style and color palette to believe that he had painted both rooms. The colors and the loose, flowing brushstrokes were the same.

A battery-powered camping lantern stood in the center of the room, casting a dim light that didn't quite reach its corners. There were no benches around the walls, just a single chair with a footstool and side table nearby, all of them wooden and simply made. The side table's surface was covered with water rings. Faye imagined the artist—Lonnie, she supposed—sitting in the chair at the end of a painting session, kicking back with a beer and studying his work.

Today, though, it was not Lonnie sitting in the chair. It was Stacy Wong.

Chapter Thirty-Five

"Sitting" wasn't exactly the right word for what Stacy was doing. She was slumped unconscious in the chair with her head lolling to one side. Her feet were propped on the footstool and her arms dangled limp with her fingers brushing the ground. Only the chair's wooden armrests digging deep in her armpits and the chain around her waist kept her from tumbling onto the floor. The chain was looped through a metal hook protruding from the brick wall, stout and strong enough to hold a heavy bucket back in the days when people had lived in these catacombs. Faye could see that Stacy was taking long, deep breaths, so at least she was alive.

A large bruise on Stacy's forehead was blue-black, shading toward green, and blood was matted in her hair. More bruises covered her hands and arms, and this made Faye wonder what bruises lurked under her clothes.

A clear plastic clamshell container holding half of a ham sandwich was on Stacy's lap, resting neatly on a dark blue napkin. An open single-serving carton of milk was in the process of adding a square to the water rings to the side table's surface. Thank God somebody was feeding her, although Faye wasn't sure Stacy had actually eaten anything in the ten or more hours since she'd disappeared. Maybe she'd only been given half of a sandwich.

Faye reached out and touched the milk carton. It was half-empty, so at least Stacy had been drinking. The waxy cardboard was still slightly cool, so she and Cully must have just missed the person feeding Stacy. Since this was presumably the person imprisoning her, the thought made Faye jittery. However, this probably meant that it would be a while before that person returned, probably hours. She and Cully had time to figure out what to do.

Cully dropped to his knees and took one of Stacy's hands in his. "Are you okay, sweetie? Stacy. I need you to open your eyes."

Stacy opened one eye, looked at him, and sighed. Then she opened the other.

"Well, that's something," he said. He took Faye's hand and put Stacy's hand in it. "You take over here. I gotta do something."

"Can you talk, Stacy? Can you tell us what happened?"

Stacy opened her mouth and said, "I was—" and her voice drifted off. She tried again and managed to say, "Tried to—" Then she seemed to give up, unwilling or unable to do anything but focus a brilliant smile on Faye.

Now Faye was worried about whether they should move her. She studied the cut on Stacy's head. It was long, but it wasn't too deep. There was a small lump beside it, but nothing dramatic. Only her behavior made Faye fear brain damage. Stacy was rolling her head from side to side without apparent pain, making this examination more difficult than it needed to be, so maybe her neck was okay.

Faye saw that Cully was still holding the bolt cutters as he walked to the metal door in the room's back wall.

"This'll be a lot easier to take care of than that other lock," he said as he examined it.

Faye saw that the lock was attached to a hasp that was little more than a flimsy loop of corroded metal. A sturdy pair of tin snips could have cut right through it. Rather than cut through the shank of the lock itself, Cully easily snipped the hasp but left it in place. The padlock hung on to what was left of it, but it was useless to stop the door from opening.

"That's in case we need to use the back door in a hurry," he said. "Even if we can get out the way we came, we might need to come back. The person who put Stacy here might not think to check and make sure that the lock's still in one piece."

"It's always good to have options."

"Yep. Besides, a smart man never lets himself get penned up in a box canyon."

"Whatever you say. We're going to have a hard time getting her out of here if she doesn't perk up, though. It seems like a bad idea to leave her alone and I doubt we have any cell reception down here."

He checked his phone and said, "Nope." Then he tossed Faye's loaner phone at her and asked, "You?"

"Nope."

He knelt next to Stacy and said, "Don't worry, sweetie, we'll get you out of here." Then he set to work hacking through her chains with a pair of bolt cutters that were barely big enough for the job. They did the trick.

Next, he started pawing around in his backpack, looking for something.

"How did you know Stacy was here, and why couldn't you just tell the FBI or the police and let them find her?" she demanded.

He ignored her.

"Because now we have to try to get her out of here with no help," she said. "Or else one of us is going to have to sit here with her while the other one goes for help, and that doesn't seem like a good plan, because the person who chained her up will be coming back. I'm thinking we have a couple of hours at most, presuming Stacy is getting regular meals. So what's going on with you, Cully?"

Cully stopped ignoring her, which was progress. He nodded his head several times. "Good questions. Those are all good questions. I can answer them. And I will answer them. Most of them, anyway." But he didn't. He just kept shuffling through his backpack.

"Can you move your right hand, Stacy?" Faye asked. The left hand twitched, but then the right one opened and shut. Stacy might be disoriented enough to be confused about right and left, but she could hear, think, and act. Faye was relieved. "What about your right hand? Right foot? Left foot?" Stacy's movements were awkward, but she followed all of the instructions.

Faye squatted on her heels and eased Stacy into an unsupported sitting position, then she watched her sit up, wavering but unaided.

"While you're answering questions...or not...here's one more," she said to Cully. "What kind of secret is so important that you're willing to go up against somebody who did this," she cut her eyes toward the semi-conscious Stacy, "carrying nothing but a toy gun?"

He chuckled. "You knew that gun wasn't real the whole time."

Stacy's back was still off the chair. She was unsteady, but her trunk muscles were firing. Maybe they could move her after all.

"I actually didn't, not until you threw it at me. But now we're in some decent light and I can see that it's a toy. Cully, who did you plan to fool if you had to pull that thing in broad daylight?"

"I'm an actor. You'd be surprised at how easy it is to fool people. If you act scary, they get scared."

"There's no waiting period to buy a gun in Oklahoma. You couldn't take a taxi to the nearest Walmart and buy a real gun?"

"If I was an Oklahoma resident, yeah. I could've been in and out of Walmart with my gun in an hour. But I'm not. So I skipped lunch and took a taxi someplace where I could get the other things I needed really fast."

"The flashlight and the bolt cutters?"

"Yep."

"The backpack and those fashionable clothes? And shoes? And a toy gun?"

"Yep. And this." He pulled a bottle of water and a box of

cheese-and-crackers out of the pack. "Stacy, honey, you need to wake up and eat."

Faye opened the water bottle, dampened her hand, and smoothed it over Stacy's face. Maybe the coolness would rouse her.

"Cully, seriously. Tell me what's going on. Why did you decide you needed to be the Lone Ranger? You could have had the help of the Federal Bureau of Investigation, plus all of their technology, training, and firepower. What part of that sounded like a bad idea?"

Cully rested a paternal hand on Stacy's head. "I didn't know she was missing until I heard people talking after I had my first little interview with your beloved Federal Bureau of Investigation—who I don't trust as far as I could throw them and their firepower. I knew I had to do something, because I had a decent idea that I could find her. And you see that I was right. It took me a while to assemble what I needed to find her, but I did it."

"I think I understand why you thought you could find her. You knew the underground passageways because of your mother—"

"Yeah, we used to come down here all the time. We'd explore and she'd tell me stories about when she was a kid. I could probably have gotten here from that staircase at the Gershwin, but the FBI's had it cordoned off while they do their CSI thing. Besides, I wasn't sure about what the bomb might have done. Maybe some of the passageways over there caved in after the blast."

Faye held the crackers to Stacy's lips. The woman stirred but would not eat. Faye tried the bottle of water and got the same response.

"Where *are* we?" she asked.

"Pretty dang close to the old part of the Gershwin, actually. See that metal door?"

"Yeah, it's like the one in the other painted room."

"Well, it opens into the same storm sewer line, only about fifty feet above the other one."

Faye remembered her trip through that sewer. She had been so happy to see the other door that it hadn't occurred to her to ask whether it was the only one. She asked it now.

"Are there more doors like this?"

"Not that I know of. Upstream of this one, the pipe gets too narrow for me to crawl through, so I can't say for sure. More importantly, we need to get this woman someplace safe. Do you think it's okay to move her?"

Faye looked at Stacy. She was wobbly, but she was still sitting upright without leaning on the chair back. She did not look like a woman with a traumatic brain injury or a compromised spinal cord. She looked drunk.

As soon as that thought crossed Faye's mind, she picked up Stacy's milk, dipped a finger in, and touched it to her tongue. The milk didn't taste like it had soured, but it did taste really bitter. "She's not like this because she has a head injury. Somebody's drugging her. Let's get her out of here."

Cully stuck a finger in the milk, tasted it, and grimaced. "You're right."

"We've got to get her someplace safe, but it makes no sense for the three of us to limp back through both of those big rooms and drag Stacy up to the surface before we call for help. I'll go and you wait here with Stacy. I'll call Ahua and tell him where we are, and he'll send some people to help us get her out of here safely."

"No, that won't work," Cully said without explaining why.

"Then you go call for help and I'll wait here."

"No, that won't work, either." His face was obstinate.

"Well, now you have me stumped. Why won't those plans work?"

"Nobody but you can know I was here. I can't be around when she's rescued, and nobody can call for help from a phone that can be linked to me. You have to do it from your phone. There are too many questions about what happened to Angela. I don't want the FBI to know how much I know about these rooms down here, not when it was the last place I ever saw her."

"That makes sense. Not a lot, but a little."

"I'm telling you. I can't be seen. Make a lot of noise when you're coming through with the Feds, so I can crawl out in the storm sewer and hide."

"Explain something to me. Until I showed up, you were going to do this alone. What were you going to do? Drag her to the surface and leave her there? See if you could find a pay phone to call for help? There aren't many pay phones left these days, Cully."

"Look. There was a big chance that I wouldn't find her. There was another big chance that I might find her dead and yeah. If she was dead, I bought a burner phone while I was out shopping this morning that I could use to tell someone where to find her body. There was only a little chance that I would find her alive and need to stay with her until help came. If that happened, everybody would start wondering how I know so much about this place. I'd have done it to save this lady, but I wasn't going to cross that bridge until I came to it."

"Why can't the world know, Cully? What's wrong with having a mother who lived down here?"

Faye watched his face change as he lost control and shouted, "There's nothing wrong about having a mother like mine! She was an angel here on Earth." Immediately, his face showed deep shame. "I'm sorry I lost my temper. That's something my mother never did, not in all her years."

"What about Angela?"

"Angela? Yes, she had a temper. She was in a powerful rage on the last night I saw her."

"Did you have an argument?"

"No, that's just it. I was all by myself in that little cell, scratching a drawing on the wall."

He stopped himself to say, "I can't believe it's still there, actually," and shook his head.

Then he went on. "If you could have seen the terrible look on Angela's face. She got that way, sometimes. I always told myself that it was the drugs and if I could get her away from that school and her son-of-a-bitch stepfather, I could get her sober. Anyway, she called me terrible names, and then she turned and ran deep into these tunnels, in the dark. I looked and looked, but I couldn't find her. I waited for days for her to come back. When my food ran out, I went up top to buy some and I saw a newspaper that said a dead woman had been found in the river. I didn't know whether she'd jumped off a bridge or whether she'd drowned in the storm sewer. I just knew it was Angela and I knew they'd be looking for me. So I ran."

Faye wondered how you told a man that he'd spent a lifetime grieving for no reason.

He mistook her silence for judgment. "You can't let 'em know that I was with Angela the night she died. Getting famous was a stupid thing for a man on the run to do, but it snuck up on me. I went to bed one night as a low-rent extra and got up the next morning a star. I figured it was all over then. I figured the Oklahoma City Police would come after me, but I guess they never put two and two together and tagged me with murdering Angela. I stayed away all these years because I didn't want people asking me where she was and maybe getting the police all stirred up again. I'd have been on trial for her murder before I knew what was happening. Still would be, I guess. Dear God, the idea of me sitting in California with a bunch of money my family needed has eaten me alive for fifty years."

Faye tried to speak, but he interrupted her.

"Faye. Help me. There has to be a way to help Stacy without sending myself to prison."

"Listen. We don't have time for me to tell you all the details. I've got to go for help while you stay here and take care of Stacy. Then I've got to tell the FBI everything I know so that we can find the person who did this to her. Just know this. Nobody's looking to send you to jail for killing Angela because *she's not dead.*"

"What?" The bolt cutters hit the hard floor.

"At least, I don't think so. I know that wasn't her body in the river in 1962. Maybe she's died sometime in the past fifty or sixty years, but the FBI knows that she was alive when you left for Hollywood. That's why they never came for you, Cully. I'll tell you more when I get back. Take care of Stacy."

"Take my flashlight and be safe. Stacy and I will be here when you get back."

Chapter Thirty-Six

Faye ran through the first long room lined with sleeping chambers, following the bright beam of Cully's flashlight through the inky darkness, and then she sprinted through the second one. The staircase waited for her at its far end. Exhausted, she told herself that it wasn't as tall as it looked. Her legs and her lungs might be tired but they would take her to the top, where she could get a cell signal and call Ahua for help.

She wobbled as she hauled herself up the old stairs and her breath came short, but she could see sunlight leaking under the door that would take her into the alley. She was going to make it.

Stooping to pass through the door leading out of the low shed that concealed the staircase, Faye stepped into dazzling daylight shining through lead-gray clouds. It was so bright and her eyes were so dark-adapted that even late-afternoon sunshine was too much for her. The alley ran east to west, so the slanting of the sun toward evening illuminated all of it. She needed a bit of shade to help her see the phone's screen.

Things might have been different if Faye had turned around and seen the shadow cast by the shed directly behind her, but she was too exhausted to even be standing, much less trying to save a kidnapped woman's life. She broke into a run again, a limping and stumbling run, heading for the mouth of the blind alley because she knew that there would be something on the sidewalk—a tree, a bus stop shelter, something—that would block the sun and let her make a critical phone call.

———

In this moment, watching Faye Longchamp-Mantooth sprint out of an alley where she has no reason to be, I know to my core that Lonnie has ruined everything. He ruined my life long ago, my mothers' lives, my sisters' and brothers' lives. He ended Gabe, Zeb, and Orly's lives, or allowed them to end, which is the same thing.

In death, he has ruined the only victory that I could ever have over him, and he has done it by simply failing to follow the plan. How hard would it have been for him to stay underground long enough for me to blow him to smithereens?

Apparently, it was way too hard. And now here I am, face-to-face with another person who needs to be silenced before I've even decided what to do about poor Stacy Wong. I know that Faye Longchamp-Mantooth needs to die, because there can be no reason that she went down that alley except because she wanted to get underground. The dust and grime coating her clothes says that she'd succeeded. And the emotion on her face says that she has found Stacy.

But there is still hope. I am armed and I have the advantage of surprise. I do not have the moral high ground as I did when I killed Lonnie, but I still have loved ones to protect. I can do what needs to be done. I just wish that the rather likable Faye Longchamp-Mantooth hadn't been caught in the ever-expanding destruction sparked by Lonnie and his evil.

———

As Faye came out of the alley she nearly ran into the shade tree that she'd been hoping to see. Skidding to a stop, she found Ahua's number and placed the call. As his phone rang in her ear, she looked around her for the first time. Less than a block away, Kaayla, Grace, and Lucia stood near a service entrance for the South Tower. They all had very serious expressions on their faces. Faye hoped the maids weren't in trouble with their boss, then she realized that the serious expressions were focused on her, not each other. She supposed that she did look a little the worse for wear, and they probably had seen her running out of the alley like wild tigers were after her.

Kaayla was holding a sleek phone in one hand, with a finger poised to scroll through whatever information showed on its face. Perhaps she'd taken notes on the maids' failings and was now using them to ream Grace and Lucia out. This would explain their body language, which was so tense that Faye worried that she'd interrupted Kaayla as she fired them.

The thin, expensive phone in Kaayla's hand held Faye's attention. A memory was tickling at her mind. It was a recent memory, but it was fogged by pain and fear. Faye worked hard to reach through that fog and was rewarded by a single image, as clear and self-contained as a snapshot. It was Kaayla's hand, and it was holding an old clamshell phone until the bomb blew it out of her hand.

Ahua had said that pressure cooker bombs were often set off remotely by cell phones. Faye realized that bombers who didn't want to be caught wouldn't use their own phones. They'd use burner phones that couldn't be traced to them and they'd get rid of them immediately. And Kaayla, who spared no money on her professional appearance and would certainly not carry a cheap clamshell phone, had been holding something that looked an awful lot like a burner phone at the exact time of the blast.

It would have made sense for either of the other two women to carry an inexpensive phone. Kaayla, by contrast, stood there in her crisp suit and holding a purse that was way too pricey for one of her employees to carry. The slim phone in her hand now was the one that matched her self-image.

Kaayla was looking at Faye intently, as if by seeing her run, dusty and filthy, out of the alley where Stacy's hiding place could be accessed, she had proof that Faye was now dangerous.

Finally, Ahua answered his phone, Fate set to work blurting out information while she could, because Kaayla's expression was terrifying. Faye was in good shape, but she was exhausted and Kaayla was probably ten years younger than she was. Faye didn't think she could outrun her.

Backing away from the three women, Faye started talking without waiting for Ahua to say hello. "Kaayla set off the bomb. Stacy's underground." As she spoke, she backed slowly away from Kaayla and the fierceness in her eyes.

Ahua was trying to talk, but she kept steamrolling right over him. "Kaayla sees me and she knows I know. We're behind the South Tower."

In one motion, Kaayla dipped her hand into her stylish leather handbag, pulled out a handgun, and let the bag fall to the ground. "She's got a gun."

Wrapping the other arm around Lucia's neck, Kaayla pulled the woman close and pressed the gun's muzzle to her head.

"Drop the phone or she dies."

———

Ahua cursed at the sound of Faye's phone hitting the sidewalk. He shouted "Come!" as he barreled out of the command center, followed by four agents who had no idea where he was taking them. Ahua didn't have much of an idea himself, but he could certainly take himself behind the South Tower and see what was there.

———

Faye never took her eyes off Lucia's weeping face, not while Kaayla was picking up her purse and telling her to back slowly into the alley, not while she was ordering her to open the door to the lean-to shed, and not while she was forcing all three of them—Faye, Grace, and Lucia—to go down the stairs by pressing the muzzle of a handgun to Lucia's head.

Some of the jigsaw pieces were starting to fit, but not all of them. Kaayla had certainly had the opportunity to mastermind the bombing. As assistant manager of the Gershwin Hotel, she was in a position to know about the hidden staircase, but Faye couldn't quite work out the reasons for the location and timing of the blast. She knew of no reason for Kaayla to bomb her own hotel on purpose.

But maybe she didn't. Maybe she had explored as far as the painted room—but no farther, based on the tracks in the dust—and had sent Alonso Smith there to set off the bomb. Ahua had said that footprint evidence on the staircase was scant. He could say that nobody but Alonso had been past the foot of the staircase, but he couldn't say much about the stairs. Or maybe she'd gone down that far, but had told Alonso to take the door to the left and go further before setting the bomb. And maybe he was supposed to walk away from it alive, but Faye doubted it. Kaayla was a dark-haired woman born in the eighties, so she fit the profile of Lonnie's daughters, probably the oldest one, Lonna. Any surviving child born to Alonso Smith might be happy to bomb him out of existence.

The note in Lonnie's pocket had addressed him as "Father," and it was written by the person who provided him with the bomb. The letter-writer claimed to be helping him obliterate evil, but the bomb given to Lonnie was a modestly sized people-killer, not something that would bring down a building if detonated below the building's foundations.

If it had blown up underground, it would have destroyed nothing but Lonnie. From Kaayla's point of view, Lonnie embodied quite enough evil to be ripe for obliteration, all by himself. She had sent him underground with a cell phone to be used as a dummy detonator, keeping the real detonator phone for herself.

When he was safely underground, she had activated it or, more likely, activated a timer right after she took Faye's picture with Cully. And Faye had thought she looked nervous because she'd just met a movie star.

Kaayla must have felt confident that he would die alone with his evil, never to be found. But he had ruined her plan by aborting his mission and coming back upstairs into the hotel lobby where Kaayla stood waiting for him to die.

Faye couldn't stop looking at Lucia's stoic face. Kaayla had given her a flashlight and ordered her to hold it. Her fear only revealed itself by her trembling lips. They were walking through the first underground chamber and Faye's steps were slowing as she worked through what Kaayla had done.

This was the key. Alonso didn't know that the bomb would kill him. Kaayla had planned the whole thing as a way to kill Alonso Smith remotely. She wouldn't see any blood gush or hear any groans. She would probably never see the body. In fact, it might never even be found.

Stacy was probably headed for a similar fate, dying underground so that Kaayla would never have to see what she'd done. Faye remembered the ham sandwich and milk carton and knew that Kaayla couldn't even bring herself to starve Stacy while she figured out how to silence her. She also knew now that the napkin she'd seen with the food, blue like the Gershwin Hotel's linens, was a clue that should have pointed her to Kaayla.

Kaayla's refusal to look at murder as she committed it was her Achilles' heel, but Faye had no idea how to exploit it.

Faye remembered the three little bodies in the painted chamber, all of them Alonso's sons and all of them born after Kaayla. If Faye had lived Kaayla's life, watching three little brothers waste and die without the help of a doctor, she might have grown up homicidal, too. And she might have a strong aversion to ever again watching anyone die.

Faye might even be willing to say that Kaayla had done the

world a favor when she killed her father, but there was no redemption for beating Stacy, drugging her, and locking her up while she hardened her heart enough to murder her. And why did she need to silence Stacy, anyway?

So that she could never tell anyone that she'd seen Kaayla defacing the paintings in an attempt to hide any clues that might help the FBI track down the family of Alonso Smith.

They stood outside the door to Stacy's prison. Kaayla was holding the gun in one hand and the padlock that Cully had destroyed in the other.

"It was a flimsy lock. No wonder you were able to break it. That's why I was on my way down here with a better one," she said, pulling a bigger padlock out of her pocket. Its shank was way too stout for Cully's bolt cutters, even if he had been on the right side of the door to use them.

Kaayla pulled the damaged lock out of its hasp and dropped it to the floor, hooking the new one into its spot, ready to use after she had pushed Faye into the room with Stacy and closed the door. And, Faye supposed, Lucia and Grace, too. She couldn't imagine Kaayla leaving witnesses able to incriminate her. Would all of their bodies—Faye's, Lucia's, Grace's, Cully's—ever be found? Only if the FBI was able to find a way into this portion of the Chinese catacombs.

Holding a gun on Faye, she said, "Open the door. Now, back in slowly or I'll shoot you right here where nobody will ever find you. I'll shoot all of you."

Faye did as she was told. Stacy was in the chair where she'd left her, unconscious and wrapped in her chains. Cully had heard them coming and had hidden any evidence that he had been there. She saw him hiding behind the open door, holding his puny toy gun at the ready and unaware that Kaayla held a real one. She didn't know what good keeping Cully's presence a secret was going to do them once that door closed, but information had power. It made sense to limit who held that power.

"Give me the hacksaw. Or the bolt cutters or whatever you used to destroy that padlock."

Faye reached into the shadow where Cully waited and picked up the bolt cutters, throwing them through the open door.

As she stood waiting for Kaayla to force Grace and Lucia through the door, she saw her drop the gun to her side, releasing Lucia. The two maids stood free at her side as Kaayla began shoving the heavy door shut. Her laugh echoed in the small room where Faye stood and in the large room on the other side of the closing door. Finally, Faye understood.

"Your sisters. They're your sisters and they helped you kill your father."

Kaayla didn't answer her. She just laughed until the closed door damped the sound, changing it into something quiet and chilling.

Faye signaled to Cully that he shouldn't speak, pantomiming that Kaayla had a gun. The old door was solid, but it didn't block all sound. She waited until she heard the footsteps fade into nothingness before she said, "His daughters killed him. All three of them. Kaayla, Grace, and Lucia."

She turned her eyes to the walls, covered with paintings of Lonnie and his family that Kaayla had never bothered to destroy because she thought they'd never be seen. Now Faye saw them for who they were.

Kaayla, the oldest, leaned against her mother's knee or stood at her father's side, watching the younger children. Lucia, with her prominent cheekbones, was easily distinguishable when Faye knew how to look, and she was discernible in many of the paintings as a small girl standing beside the slightly older Grace. The babies' identities shifted, but Faye could usually tell by the context whether she was looking at Grace or Lucia or one of the frail boys. The doomed family's history was splattered all over these walls. No wonder Kaayla had wanted to obliterate it.

"Are you finished looking at the pretty pictures?" Cully whispered. "Because we need to get out of here."

Faye looked at the door's iron hinges. They might be able to cut leather straps with Cully bolt cutters, but they would be no match for the stout ironwork.

"Not that door," Cully whispered. "The other one."

His eyes traveled to the little metal door in the wall that led into the storm sewer that would take them to the river and safety.

"You already cut the padlock," she said. "I saw you."

"Yep. 'Cause a smart man never lets himself get bottled up in a box canyon."

———

Ahua stood behind the South Tower on a public sidewalk that offered no clue to where Faye was. He wished he was standing in a deep quiet forest, where her path would have been marked by scuffled leaves and mucky footprints. Instead, he had a concrete sidewalk, a heavily traveled city street, and a nearby alley paved in asphalt.

Thanks to Faye, he had the name of the person responsible for the bombing, presuming that she was right about that, and Faye Longchamp-Mantooth had not struck him as a person who would claim to know something unless she was absolutely sure. She had also given him a lead on Stacy's location and, even better, she had given him real hope that Stacy was alive.

But had Faye given him enough information to ensure her own safety? It didn't seem so, and that made him want to break something.

"You," he said, pointing at the agent nearest him. "Find out where the call that just came to my number originated."

That would be useful information but getting it would take too long. Faye had been taken by a known killer. He had to do something quickly, but what?

Faye had said that Stacy Wong was underground and now

Faye, too, had vanished. Maybe she was underground now, too. If so, Ahua only knew one way to get there, down a staircase in the bombed-out lobby of the historic Gershwin Hotel.

"Come," he said, taking off down the sidewalk, trusting that the three agents who weren't working on tracing the location of the killer's phone would follow in his wake. They did.

———

Joe couldn't think of any more places in the Tower Annex where he wasn't supposed to be. He had snooped into all of them. He couldn't think of any more places to look for Faye, but he was undaunted because Faye was hardly ever where anybody would expect her to be.

Thinking that maybe she was hanging out on the loading dock or beside the dumpsters—because why not?—he slipped out a door labeled "Employees Only" to take a look out back. Faye was not there but four FBI agents were, and they looked totally stressed as they ran past him. One of them was Ahua and another was Bigbee.

Joe called out to him, "Have you seen my wife?"

Ahua said only, "No," but Bigbee managed to convey the truth to Joe with eye contact, a cocked head, and raised eyebrows. Joe followed them at a generous distance, figuring that it was a free country and he could jog where he pleased. If Ahua noticed, he didn't let it show.

———

I linger outside the door to Stacy's cell, listening to Faye and Stacy whisper. They are certainly talking their way through a set of options that are uniformly poor. I'm not crazy about my options, either.

I have to kill them, of course, but the idea that Lonnie is reaching back from the grave to destroy two more lives makes me incandescent with rage. Stacy and Faye have done nothing wrong, but their continued existence will violate the only rule that Lonnie got right: Protect family at all costs.

I have to protect Grace and Lucia. They have nobody and nothing but me. Because of Lonnie's paranoia about the government, they don't actually exist on paper. They have no legal identification beyond the fake passports I had someone forge to make it possible for me to hire them. Those passports could never stand up to the scrutiny of immigration agents. We were all homeschooled, but their birth mother, Sandra, never finished elementary school and her first language wasn't English. Despite my best efforts over the years since I moved them into my apartment and set about helping them build lives in the real world, they are still functionally illiterate.

My birth mother, on the other hand, was a high school math teacher and she taught me well. A GED and community college were options for me, but not for my sisters. If I were to go to jail—or to the electric chair, and I don't much care whether it is one or the other—my sisters would immediately be jobless and soon homeless, and they would be vulnerable to deportation to...somewhere. There was once a time when immigration officials could have been made to understand my sisters' situation, but that time is not now. Where does the U.S. send people these days when they quite literally have no country?

The gun is heavy in my shaking hand. I don't want to shoot Faye and Stacy. I don't want to see the looks on their faces when they realize what is about to happen to them. I don't want to see the spraying blood. I don't want to hear them scream or groan or gurgle, but I don't have it in me to let them starve to death. I need to think of something quick and painless.

As I linger outside the padlocked door for a long time, my head is bowed and my eyes are closed as if I am praying over the matter, but I am years past being able to pray. My sisters keep saying "Kaayla?" in those soft, sweet, dependent voices that I love so well, despite the terrible burden that comes along with them.

Finally, the answer comes and it is poison. Surely there is something in the hotel's maintenance closet that will solve the problem of Faye and Stacy. Rat poison? Maybe. If the two women get hungry enough, they will eat what I give them. Their bodies will stay where they are and my sisters will finally be safe. In a way, their corpses will mirror my three little brothers' bodies, resting for decades. Even if they are found, they will be found too late for their killer to be found and punished.

My cherished sisters will only be safe when Stacy Wong and Faye Longchamp-Mantooth are silenced, so that is what I will have to do.

Chapter Thirty-Seven

Cully eased Stacy to her feet and the chain that had held her clattered to the floor.

Faye crossed the room and opened the metal door that led into the storm sewer. She was surprised to see that the water level was less than a foot below the door opening, and she was also afraid. She hadn't had a chance to think about what the rain that had been spattering on her head aboveground would look like down here.

"I'm not sure we can do this, Cully. There's a lot of water and it's moving fast. And it's still raining up there."

She would have added, "And it's only going to get worse downstream. Those lateral lines are all going to be bringing in more water," but Cully interrupted her because he didn't want to hear it.

"We got no choice. The water might kill us and Kaayla might kill us. The difference is that Kaayla needs to shut us up. She wants to kill us and the water just don't care."

Stacy looked more alert. Maybe the drugs were wearing off or maybe Cully had charmed her into consciousness. He had to grasp her elbows to support and guide her, but she was walking unaided otherwise. When he got Stacy to the open door, he motioned for Faye to grab her elbows. Then he crawled through the door and stood in the water, reaching back into the room to help Stacy make the awkward climb through the portal.

It was a good plan and it should have worked. Even in the flowing water, they should have been able to make their way to the river outfall and, once there, find a way to get some help. Unfortunately, two things happened simultaneously that torpedoed the plan.

The first torpedo was launched by clouds that they couldn't see. Those clouds erupted into the kind of thunderstorm that was a routine rain event for Oklahoma, and the stormwater control system dealt with it, operating as it was designed to operate. Unfortunately, the presence of human beings deep in the bowels of the system was not one of its design parameters.

The second torpedo was launched personally by Stacy Wong, who looked at the man trying to drag her into a confined space, pitch-dark and half full of water, and did the only rational thing. She screamed as if there were no tomorrow.

———

When I came to grips with the realization that two innocent women must die by my hand, I lifted my head and smiled at my sisters. Everything was going to be okay.

They must not have understood that everything was going to be okay, because they didn't seem comforted.

"Sister," Grace said, "what are you going to do? Those two women—"

She was interrupted by a woman screaming as if there were no tomorrow.

And then the screaming woman started shouting about how she didn't want to go into the water. Bounding toward the padlocked door, I shook off my sisters' hands. The most critical thing in my world at that moment was silencing Stacy and Faye before they emerged from the storm sewer outfall and started telling the world what they knew.

———

Joe kept his distance from the FBI dudes. They were, after all, heavily armed, and they had dozens of heavily armed friends within shouting distance. He loped behind them, wishing that Faye wasn't involved with whatever it was that had the feds in such a lather, but knowing that she was. He had heard Ahua turn to the man beside him and say, "Make sure there's an ambulance on its way. No, two. Either of the women might need medical care when we find them. Maybe both."

So they were looking for two women. One of them was probably Stacy Wong. The whole town probably knew she was missing by now, but Joe had heard no news reports of a second missing woman. He did know, however, that his wife was nowhere to be found.

When Ahua and his friends barreled through the door of the bombed-out lobby of the Gershwin Hotel, ignoring the fact that it was supposed to be off-limits for everybody who wasn't an evidence technician, Joe knew that there was a crisis happening. He took advantage of the confusion surrounding that crisis to follow Ahua and his agents right down the staircase into the underground chambers that he'd been hearing so much about.

As Joe descended, he saw Ahua take a few steps into the room at the foot of the stairs then come right back out and go through a door to the left. The other agents followed. Just a few steps behind them, Joe stepped into the first room and found himself surrounded by colorful paint in a room where his wife was not. A small metal door in the wall in front of him stood slightly ajar, as if Ahua had peeked through it before abandoning the room. Joe felt that he should peek, too, so he did.

Water lapped at the bottom of the opening, splashing over into the room. Joe looked at its dark, oily surface and thought of Faye's mysterious trip under Oklahoma City. She hadn't been allowed to talk to him about it, but she'd mentioned hip waders, and he'd seen the water splashed on her shirt. He had asked himself where the water came from and where it was going, but he'd never had time to think the question through. As he stared at the flowing water, he was jolted into action by the sound of a woman screaming as if there were no tomorrow.

Joe hoped and also feared that the screams came from Faye, but he saw that it wasn't her when the rushing stormwater swept Stacy Wong past him. He was through the door and in the water in a heartbeat.

———

Cully had dragged Stacy through the open door before the scream was out of her throat. She had clung to him, shouting, "No, no, not the water. I don't want to go in the water. Don't make me go in the water," but she had been too drugged to fight him off. She'd gone headfirst into the rising current.

And it was indeed rising. Cully had no doubt of that. He just hoped it didn't fill the pipe so completely that there was no air left to breathe. He dragged himself back through the door into the painted room where there was another woman who needed rescuing.

Faye had lots more fight left in her than Stacy did, but Cully was bigger and he knew all the dirty tricks of two generations of stunt men and women. He dismantled Faye's last objection by saying, "You have to get to Stacy. She's still pretty stoned. I don't know if she can swim." Then he stuffed her through the opening.

A noise behind him made him turn his head in time to see the heavy door twitch on its hinges. Over the noise of the rushing water, he heard the heavy click of an opening padlock and the grinding sound of wood on brick as someone worked hard to shove it open.

He needed a weapon. The only thing he saw was the chain that had bound Stacy. Still standing against the back wall, he leaned down and picked it up.

Stacy and Faye were out of the room, and that was good. Even in a flooded storm sewer, they were safer than they would have been if they were facing Kaayla and her gun. His plan was to keep doing whatever he could to slow Kaayla down. Every second that he bought Faye and Stacy took them further from a loaded gun and closer to safety.

The chain was heavy in his hand. In these close quarters, he might be able to sling hard and connect, then keep connecting until he knocked Kaayla out or she shot him.

Out of nowhere, he felt a small, strong hand grab him by the right shoulder. It threw him off-balance and he stumbled. He would have fallen, but a second hand grabbed him by the other shoulder and guided that fall through the door into the storm sewer. He hung for an instant with the metal rim of the doorframe digging into his back, but Faye never let go. She maneuvered her feet to the pipe wall below him and pressed hard, using the leverage to pull him into the water with her. She had told him that she lived on an island. She sure handled herself in the water like an island dweller.

The current was strong. It grabbed them and pulled them downstream. They were just clear of the opening when he saw a bullet slam into the sewer wall just inches from Faye's head. A puff of orange dust erupted from the brick that took a bullet for her.

Her name came out of his mouth, unbidden. "Faye!"

The sound of the gunshot was deafening and Cully recognized a dangerous kind of terror on Faye's face. It was the kind of terror that could make someone do fatal things like crawl back into the room where a woman waited with a gun. He slung an arm under Faye's armpits, making sure to keep her face above water, and making sure his footing was secure. Then he started dragging her downstream like a lifeguard saving a swimmer from drowning.

Ahead of him, he heard Stacy still shrieking her displeasure as the water washed her farther from danger. He was grateful for her shouting, because it reassured him that she wasn't drowning.

In the darkness ahead, he heard a splash and a man's voice, but he couldn't spend any time figuring out who was barreling out of the other painted room, because another splash sounded, and it was much closer to him. Kaayla had come into the storm sewer, bellowing, "Grace. Lucia. Stay where you are." More splashing ensued, so Cully wasn't sure whether either of them followed her orders.

In the lantern light spilling out of the room he'd just escaped, he could see Kaayla maneuvering into an upright position, holding her gun above the water. If she managed to get enough traction on the pipe's bricks to stand up straight and aim a shot properly, it was possible that she might be able to kill them before they'd made it out of range.

Cully slung the arm that was dragging Faye and he slung it hard, tossing her a few feet downstream from where he stood. He hoped she'd regained her senses well enough to swim or at least keep her face out of the water while it carried her away from Kaayla and her gun. He also hoped that Stacy, barely visible ahead of them, had been sobered up enough by the chilly water to be able to swim. By letting them go ahead, he risked letting them drown, but Kaayla and her bullets seemed like the more immediate problem. All he had to buy them was seconds for the water to whisk them farther downstream in the dark.

Dim light shone through the door of the other painted room, the one in front of him, and it illuminated a bend in the pipe. Faye and Stacy could be around that bend in seconds. So, of course, could Kaayla, but once she lost her footing, the torrent of water buffeting them would keep her from finding it again. This was her last chance to stand still and coolly draw aim, and he knew that he could stop her.

Cully admired Faye and Stacy a great deal. He figured that they each had forty or fifty good years left to them, while he had ten or twenty, tops. And that was if he was lucky. It seemed like a good trade to buy eighty or a hundred years for them with ten or twenty of his own. The characters he had played on-screen liked to think of themselves as excellent horse traders, so he was at peace leaving the earth as part of a good trade.

Cully reached down with his feet and used the rubber soles of his new sneakers to grip the bricks on the bottom of the pipe. Standing up tall, so tall that his head bumped the pipe above him, he did his best imitation of a human shield and waited for Kaayla to fire.

———

Ahua stood at the foot of the stairs, looking into the room to his left. The dust on the floor was still deep and undisturbed, and this is how he knew that he was looking for Stacy in the wrong place. In all likelihood, Faye was with her. And so was Kaayla, the woman Faye had accused of sending Alonso Smith to set off the bomb that killed him. If they were underground, it was in a part of the abandoned network of rooms that was accessed by another stairway. Ahua had no idea where to begin looking for it.

He was facing the futility of looking for an entrance that had been hidden for eighty years while the clock ticked on two women's lives, when he heard a scream. The sound seemed to be coming from the painted room, so he wheeled around to step through that door. Pushing his way through the agents accompanying him, he arrived just in time to see Joe Wolf Mantooth's bottom half disappear as the big man threw himself into the storm sewer.

Ahua was very proud to see all of his agents preparing to follow Mantooth into the water that was slopping over the bottom rim of the open door, but it made no sense for all of them to go in. Too many bodies in such a narrow pipe was a recipe for a logjam that could drown them all.

"Stand down. Nobody's going in but me. That pipe's not wide enough for all of us to go in." He pointed a finger at the nearest agent. "You. Call an ambulance to meet us at the spot where this pipe dumps into the river. Agent Goldsby can tell you where it is."

He pointed to another agent. "And you. Alert the Agent in Charge."

As he launched himself into the water, he said to the last one, Agent Bigbee. "Find a vehicle and get yourselves to that outfall. I'm going to need backup when I get there." He could see that Bigbee wanted to ignore the order and go after a screaming woman who might well be his friend Faye, but Bigbee was an excellent agent. He stood down and watched Ahua dive through the opening.

Then Ahua heard a gunshot and he heard Cully Mantooth's voice bellow Faye's name and he knew that, somehow, he'd succeeded in following her cryptic clues to the spot where he was meant to be.

—

Cully felt an impact when the gun fired a second time. It wasn't painful, but it knocked him off his feet. Maybe getting shot wasn't so bad, after all.

Then he realized that it was no bullet that hit him. It was Faye, who could apparently swim with the speed and force of a barracuda. She slung an arm under his armpits and began pulling him downstream with the same lifeguard's technique that he'd used on her.

He was floating on his back, so he saw everything that happened upstream, dimly lit as it was by the light coming through the open metal door that he'd just passed through. Kaayla was still on her feet, steadying herself to take another shot at him, and Grace was tugging at her arms, begging her not to shoot. Kaayla pushed her away like a big sister keeping a little sister from messing with her dollhouse. Grace wasn't going to be able to stop Kaayla from shooting to kill.

———

Joe could hear Stacy screaming downstream. In the darkness, it was hard to tell which way was up, but he focused on maintaining an awareness of the water's surface. It was rising, and the time was coming when there might be only a bubble of air at the top of the pipe where he could breathe. And where he could take Stacy for air, if she turned out to be unable to do it for herself and if he could find her. Or any of the other people he heard struggling in the rushing water. After that, the time might come when there was no air at all.

Joe stretched himself to his full-length, stuck out his hand, and was rewarded by the feel of sodden leather. He grabbed the shoe and gently pulled Stacy Wong toward him so that he could help her keep her face above the surface while there was still air to breathe.

———

Everyone in the sewer—Stacy, Joe, Ahua, Faye, Cully, Kaayla, Grace—had been knocked off their feet by the water or by each other, and they were now helpless to slow their rate of travel. The rainfall outside had increased suddenly when the thunderstorm struck, sending a slug of water that rapidly raised the water level in the storm sewer pipe, moving them along even faster.

Stacy passed the point where two lateral lines entered the pipe first. They brought still more water into the main line, and they brought it with such force that Stacy was buffeted by turbulence. Joe, who was still clinging to her shoe, lost his grip as the water tumbled him until all sense of direction was gone.

One by one, the others passed that point and found themselves banging into the pipe's brick walls and into each other. The remaining air at the top of the pipe was only inches deep. Each time their faces surfaced, water splashed into their mouths and noses. All their flailing to find the surface did nothing to help.

Life and death hung on the question of finding air in utter
darkness while tumbling through moving water. Periodic crashes
into the pipe's rough brick walls brought blood and bruises, but
nothing to breathe.

———

Faye took a punishing crash into the pipe wall. She had lost Cully
somehow. Maybe he was ahead of her and maybe he was behind
her. When the water went turbulent and they passed into a pipe
that was six feet across, bodies had tumbled through the water
in every direction.

She had learned the hard way that she needed to protect her
skull, so she was curled into a ball with her arms and hands cradling her head and face. Soon, she would need to uncurl and find
some air to breathe.

Two hands grabbed her and dragged her down, exactly like a
drowning person in a swimming pool would take down anyone
in the vicinity without meaning them a scintilla of harm. Only
here, in this place, the concept of "taking down" someone was
heavily dependent on whether either the attacker or defender
had any notion of where "up" was.

The person attacking Faye was trying to walk right up her
body like a ladder, digging her feet into Faye's groin, abdomen,
chest, face. Faye turned the tables by reaching up and grabbing
at her attacker's face and throat. She felt a metal name tag on the
person's lapel and long straight hair wrapped itself around her
hand, so she knew she was dealing with Kaayla. What she didn't
know was whether Kaayla's attack was a premeditated attempt
to drown her or whether the woman was out of her mind with
panic. Either of these things would make Faye equally dead.

She struck out at Kaayla with both hands and feet, but the
woman hung on. In desperation, Faye held her at arm's length,
flailing with her feet in hopes of finding the pipe's walls and

figuring out which way was up. Her foot struck bricks with bruising force, but the pain felt good. Faye struck the bricks hard and used the force to ram Kaayla into the opposite wall. In the moment of impact, her assailant went limp.

Still longing for air, Faye used the bricks to push off again, this time heading downstream.

———

By the time Faye slammed me into the sewer wall, I had long since dropped the handgun. It had become a burden that weighed me down and left me only one hand to use to save myself. And to save Grace. And maybe Lucia. I have no way to know whether she flung herself into the water after us.

The gun was drowning me and I had to let it go. This might mean that Faye and Stacy will live to testify against me. It might mean that I am convicted of killing my father, which is something that I in fact did. And perhaps I deserve it. Evil must be obliterated. I refuse to call myself evil for ridding the world of Lonnie, but the things I did to Stacy and Faye…the things I planned to do them… those things are evil.

Right now, though, the question of evil in my soul does not matter. The thing that matters is finding Grace. And maybe Lucia. Even finding air to breathe means nothing if I can't find air for them.

In truth, my love for my sisters is all that has ever mattered. Except, of course, for obliterating Lonnie.

———

Cully saw daylight ahead, and this meant that he might just make it. He had no idea what had happened to Faye. Somehow, it was now Stacy's head that he was holding out of the water. He thought, but was not sure, that she was still alive, so she too might make it. He didn't know about the others. At some point, they had become nothing more than bodies bashing him with arms, legs, fists, feet, flailing in desperation.

Maybe some of them were still alive. He hoped so.

As this hope began to grow, Cully felt rather than saw a long, strong body leap out of the darkness. The gray light had grown just strong enough for him to recognize the man's face and strong shoulders as Joe's.

If Faye swam like a barracuda, her husband was a killer whale. Joe wrapped his arms around Cully and Stacy, gently guiding them toward the light. For the first time in real life, Cully understood the joy in a besieged frontiersman's heart when the cavalry appeared over the crest of a hill, poised to sweep down and save the day. Sometimes, they even saved people like him.

Chapter Thirty-Eight

The gushing water at the storm sewer outfall wasn't quite enough to carry Joe all the way to the Oklahoma River. He crashed and rolled along the cement ditch and into the riprap at the water's edge, releasing Cully and Stacy from his fierce grip. The water was still carrying him riverward. He was accumulating scrapes and bruises over his entire body but he didn't care because he could breathe.

There wasn't much left of the rainstorm that had nearly drowned them all, only scattered raindrops and a steel-gray cloud moving away from them toward the eastern horizon, so there were no raindrops in the air he was sucking into his lungs. The air was fetid with the odors of everything that the storm had washed off Oklahoma City streets, but it tasted glorious.

Cully lay in the ditch a few feet away. Joe crawled over to make sure he was breathing. He was.

Where was Faye?

He found her in the river, bloody-faced but alive. She was treading water and dodging floating logs and trash, cradling an unconscious Stacy's head above the surface.

Kaayla was an arm's length from Faye. She was near-drowned but unwilling to save herself by letting go of Grace's limp body.

Time and again, she struggled to the surface, bringing Grace with her.

"Breathe! You have to breathe. Sister. Please breathe." Again and again, she pleaded with her sister to breathe and begged anyone who could hear her to look for Lucia, but Grace was beyond hearing and Lucia was nowhere to be seen.

Ahua was staggering along the grassy shore, waving his arms and calling out to an ambulance that was just coming to a stop, sirens blaring. Two agents ran to his side and one of them caught him before he dropped.

"Arrest the woman in the water" was all he could say, but there were three living women in the water and one dead. Ahua couldn't answer their questions, so he'd been reduced to pointing a hand of judgment at Kaayla.

Another car skidded to a stop behind the ambulance. Liu was out of it in the same instant that she slammed it into park. She ran past Ahua, full-throttle into the neck-deep water.

Joe thought that Liu was going to grab Stacy Wong hard enough to hurt her, until she stopped stock-still. Her whole body relaxed at the sight of Stacy, relaxed, unharmed, and not dead.

"May I?" she asked Faye.

Faye released Stacy and stepped away as Agent Liu wrapped both arms around her, gentle but firm, and pulled her toward shore. She eased Stacy up onto the riverbank, lifted her over the riprap and onto the grassy shore. Then she laid her head on the groggy woman's shoulder and wept.

"I'm so happy you're alive, Stacy," she said between great shuddering sobs.

When Joe finally got to Faye, he wrapped her in both arms, holding her just as tight as Cathy Liu held Stacy Wong.

She was weeping, which was not unexpected. Joe had been through the same nightmare as Faye and he knew exactly how bad it had been. He asked why she was crying anyway.

"Grace. Oh, Grace. She never had a chance."

Joe didn't know exactly what she meant. Maybe she meant that Grace had never had a chance to avoid drowning and that may have been true, because Kaayla was wailing, "Why did she do it? I told her to stay. She can't swim. Neither of them ever learned to swim."

But Joe thought that Faye meant something more. She knew more about Grace's life than he did, because she took it seriously when the FBI told her not to tell a soul, but Joe saw how it was. Being a hotel maid was one way not to ever have a chance in the world. Having a sister who was a stone cold killer was another.

When Faye said "Poor Grace" again, he kissed the top of her head and held her even tighter.

Chapter Thirty-Nine

Cully didn't want to be alone. Faye understood that.

When he'd invited Joe and Faye to come up to his penthouse with him, she knew that the only kind thing to do was to say yes. They had showered and come right up. Now they were sprawled across one of the penthouse's expensive leather couches. Part of her would rather be resting in their own quiet room, but the part of her who had never had a father was warmed at the thought that Cully was treating them like family.

Jakob was snoring in the easy chair beside Cully's. Every once in a while, he woke up, punched his friend on the arm as if to say, "Glad you're alive, buddy," then drowsed off again. Faye was seriously short on relatives, so she thought maybe she'd make Jakob an honorary uncle.

"I'm going to call a bellhop and get your stuff moved up here," Cully said to Faye and Joe. "There's a bedroom at the end of the hall, next to the sauna."

Faye thought that being next to a sauna sounded seriously awesome. She felt wet through and through, and she wanted to bake herself until her bones finally dried out.

Cully reached for the phone to call a bellhop but it rang before he picked it up.

"Well, that's service," Faye murmured.

When he hung up the phone, he said, "That was Ahua. He's coming up and says that he's bringing a man who's been looking for me all day."

"It's been a weird day," Joe said. "You sure it's safe to let a stranger come up here?"

"Ahua's coming with him. He's a fed, so it's not like we'll be defenseless. Also, he says he's pretty sure I'm going to want to talk to this guy."

Within minutes, there was a knock at the door and Cully answered it.

Ahua entered. Faye recognized Ben McGilveray at his side, but she could tell that Cully had no idea who he was.

Ben introduced himself to Cully by saying, "I brought you a gift. It's from an old friend."

He handed Cully a fat, yellowed envelope. Ahua reached in his pocket and handed him a slimmer one that was damp, as if maybe it had spent time in the pocket of a man trying not to drown.

"Ben gave this to Carson, who came straight to me with it, because he thought something was fishy about the way he said to give it to Cully and only Cully. It can be dangerous to be a celebrity. Unfortunately, I pretty much went straight from Carson to our adventure in the storm sewer and the letter is still wet."

Faye could see that Cully was intrigued, because he settled back in his chair next to Jakob and motioned for Ben to sit in the empty chair on his other side. He gestured at another chair for Ahua, but the agent stayed standing, watching Ben's every move.

Cully slid a stack of old photos out of the dry envelope. As soon as he saw the top photo, he dropped it and the other envelope and all of the photos, except for the one he held in his hand. Tears ran down his face and dripped off his jaws, but they didn't wet the photo because he held it so carefully away from harm.

Faye was burning with curiosity, but a loud knock sounded on the door before Cully could say anything.

"Cully Mantooth! Are you in there? And do you have my son and my new daughter in there with you? Open up!"

Cully was on his feet and across the room in a single stride. He threw open the door and threw one arm around Joe's father Sly, but just one arm. The other one was holding the old photo at a safe distance. Amande and Michael rushed past them to throw their arms around Faye.

"It's been a long time," Sly said. "I really missed you, man."

"Missed you, too, Little Guy. Now would you look at what this young man just brought me?" he said, pointing at the fifty-something-year-old Ben and showing the photo to Sly.

Sly had to look twice. "Good God. That's Angela. Only she's got some meat on her bones and she's smiling. She's just beautiful."

Cully looked at Ben. "This picture was taken a long time ago. Do you know what happened to her?"

Ben stooped to pick up the photos and the wet envelope that Cully had dropped. He sorted through them silently and chose another one to show Cully.

"This one's Angela, too," the older man said, looking at the photo as if he would kiss it if he weren't afraid he might damage it. "But it's before she picked up that extra weight. And—" He brought the picture closer to his eyes. "Is she pregnant?"

Ben handed him another photo and Cully's face softened as he stared at it. "She was so very lovely. Such a beautiful mother. And that baby's near as big as her."

Ben's face softened, too. "That's me. I was born in December of 1962."

The photos went to the floor again. "1962? Why didn't anybody tell me?"

"She didn't even tell *me* who my daddy was until she saw that article in the paper last week, saying that you were coming to town. She thought it might finally be time to tell you everything. She knew she was pregnant when you ran away from the school, but the two of you only got as far as Oklahoma City before she knew that she'd never get much farther. She was bad into heroin."

"I knew it. That's why I was trying to get her away from the people what sold it to her."

"Yeah, but neither of you knew how bad withdrawal would be. Especially with her being pregnant. She was in a bad way, but she didn't want to go home to that bastard of a stepfather. And she didn't want to slow you down. She told me that the time came when she just had to run."

Cully took a long, deep breath. "Yeah. That's exactly what she did."

"She found a homeless shelter and they found her some help, helped her start over. When I was just a baby, she married the man I thought was my father." Answering the question on Cully's face, he said softly. "He was a good man. They were happy together."

Cully made a quiet sound like a stifled sob.

"She didn't know where you were for years. When she started seeing you in the movies, she held her peace. Her life was good. Your life was good. I was a happy kid. Why stir up trouble?"

"Maybe because I've lost fifty-some years with my only child?"

Out of the corner of her eye, Faye saw Jakob lean forward, ready to come to Cully's aid if needed, because in movies of the old West, that was the job of the hero's sidekick.

"We've got some years left, don't you think?" Ben said, sticking out a hand to shake Cully's. Cully ignored the hand and seized his son with both hands.

Enveloped in his father's arms, Ben asked, "Do you want to see my mother?"

"More than anything. But only if she wants to see me."

"She said to bring you to dinner tomorrow. That's what's in the other envelope. A letter from her and an invitation."

Cully tried with shaking hands to get the letter out of its envelope without tearing the wet paper. He finally gave up and said,

"I'll dry it out in the sauna and read it tonight. Please tell her that I would be honored to come to dinner."

"I don't know what else she's making, but she says you always did love her fry bread."

Faye leaned against the well-padded back of the couch, her son on her lap and her daughter standing behind her, draped over her shoulders. Encircled by her children, she listened to the sound of five male voices trying to outtalk each other. Any single Mantooth man had enough personality to fill a room. Cully, Sly, Ben, Joe, and little Michael possessed enough personality, cumulatively, to fill a penthouse and then some.

Ahua walked over, perched on the coffee table in front of her, and said, "Guess where Cathy is?"

"With Stacy?"

"Yep. She'll be sitting in that hospital room until the doctors decide to let Stacy go. She needed a few stitches and that concussion's going to slow her down for a while, but she'll be fine. Liu tells me that she's taking Stacy to her favorite restaurant as soon as she's able to go, deep in the Asian District where the chefs know how it's done in the old country."

"Dinner date?"

"Dinner date." She thought his joyful smile might crack his face right open.

"Does Liu still have a job?"

"She'll suffer some consequences, but I think she'll keep her job. Our Special Agent in Charge is a sucker for romance. Liu's career will take a hit, but it's not over. I thought you'd want to know."

Faye's joyful smile was probably just as wide.

"I suppose that Kaayla's in custody."

"She's told us everything. About finding Lonnie. About luring him into a fake plot to blow up the IRS when she really meant to blow him up. About panicking when Stacy found her vandalizing the paintings. About locking her up and trying to decide what to do when everything snowballed out of her control. Everything."

"Were Grace and Lucia involved?"

"She says no, but her instinct is obviously to protect them, so it's hard to be sure. She says that she assigned them to mop the area around the door and told them where to put the 'Wet Floor' signs so nobody would come near, except a man in a cowboy hat. They were supposed to let him pass. She claims that they were in the dark, otherwise."

"She had to have told them more than that. What if they recognized him?"

"As it turns out, they did, and it saved their lives. Grace recognized Lonnie when he came out of the wall. According to Kaayla, Grace was still terrified of him even after all their years apart, so she called out for Lucia to run. Seconds later, the bomb blew. Despite that, Kaayla is adamant that her sisters were innocent, just doing as they were told. And they did that, up until the very end when Grace defied her by going into the sewer to stop her sister from killing again."

Faye tried not to think of Grace and a fistful of candy on her pillow. "What about Lucia?"

"We don't know where she is. If she went in the sewer with the rest of you, she washed out into the river without anybody seeing her. Maybe she drowned and we'll find her body downriver. Or maybe she could swim enough to get away during the confusion, but Kaayla says no. More likely, she escaped into the catacombs, coming aboveground at the entrance you found or maybe at another one that we don't know about. On one hand, it's going to be hard for her to get far with no money and no car. On the other hand, it's hard to track a woman without credit cards or ID."

Faye thought of another woman who was once on the streets of Oklahoma City with none of those things. "Somebody helped Angela Bond find a new life. Maybe somebody will help Lucia."

"I don't think you want her to get caught."

Faye wasn't sure what she wanted.

Ahua gave her a close look but said only, "You do good work. If you ever need anybody to vouch for that, send them to me." Then he shook her hand and let himself out.

Faye spent the rest of the evening sitting quietly on the couch, watching her kinfolk, old and new. They told stories and, after the sauna had done its work, they read a damp letter from Angela to Cully that had passed beneath Oklahoma City in an FBI agent's pocket. They pored over a yellowed envelope full of old photos. And they did a lot of laughing.

Eventually, the Mantooth men remembered that she was alive and Cully announced, "Cousin Faye. It's time for your first lesson. Go get your flute."

Notes for the Incurably Curious

The parts of this book's historical backstory that are the most difficult to believe are true. There really was a Chinese community living underground in downtown Oklahoma City in the early twentieth century. The health department really did perform an inspection down there in 1921 and report that they found "the 200 or more inhabitants of the submerged quarter in good health and surroundings and as sanitary as all get out." A staircase really was discovered in 1969 during convention center construction and part of the underground system of rooms was explored at that time. Even the photograph that I described of a man holding a flashlight on an old stove was, and still is, real.

Here is a 2007 article from *The Oklahoman*'s website, summarizing much of what is known and rumored about the underground community: https://newsok.com/article/3069770unlocking -the-secrets-of-oklahoma-citys-mysterious-city?

If you scroll to the bottom, past the broken link to the article's slideshow, you will see the flashlight photograph and a photo of Chinese language flyers like those Faye encounters in *Catacombs*.

The chambers uncovered in 1969 are presumably still down there. Why would anyone go to the time, trouble, and expense of destroying them, if they were planning to seal the entrance? I feel confident that intrepid urban explorers have invested a great deal of time over the years in looking for another entrance but please, Dear Reader, do not attempt this yourself.

First of all, trespassing is against the law. Second of all, the kind of trespassing that would be required to access underground rooms that have been abandoned for a century is incredibly dangerous. The danger inherent in being trapped underground without a cell signal to call for help is obvious. If you're thinking of trying Faye's strategy of using storm sewers for access, remember that they have an additional risk baked into their design—water that comes in in large quantities and at unpredictable intervals—so stay out of them. People have drowned in storm drains when surprised by sudden storms, here in Oklahoma and elsewhere.

It's far safer to let this piece of history remain in our imaginations, a time capsule safely buried with its secrets...unless someone once again stumbles on it accidentally.

The convention center that was being built in 1969 is coming to the end of its useful life, and it is soon to be replaced by something more up-to-date. As I write this, plans are afoot for demolition and redevelopment of the old convention center. Proposed plans include restoration of the mid-twentieth-century street grid or replacement with a high-rise building, as described here: https://kfor.com/2018/07/12/whats-the-future-of-the-cox-convention-center/.

Our best bet for getting a look at what the Chinese community built a century ago is to remain comfortably (and safely) aboveground and wait to see what the bulldozers of progress turn up this time.

Acknowledgments

I'd like to thank all the people who helped make *Catacombs* happen. Tony Ain did his usual scour of the manuscript, and you would not believe the number of unclosed quotes, errors of fact, plot holes, unclosed parentheses, and omitted punctuation marks that I can leave in a manuscript that I think is pretty close to finished. This wouldn't have been the same book without him.

My children—Michael Garmon, Rachel Broughten, and Amanda Evans—also offered their insightful commentary.

This was my first book featuring a significant FBI presence, and I am hugely indebted to Angela Bell with the FBI's Office of Public Affairs for patiently answering many question that, truth told, were a bit odd. When FBI agents in *Catacombs* behave as FBI agents in real life do, it is due to her experience and expertise. When they do not, it is either due to my failure to ask her the right questions or to the necessity of bending reality to fit the needs of a good story.

I'd also like to thank Raymond Melton and Derek Johnson with Oklahoma City's Department of Public Works for helping me imagine the world beneath the feet of everyone who walks through downtown Oklahoma City. And I'd like to thank Lieutenant Medley of the Oklahoma City Police Department for believing me when I told him that I did not ask Public Works for information on moving around under the city because I had any intention of doing anything untoward down there. I've been writing crime novels for more than fifteen years now, and this is the very first time that my quirky questions have triggered a call from law enforcement. I feel oddly proud.

I'm grateful to Ember Ahua for helping me get a feel for my Nigerian American FBI agent and for telling me about egusi soup with bitter leaf, because it is just the kind of sensory detail that brings stories to life. She was so helpful that I gave my FBI agent her beautiful surname.

Cully Mantooth's first name owes a debt to Leroy Cully, my friend and the maker of my beautiful cedar flute that I don't play very well. His flutes were the inspiration for Cully Mantooth's career as a musician and composer. If you see me wearing a cowboy hat with a beautifully beaded band, know that the band was a gift from Leroy. His daughters Kelley Morrow and Vinci Cully Barron have also been very generous with their knowledge of tribal issues and of Oklahoma.

As always, I am grateful for the people who help me get my work ready to go out into the world, the people who send it out into the world, and the people who help readers find it. Many thanks go to my agent, Anne Hawkins, and to the wonderful people at Poisoned Pen Press, who do such a good job for us, their writers. For *Catacombs*, I'm proud to add the wonderful people at Sourcebooks to my list of folks to thank. I'm happy to be a part of the Sourcebooks team and I'm excited by the synergy that will help Sourcebooks and Poisoned Pen Press get Faye's adventures to a new audience. Because I can trust that my editor, Barbara Peters, and the rest of the hardworking Poisoned Pen Press staff will ensure that my work is at its best when it reaches the public, I am free to focus on creating new adventures for Faye. I'm also grateful to the University of Oklahoma for providing the opportunity for me to teach a new generation of authors while continuing to write books of my own.

And, of course, I am always (always!) grateful for you, my readers.

About the Author

Mary Anna Evans is the author of the Faye Longchamp Archaeo-logical Mysteries, which have received recognition including the Benjamin Franklin Award, the Mississippi Author Award, and three Florida Book Awards bronze medals.

Mary Anna is the winner of the 2018 Sisters in Crime Academic Research Grant and is an assistant professor at the University of Oklahoma, where she teaches fiction and nonfiction writing.

Check out her website, enewsletter, Facebook author page, and Twitter.

Photo by by Randy Batista at Media Image Photography